SECRETS
and
SONGBIRDS

SECRETS
and
SONGBIRDS

N. J. RODMAN

ENTHEAS
THORNCRE
PATRIVAH
TEMPLE OF VEDAS
BRAEXMIRTH
OLDCASTON
ELDKIN
STELONBRIAR
IREFELD
OBSIDIAN SEA

N
W
E
S
NURAKA
XIAN DAO
EMPIRE
SAIPRI
ILASTEAD
TELAR
DRAESTEL
VEBELEN
ESIMIAN ISLES
VAKARI
DYNASTY
DHAMTRA

CONTENT WARNINGS

PROLOGUE

Soren rolled out of bed and headed for the kitchen to put the kettle on. She needed caffeine, and she needed it now. She guzzled down the boiling liquid, wincing as the coffee burned her tongue. Regardless, she ignored her mouth's cry for help and refilled her ceramic mug before settling in to eat her breakfast. She eyed the wood stove, insuring the flames had settled before biting into her toast.

The cinnamon raisin loaf from the bakery down the road was amazing, but it was almost gone. She mentally added it to her grocery list as she put her dishes away.

Dishes were a monotonous task. She always loathed having to heat the water. The well was not far from the back door, but in winter, they kept jugs in the cellar for convenience when it was too cold to pump. Soren hated lugging the large pot across the lawn, often soaking her shoes as the liquid sloshed out. Drying them was the bane of her existence and something her and her father constantly tiffed about.

He had been away for work for a couple of weeks and was due to be back in a few days, so she was soaking up having the house to herself since it was her day off.

She put her plate away, the dish clattering on the shelf before she settled down by the fireplace with her most recent read. She was just getting to a particularly exciting part of the story when a knock interrupted her.

"Of course," she grumbled, slamming the book shut. There was no way for her Father to be back this early, and she had heard Enara leave already, so whoever was here was not invited. *Baz did say he might stop by today.* She was going to beat that boy if he was here this early. "Maker forbid I try to enjoy my book in peace!"

Yanking the door open to find one of the heads of the town council, she adjusted her posture. "I'm sorry, you're not who I was expecting. Is there something I can do for you?" She bit her lip. She hated dealing with people of authority. The council only made house calls when it was an emergency.

"I am sorry to have to inform you of this, but your father was found dead this morning." His tone was sympathetic as he adjusted the collar of his cotton suit.

The air was sucked out of her lungs as she attempted to comprehend the foreign information. "What do you mean, *he's dead?*" She wasn't sure why she was asking. She knew what the word meant.

She could feel her heartbeat in her ears, and tears blurred her vision.

"Do you want to sit?" The older man reached out to her, but she batted his hand away.

Through gritted teeth, she said, "Just tell me."

"They found him out near the end of the Boreal River, just before the falls."

She sniffled. "What happened?"

"They are still examining the body, but it seems he sustained multiple injuries and succumbed to them before he reached town. Most of the injuries were defensive wounds, leading us to believe that this was no accident. I'm so sorry."

"*You're sorry*? You're sorry!" she yelled. "My father is dead, probably murdered, and you're sorry?" She tried to force down the knot in her throat.

"I wish I had better news. You will have access to his body by the end of the day. The city watch's coroner will have finished the autopsy by then. Since you are his next of kin, you will be in charge of the funeral arrangements."

"Are you fucking kidding me right now?" Anger filled her entire body as she lashed out at the poor man. "I don't know how to plan a funeral! What the fuck am I supposed to do with his body?" Tears slid down her face as she continued her assault. "How dare you? How could you come here and just drop this on me like it's an item off your damn checklist?"

The man was obviously uncomfortable, but she didn't care.

"I am sorry for your loss. If you need help with the arrangements, contact the city watch's main office; they can help you coordinate with the funeral home. I would do it soon so they can prepare his body for the service. Again, I am truly sorry, but I must be going."

"Oh, go fuck yourself!" She slammed the door in his face then fell to the floor, sobbing. Her heart was out of her chest and bleeding out on the floor, the open cavity sickeningly empty. She shook, gasping for air, coughing so hard she got sick right there on the hardwood.

She wiped her mouth then crawled to the bathroom where she laid her head on the woven rug, leaving a trail of tears in her wake. She held her breath and counted to ten, trying to slow her breathing. Her whole body vibrated with the effort, and she could feel her heartbeat in her temples.

As she stood, wobbling her way back to the living room, her vision got fuzzy. She dropped down to crawl to the rug in front of the fireplace where she curled in on herself, her chest aching from her manic breathing.

Her body seemed to be rejecting oxygen as she held her breath again. Her head swam as she felt the heat from the embers warm her face.

She lay there, staring at the flames, utterly shut down to the world until she was empty of tears. She wasn't sure how long she had been lying there. It could have been minutes. It could have been hours. It didn't matter. Nothing mattered. She had grown up without a mother, so the loss of her father left her feeling utterly alone in the world.

She watched the flames flicker, the shadows dancing off the back of the fireplace as exhaustion creeped up her body.

The door swung open, and Enara came rushing in. Her best friend from Voxridge Academy was not one to coddle, but when she saw her on the floor, she did not question it. She grabbed a blanket off the couch and put it over her, leaving for a moment before returning with a glass of water. The cylinder clinked as she placed it on the floor.

Soren watched as sweat beaded down its side. Then she reached forward with a shaking hand and took a sip. Gingerly, she placed it back down.

"He's gone," she finally said, voice cracking.

"I know."

They sat in silence for a while. Enara added a few more logs to the fire as night fell before placing Soren's head back in her lap and stroking her hair gently.

"I'm supposed to plan a funeral."

"I'll help you; don't worry about that now."

"They said he had defensive wounds. I want to know what that means. Who would have done this to him, Enara? I should have asked more questions … but I was just so angry. It all felt like a sick joke."

Her friend shifted her vision downward, looking into Soren's red-rimmed eyes. They were a deep chestnut brown but flashed orange in the firelight. "I heard the gist of it. The unfortunate thing about living in a small town like Vreburn— news travels fast."

"Enara?"

"Yeah?"

"It's just us now," she said solemnly, the tears returning.

"We are all we need," she replied.

No one told their kids how to plan a funeral. They never spoke of all the decisions you were forced to make amidst the cloud of grief. By the time they were old enough to dwell on these considerations, they expected you would just know what to do. When a parent passed earlier in a child's life, they were left to make these decisions on their own.

Do you want to cremate the body? Open-casket or closed? What type of casket? Do you want to purchase or rent? Do you want a wood or cast urn? What type of flowers? Do you have photos you want to display? What do you want him to wear? Do you want to be a part of the body preparation? How many will attend the service?

She was asked these questions as if she already had the answers. She was thankful that Enara had known her father decently well and helped make suggestions along the way.

"Remember how he liked purple irises because they were your mother's favorite. He used to keep them out back," Enara offered softly.

Soren remembered with fondness. He had grown them when she was younger but had stopped when he'd begun to travel more for work.

She nodded. "Yeah, let's use those. And I think we should put him in the gray suit. It looked nice on him."

Her friend grabbed her hand and squeezed, knowing how hard this was for her.

"Can we go now?"

"Yes, of course," the funeral director replied, closing her notebook. "If we have any further questions, we will get in contact with you. Take all the time you need."

"How are you feeling?"

"How do you think I'm feeling?" Soren scowled, rubbing her hands down her face. "I can't get the image of him out of my head. He was so cold. There were so many ... How could someone do that to him?"

"I don't know, but I promise we will do our best to find out. Come," Enara said, standing and extending her hand. "Let's get you home. Baz is standing by with some of his mother's minced pie." Laraline had made them with ground elk, and it was one of their all-time favorites.

"I'm not hungry."

"Well, I am, and you have hardly eaten in the last two days. Come on."

THEY SAT AROUND THE DINING TABLE, DIGGING INTO THE ASSORTment of food that Baz had delivered. It was unsettling to see a mask of sadness covering his normally cheery face.

"I'm sorry about your father, Soren. He was a great guy," he said, embracing her tightly.

She squeezed back, nuzzling into the warmth of his chest.

Baz was a good friend, and she was happy to have a male presence in the house.

She pushed around the food on her plate, trying to eat, but her stomach rejected the nourishment. "Thank you guys, for being here."

"There's nowhere else we would rather be."

"Yeah," Baz replied. "You know we would never leave you hanging."

"I know." She turned her lips up in appreciation. They truly were the best friends she could have ever asked for.

"It's okay if you need time to process it all, but if you want to talk, we're here," Enara said before she bit into her mashed potatoes.

"I know the situation is a bit different, but I know what it's like to lose your parents, so if you need some insight, I got you."

Soren furrowed her brow. She had nearly forgotten that Baz had been orphaned prior to moving to Vreburn.

"I don't think you ever told me what happened," she replied. "I knew you were adopted, but you never mentioned what happened to your birth parents."

He shifted uncomfortably. "I'm not sure it's the kind of story that would make you feel better."

"I promise it's okay … Go ahead, I could use the distraction."

"Well, you know how, back home in Nuraka, they would persecute anyone who protested the law of the empire?"

Soren nodded.

"Well, my parents were activists during the civil war when Bao-Ren first came into power. His authoritarian rule caused unrest amongst the people, and they rallied against him."

"They must have been so brave," Enara said, looking at him intently.

"Yeah." He smiled fondly. "They were. I mean, until they had me. When my mom found out she was pregnant, they stopped attending rallies for safety reasons. They continued to assist the rebellion from the sidelines, but Bao-Ren was building a following and things were getting dangerous. They ended up going into hiding, picking up work on a small rice farm outside of Saipea. They used forged papers with different names to avoid suspicion."

"Do you remember much from back then?" Soren asked.

"Little things. I was six when we left, so most of the earlier years are lost on me, but I do remember that my mom would always sing to me when I was upset."

"My dad said Mom used to sing to me while she was pregnant," Soren commented. "He said she favored sea shanties."

Enara laughed. "Well, that explains your love for the tavern then."

"You're not wrong." Soren shrugged.

"My mom used to sing folk songs. We would dance around the rice fields, water sloshing in my boots. We were happy there for a while."

"Then what happened?" Enara asked.

Baz straightened. "Bao-Ren had secretly continued his investigation into anyone who was involved in trying to overthrow the empire. Anyone found to be involved with the resistance was forced to stand trial for treason. As you can imagine, they were all found guilty and hung for their crimes."

The girls sucked in a breath, shocked at the brutality.

"I didn't think they were still allowed to employ those methods … even for the death penalty," Enara said, shaking her head with disbelief.

"I'm not sure how it is now, but no one questioned it back then. So, anyway"—he paused to gather his thoughts—"my parents caught wind of this through a friend from their rally days and heard that empire loyalists were coming for them.

"All I remember is them waking me up in the middle of the night and throwing me in a small boat. They told me to stay down and keep silent until we passed the guard towers. When we reached a safe distance, I asked where we were going, and they just said somewhere safe. Three-quarters of the way through the crossing, a storm broke, capsizing the boat. I lost both my parents that day. Luckily, a sailor from Ilastead found me, or I would have been shark bait."

"Baz, I had no idea. That's horrible." Soren's eyes filled with sympathy for him.

"It's okay. I mean, yeah … it's really shitty. But if it weren't for my tragic circumstances, I would have never met the two of you." He nudged Enara's shoulder.

"Well, that makes us quite the group," she said. "You two lost your parents, and I don't want anything to do with mine. Guess that means we're stuck with each other."

"Guess so." Soren smiled.

"I mean, I'm not complaining," Baz added.

They finished their meal then retired to the living room, sharing more stories from their childhoods. When it was time for bed, they said goodnight to Baz.

As he headed out the door, Soren turned to Enara, her eyes glossy with tears. "Can you stay in my room tonight?"

"Of course, lady, whatever you need."

"I just … I don't want to be alone," she stammered. "I … I know he was gone all the time, but the house just feels hollow now." She looked down, tasting salt on her lips.

"You don't have to explain. Let's go to bed."

They walked down the hall and washed up in silence. Then, crawling under the blankets, Soren settled in, taking a deep breath, feeling calmer with Enara passed out beside her. The woman could fall asleep anywhere instantaneously, a skill Soren could only wish for.

Before sleep took her, she looked out the window, tear-drops darkening her pillowcase. "Goodnight, Dad. I love you tons."

Soren gazed down at the procession, her eyes blank. Grief settled in the pit of her stomach like spoiled milk. The horses shuffled around anxiously as their owners hopped out of their carts to join the other guests who had already been seated.

Just weeks ago, they had been laughing and sharing stories around the dying embers of the hearth. Their home had been so full of love and warmth. Now she stood on the hilltop above the cemetery in her alabaster mourning dress.

A rustle in the overgrowth made her turn.

"It's time," Enara said softly. She stood a few footfalls away, a solemn expression on her face.

Soren turned back just in time to see Baz and a few men from town remove the ebony casket from the elongated hearse cart. Her heart sank.

"I don't know how to do this." She picked at her nails. "They expect me to know what to say, and I don't have the words."

"We could just skip it. There are no rules here, lady. I wouldn't blame you." Soren smirked.

A whisper of a laugh tugged at the corners of Soren's mouth. "We both know I would be all too tempted." She reached out her hand, and Enara reciprocated, entwining their fingers.

"You know he was more a father to me than my own ever was. I will miss him."

"He loved you, too, you know."

"I know."

Soren sucked in a breath, taking one last moment of solace for herself. "Okay, I'm ready."

CHAPTER ONE

It was five weeks to the day since Soren had buried her father. Five weeks since she had stood in front of all his peers and spouted whatever sappy stories she could muster while her grief threatened to swallow her whole. She had smiled and nodded while they had expressed their condolences, shying away awkwardly when they had embraced her. Enara had given her sympathetic looks from across the room as the thirty-fifth attendant had held on for longer than was necessary.

Never in her life had so many people said, "I'm sorry for your loss," like the words actually meant something. She had been glad to have had her friends by her side. If not for them, she would have let the panic take over and resorted to sucking face with a paper bag for the rest of the evening. She had just wanted it to be over so she could lament in peace. And lament she had.

When the last of the mourners had said their goodbyes, she'd requested to have a moment alone.

"No problem, hon. We will go wait by the entrance." Enara linked arms with Baz, and then they walked down the narrow path toward the gate of Vreburn's town cemetery.

Soren watched them go, waiting to say her piece until they were out of sight. Then she picked up a handful of earth that was damp and cool between her fingers. It had rained that morning, and the ground was still soft under her boots.

She sprinkled the dirt over the coffin that had already been lowered into the ground as tears sprung to her eyes. She had held them in throughout the whole ceremony, not wanting to break down in front of everyone. She hated other people seeing her cry and did not want their pity.

She looked down at the coffin spray, the irises marred with dirt. The whole scene was unsettling. Images of her father's injured body flashed through her mind, making her stomach churn. She shook them away and took in a steadying breath.

"I'm going to miss you, Dad." She choked on the words as the charcoal under her eyes made small, black rivers down her cheeks. "It's not fair. I don't know how to do this without you." She wiped her eyes, grabbing the tissue from the pocket of her dress that Baz had offered her during the service. "Who would do this to you?" she whispered, a million questions running through her mind. She used the cloth to wipe the remaining dirt from her hand before stuffing it back into her pocket. "I love you tons." She sniffled. "And I promise I'll make you proud." She looked down at the coffin, another wave of grief threatening to pull her under. She wished she could hug him one last time.

She steeled herself, knowing if she allowed the panic to set in, she would likely do something reckless. Squeezing her eyes shut, she pushed the wave away and swallowed back the lump that had built up in her throat. Then she turned on her heel, refusing to look at the hole in the ground, and went to find her friends, leaving a trail of boot prints in her wake.

THE FIRST FEW DAYS HAD BEEN UNIMAGINABLY HARD. IT WAS THE little things you didn't think about when someone passed away. She could feel the emptiness of him everywhere she looked. His jacket still hung on the rusty hook beside the front door. His bed sheets still slept in. She never understood why he hadn't made it before he'd left.

She'd spent her days sitting in silence, staring at his drawing room door, not having the courage to enter it. At night, she would go to The Crow's Nest to drown her sorrows. After she was well and truly intoxicated, she would find comfort in the arms of whatever lucky bastard she had brought home that night. Grief was a cruel mistress. A deadly companion.

Everyone grieved in different ways. Soren went dark, pushing away her friends' attempts to make her feel better.

"A few home-cooked meals aren't going to bring him back!" she'd yelled when Baz had shown up with more food that his mothers had prepared.

"Soren, you need to eat," Enara had jumped in, defending him.

"What I need is a stiff drink," she shot back, pushing past them.

"Don't you think you have been going out too much?" Enara asked, concern ripe on her face.

"You are not my mother! If you hadn't noticed, I don't have one of those, either!"

Enara stepped back, the words feeling like a slap to the face.

"That's what I thought." Soren turned, not wanting to see the hurt she had caused. "And don't even think of coming after me." She stomped away, leaving her friends standing at the door, mouth's hanging open in shock.

They had left her alone after that.

Enara walked on eggshells around the house, trying to stay out of her way to let her grieve how she saw fit. Soren knew she would feel terrible later for treating them so badly but, right now, she didn't care.

On the first morning of the fifth week, Enara had finally had enough. She barged into Soren's bedroom, unbothered by the naked man in her bed. "You," she said, throwing trousers at the doe-eyed boy, "get out."

Soren had never seen such surprise run across someone's face as he quickly gathered his things and, with an awkward, "Um … thanks for last night," was out the door.

"You have exactly ten minutes to get your shit together before I come in here with the water bucket."

"*Ugh*," Soren groaned. "Can I at least have a tonic for my hangover before you start giving orders?"

Enara rolled her eyes and responded with a curt, "No. Now get your ass out of bed."

No less than ten minutes and forty-seven seconds later, Soren was dressed and out the door. She couldn't be too mad at Enara. She had known this was coming, and she couldn't keep this up forever. She was going to have to tuck her tail between her legs and apologize at some point.

She breathed in the morning air. The rising sun had just settled itself amongst the trees. It warmed her cheeks as she looked back at the home she shared with Enara … and once her father.

They wouldn't consider themselves rich by any means, but they were well off. Her father's archeological finds were usually donated to the Vreburn Institute of Archaeology, but every now and then, he would auction off an item or two. Soren was constantly disgusted by how much wealthy people were willing to spend on an old clay pot or a crusted piece of parchment.

It wasn't that she didn't have an understanding of her father's work. In fact, it was quite the opposite. She wanted the items to be appreciated for their history, not used as a display of status. Soren was happy with what they had and knew she was more fortunate than most.

They had a decent-sized property, and the rustic home was nothing to scoff at. It was made entirely of spruce logs, stacked in row upon row, with a large, geometric window in the center. The entrance was flanked by large stone pillars on either side, holding up the gabled roof. The chimney mirrored the stone, and the front door was painted a misty teal that reminded Soren of the river a few miles west, where her father had taught her how to fish.

She loved this home. They had finished the build seven years prior, and Enara had moved in three years later after a final, devastating blow from her abusive father. Soren had been overjoyed to have her companion just down the hall. At night, they would slip out while her father slept and lay under the stars, talking about their recent love interests. During the warm summer days, they would lounge on woven blankets, drinking loxberry tea in the shade of the large red oak trees. Those trees were massive and surrounded the entire property. Her father would join them out back, swinging his axe by the firepit to add to his never-ending stockpile of fuel. She had so many good memories here.

A friendly voice drifted from behind her. "I see someone had a good night." Baztien sauntered over, giving her a wry smile, his auburn hair still tousled from last night's sleep. He gave her a once-over and smirked.

"Fuck off, man," Soren replied, shoving him playfully.

"Hey now! I got a rude awakening this morning, too!"

Soren grinned.

"Enara practically gave me a heart attack, creeping outside my window. I'm pretty sure she was trying to see if I sleep naked."

"Gross." Soren screwed up her face in mock disgust.

"Come on; you know you want this," Baz said, attempting to gyrate his hips. However, he tripped over an unseen root and landed hard in the dirt.

Soren burst into a fit of laughter, slapping her knees. It felt good. She couldn't remember the last time she had laughed like that.

Baz stuck out his tongue as he stood up, wiping the dust from his pants.

"Okay, you two," Enara chimed in, exiting the front doorway. "I am calling a family meeting."

Soren and Baz looked at each other and groaned.

"We have things to do, in light of recent events. Case in point: Soren traipsing herself all over town. I think it's time we, meaning *you*"—she eyed Soren—"need to get your shit together."

Soren looked down, clasping her hands together in embarrassment.

"Not to mention, the curators have been up my ass about a few items in your father's collection that they desperately want." Enara had started volunteering at the institute years ago to avoid spending time at home, but she stayed because she enjoyed it. Cataloguing things in a quiet dusty room gave her peace. Soren never understood why. She avoided paperwork at all costs. She was more of a hands-on type of girl.

She sighed, knowing her friend was right. "I know I have to stop putting it off …" A solemn look passed over her features. She shook it off, saying, "But if we're doing this, I am going to require about ten doses of tonic for my raging headache and a carriage load of depression snacks."

Baz chuckled. "This day is getting better already."

AFTER A QUICK VISIT TO THE LOCAL MARKET AND A FEW NECESsary herbal remedies later, the trio got to work. Soren had apologized on the way to town for her recent behavior, and her infractions were quickly forgotten. She was happy to be back in their good graces and walked a little lighter on the way home.

It didn't take long to pack away Tarak Nightsong's possessions. He had been a simple man. Apart from a few archeological finds from his personal collection, he hadn't needed much. Soren always appreciated her father's love for the mundane. The simplest things had brought him the most joy. "All I need is the light of the moon, and the stars will lead my heart home," he'd said as they had watched the remnants of the fire die down.

She smiled at the memory, letting it warm the parts of her heart that were still frosted with sorrow. They had spent countless nights staring at the night sky, studying the constellations.

"I think we're almost done," Enara said, bringing over one last crate from the reading nook.

Soren's mind returned to the present.

"Baz just finished packing up the artifacts for the institute. Did you want to double-check them?"

She shook her head. "No, I already set aside the ones I want to keep for myself, plus a few that would do well at auction." It pained her to think of giving anything of her father's away, but she couldn't hold on to it all forever.

Enara shifted the box up to adjust her grip. "Okay then, that's everything out here. The only room left is the—"

"Drawing room," Soren said quietly.

Enara put a hand on her arm. "We can do it another day, if you're not ready. It's okay."

Soren squared her shoulders and gave her a small smile. "No, it's okay. It's time. Can …? Can you and Baz just give me a few moments? It's just … this was his space, you know. We used to joke that he spent more time in here than he did sleeping, and I just need to see it one last time before we pack it all away."

"Say no more. Just come grab us when you're finished. Take all the time you need." And with that, she was gone.

Soren suddenly felt small without her friends by her side. Her fingers trembled as she reached for the handle, her heart fluttering in her chest like a caged bird. She took a deep breath and stepped through the doorway.

It was just as she remembered. It smelled of sand and parchment. His trowels and brushes were laid out meticulously on the table, as if he'd just cleaned them. Maps littered with coffee stains, different symbols marking the type of dig site. Soren used to love sitting in here with her father and drawing up maps of her own, making him laugh with sordid tales of her adventures. "Come now," he would say, ruffling her hair as the sun fell below the tree line, "let us see what the stars have to say tonight."

She missed those days.

"Well," she said to herself, "better get to it."

After an hour or so of packing away various tools, rolls of parchment, and a jar of suspicious origin, Soren wiped the sweat from her brow. Who knew paper products could be so heavy?

She took a swig from her canteen then wiped the contents that had dripped down her face with her sleeve and let out a heavy breath. She squinted as the sun caught her eye, reflecting off an old photo of her and her father. She picked it up and smiled fondly.

It had been taken on Soren's first trip to her father's childhood home in Vakari. She had just turned ten, and her father had gotten approval for her to join them on a dig south of Dhamtra. She had loved seeing where her father had grown up. Everything was so different over there, more colorful somehow.

His given name was Tarakesh Raatkageet, but the locals in Draestal had trouble pronouncing it, so he had gone by Tarak. When you translated Raatkageet to the common tongue, it meant Nightsong, so he had used the latter. Soren was secretly thankful. It wasn't that she didn't want her father's Vakari last name, but taking the westernized version made filling out forms a hell of a lot easier. Eastern food was still her favorite, though. She vaguely remembered trying to convince him to let her bring home a pet monkey once, but it was a no-go.

"Hey, Sor—"

The sudden interruption made her jump, and the photograph slipped from her fingers. "Fucking hell, Baztien!" she shrieked.

"Shit, I am so sorry," Baz said, looking sheepishly at the shards of glass littering the floor. He quickly bent down to help pick up the pieces.

"Idiot." Soren smacked him on the back of the head. "You scared the shit out of me. Literally. I might require new undergarments." She reached down to pull the image of her and her father from the debris when she noticed something was attached to the back.

"We were going to wait for you, but—"

"Shh!" Soren silenced him, her eyes widening as she turned the photograph over in her hands. Affixed to the back of the picture was a letter with some black script on it. She would recognize the muddled handwriting anywhere—it was her father's.

She fingered the dried ink, tears pricking her eyes as she read it out loud with a shaky voice, "*The stars are speaking, and you must listen.*"

CHAPTER
TWO

Soren looked down at the letter, tears pooling in her eyes as she brushed her long hair out of her face. The blue hair dye had begun to fade, and the natural brown was starting to show through. Her father had always been disappointed when she dyed it. Virgin Vikarian hair was well sought after for those who had less fortunate genealogy.

She stared at the parchment, her teardrops causing the paper to swell and pucker. *He left this for me.* Her arms prickled. *How did he know I would find it?* Her heart hammered in her chest. It felt like it was collapsing in on itself.

The autopsy report had said that the death had been ruled an accident. According to them, it had been caused by an unfortunate animal attack. Soren wondered if he had ever seen it coming. The details weren't adding up, though, and her mind spiraled. Her pupils dilated as the chemicals in her brain thrust her into fight or flight mode.

"Earth to Soren!" Baz flailed his arms in front of her face. "Are you in shock? Is this what shock looks like? I'm not sure what to do here." He shook her shoulders, a look of concern in his eyes. "Soren, dammit, snap out of it!"

At that, Soren shook her head to clear the haze, looked up into his hooded eyes, and started mumbling through her confusion. "It's a letter from my father … It's for me. I know it. But … he … His death was an accident." She sucked in a breath. "I don't understand. I … I don't … I …" Her breaths coming quicker now, she sunk to the floor, her panic dragging her down like an anchor at sea.

"Enara, I could use your help in here!" Baz shouted as he kneeled in front of Soren.

"I can't… I can't …" she whispered, tears streaming down her face. She was hyperventilating now and would pass out soon if she didn't get her breathing in check.

"What the hell is taking so—" Enara stopped in the doorway. When she noticed Soren on the ground, she rushed to her side. "What happened?" she asked, fear-stricken.

"I think she's having a panic attack."

"Soren? Soren? Hon, I need you to breathe for me. Soren, look into my eyes, okay? It's all going to be okay. We're here," Enara coaxed, kneeling in front of her.

Soren had been diagnosed with a panic disorder when she was a child, but it had been years since she'd had an episode this bad.

"Baz, get some water and grab her meds from her bedside table. Quickly! Go!"

Baz exited the room in a hurry.

Soren rocked back and forth, shallow breaths dragging from her throat. Her eyes were fixed on the piece of parchment in her hands, the paper creasing under the pressure of her fingertips.

Enara moved to her side and rubbed her back gently. "Breathe with me," she whispered. "In …" She breathed in. "Out …"

Soren exhaled slowly.

"Good," she praised as Soren took a shuddering breath. "That's it."

It took another twenty minutes for her erratic heart to finally settle. When she was able to speak in full sentences again, she said, "I'm too scared to open it." She sat across the dining room table from Enara and Baz, tracing the edges of the letter with her fingers.

"Well, you have two choices," Enara offered. "You can stash it away in a box somewhere and forget it ever existed, or you buck up, put on your big girl trousers, and see what your father had to say."

Soren knew she was right but was terrified. She loved her father, had looked up to him. Whatever scrawl was on that paper had the potential to change everything she knew about him.

Baz reached a hand across the table. He usually resorted to bad humor, but he had read the room and had decided against it.

Soren squeezed his fingers and gave him a small smile. Then she looked back and forth between the two and steadied herself. Her hands shook as she reached forward and broke the wax seal before slipping the parchment from its paper jacket.

"*My dearest Soren,*" she started reading aloud, her voice ragged from crying.

"I am writing this letter as a fail-safe in the event of my death. I hope you will never need to read what I am about to say, but I must say it.

I'm sure you have so many questions. I will try my best to answer as many as I can. I am writing under the assumption that my death was sudden. I am sorry that you are having to read this through your grief, but I know that Enara will take good care of you. It eases my heart greatly to know that she will be by your side. She is a good friend. Please, tell her I will miss her dearly."

Enara's eye's misted as she whispered, "I miss you, too."

Baz rubbed her back, and she nodded for Soren to continue.

Soren coughed to clear her throat, finding the point where she had left off.

"In my early years, I discovered an artifact that held great value to a powerful being formally known as the King of Ravens. I hid it away so that its power could never be used. My death means they are getting close to finding it."

Soren choked back a sob.

"Do not underestimate him. He is not of our world and will not hesitate to send his unkindness after you.

My sweet, smart girl, I know this is too much to ask, but I must ask it of you. You need to retrace my steps and find a way to destroy it before it falls into his possession. He is cunning and cruel; you must be on your guard at all times. I should have removed the threat long ago, and I will be sorry into the next life that I let this burden fall upon you.

I have enclosed a map. Let it be your guide, and don't forget when you are lost, you can find the answers you seek amongst the stars. Death is not goodbye. It simply means I'll miss you until we meet again.

Love you tons,

Dad."

Soren blinked the tears from her eyes, letting out a strained breath.

"No pressure," Baz quipped as he gawked at the letter.

Soren released his hand, and Enara shifted in her seat, the gears in her head turning.

Unexpectedly, Soren started laughing hysterically. She doubled over, holding her belly.

"I think she's finally lost it." Baz furrowed his brows, sharing a look of confusion with Enara.

Soren's giggling continued as she blurted out, "Are you fucking kidding me?" She got up, using a cloth handkerchief to wipe the snot from her face. "My dad was murdered … and wants me to go on a quest … for some artifact that some guy called the King of Ravens is after?" She waved her arms up in defeat. "To what? Save the world?" Her howling subsided as she straightened herself. "This is a joke, right?" she asked, looking up at her friends.

They felt sorry for her but knew she wouldn't want their pity.

Enara shook her head and wiped a tear from Soren's flushed cheek. "Well, hon, we were due for an adventure."

"I call the front bench of the carriage!" Baz said excitedly, pushing up from his seat and sprinting for the door.

The girls' mouths dropped open as they looked after him.

"Last one out pays for the first night's lodging," he yelled from the front lawn.

"Should we tell him?" Enara asked.

"Nope," Soren replied, her mood lightening just a little.

"Look, lady, I know this is crazy … but we owe it to your father to at least find the truth in all this. You know he wouldn't have written that letter if he didn't mean every word."

"I know. I'm just in shock. I barely have myself together, and now I'm supposed to go into all this blind? Nothing makes sense to me right now." She picked at a hangnail, hissing when it drew blood.

"You know I stand by what I said before—you can put it in a box and pretend it never existed, or we can deal with it and move on. That choice hasn't changed."

"You know I can't do that." Soren sighed, biting her lip.

"I know."

"Well then, saddle up, bitch. I have a feeling we're in for a hell of a ride."

THE GIRLS WENT OUT FRONT TO DRAG BAZ BACK INSIDE. HE WAS practically vibrating with excitement but deflated when they reminded him that they had yet to know their destination.

The trio worked together to make some semblance of dinner, the map splayed open on the table. The parchment was inconsequential, showing the same islands and territories that they had all learned about in school. Everything was as they remembered. They were stumped.

"I got it!" Baz screeched, running in from the kitchen, causing Soren to choke on a grape as Enara coughed, inhaling her wine.

"The coffee stain!"

They raised their eyebrows in confusion.

"Look," Baz said, ecstatic. He flipped the map around and pointed to a brown smudge on the bottom left corner of Stelonbriar. "It's clearly marking a location," he finished, standing proudly.

Soren snorted, covering her mouth. "Sorry to break it to you, Baz, but I spilled coffee on that a few months back."

He looked at her, dropping his shoulders, and sat down with a *humph*. "Clearly, I need to work on my investigative skills."

Enara patted him on the back, knowing he was trying his best to help.

"Anyone else got any bright ideas?" Soren asked, wandering over to the front window and soaking in the last few bits of warmth from the day.

The sun was just starting to fall as the moon sang it a lullaby. The shadows from the trees stretched and moaned, rubbing their tired eyes. *It will be dark soon.*

She looked at the tree line, something clicking into place. "The stars!" she proclaimed, practically bursting. "Dad said something about the stars! Look!" she enthused, pointing to the letter. "Find your answers amongst the stars. That's it! That's the first clue! Dad would bring me out at night all the time to study the stars. He used to say they held secrets. If you listened hard enough, he said they would whisper them to you." She bounced up and down.

Enara smacked herself on the forehead. "I should have thought of that! I remember you mentioning it to me." She stood up, her chair sliding angrily across the floor. "There was an astronomy book on your father's shelf that I packed up earlier. Let me go grab it." She was halfway out the door before they could respond.

"I thought my idea was cooler," Baz huffed.

"Oh, don't be so hard on yourself." Soren chuckled as she ruffled his wavy hair. "I appreciate the effort."

Enara ran back in. "I got it!" She waved the book around triumphantly.

Soren snatched it out of her hands and rifled through the pages before coming to an abrupt stop.

Baz peeked over her shoulder and read out the chapter title. "*Avaris*. What's that?"

"Yeah." An affectionate smile spread across Soren's face. "It's my favorite constellation. Dad's favorite, as well." She flicked away a tear that had escaped its cage. "Avaris correlates with the old Vikarian saying of 'The Moment of the Universe,'" she explained. "There is a specific time of day, between four and five in the morning, that makes one feel closer to the heavens. It's also a good time to meditate, if you're into that sort of thing." She shrugged. "I always liked it because its tail is one of the brightest stars in the sky."

"Sounds cool," Baz mentioned.

"That's beautiful, Soren." Enara touched her shoulder as Soren pulled out a slip of paper that had been tucked between the pages and began reading aloud.

"Looking inward, you will find,
The hidden eye of your mind,
A secret story buried deep,
Whispered to you in your sleep.
The spoils will be found below,
By the blazing torchlight's glow.

This ancient power holds a price,
Multiply the sacrifice.
A pool of tears holds the key,
The answer to the prophecy.
Practice caution in all things,
As evil follows on gilded wings.
Before the darkness can take flight,
Bathe in the oracle's light.
To find where you must begin,
Go to where the roots dig in."

As the last line tumbled out of her mouth, Soren knitted her brows. Her face was a mask of fierce determination. "I know where he wants us to go," she stated, sliding the map across the table. With a smug smile, she pointed to a city on the map that was littered with pictures of little trees.

"Eldrin?" Enara queried. "What's so special about Eldrin? I mean, other than the fact that it's the capital of Estelar."

Soren smirked. "I see your geography skills haven't faded much since the academy."

"My mother orders bandages for her shop from there. They have some of the best hemp weavers on this side of Entheas," Baz chimed in.

"Look at the surrounding waterways," Soren said, tracing the ink that wound down the parchment. "They look like the roots of a tree, and they all meet at the lake surrounding Eldrin. My dad once told me they call the city The Tree of Life. All the waterways are trade routes."

"Ah …" Baz nodded. "Routes, not roots."

"Of course," Enara said, "I heard they trade in more than just physical items. There is talk that they trade in information, too. I think he means for us to consult with an oracle there, maybe someone he knew before he died."

"That's my guess, too …" Soren picked at her nails. "So, what do you guys think?"

"What do you mean, *what do we think*?" Enara narrowed her eyes.

"You know you guys don't have to come. The burden was left to me by my father, and it will be dangerous. We have no idea what this Raven guy is capable of."

"Soren?"

"Yeah?"

"Shut up."

Soren smiled up at her best friend, a knowing look on her face. "You're not going to sit this one out, are you?"

"Not a chance in hell. Besides, one of us has to look after your sorry ass."

Soren laughed at that, plucking away at the food on her plate that had gone cold.

Baz started to speak with his mouth filled to the brim. "Hwey ugmm … Cwan I come twoo?" He suppressed a cough and chugged the remainder of Enara's drink.

"What about your moms, Baz? This isn't just a day trip to Estelar."

"We have been talking about me leaving the nest for a couple of months now." He shrugged. "You know, sow my oats and all that."

"You mean, spread your wings?"

"Yeah, that."

"And if we have to fight?"

"I'm not just all good looks, you know," he said seriously. "Unless you two forgot," he said haughtily, "I aced my hand-to-hand combat courses as well as melee weapons training." He stood tall and puffed out his chest to prove his point further.

He was only an inch or two taller than Enara, but they had to admit he had filled out nicely in the last year or so. Soren was the smallest of the three, standing at a whopping five-foot-three and weighing a little over a hundred and thirty pounds. She had often been the victim of short jokes, her petite frame earning her nicknames like "Pixie" or "Little One." It wasn't until after graduation that her curves had decided to present themselves, earning her attention from many of her previous classmates.

Enara was the only one of the three who never had any issues in school. She was top of the class in every academic course and was, without question, the best fighter. Male and female alike, she bested them all. In the first year, she'd sent the combat master's son to the medic's office after their first sparring match.

Soren's fighting skills, on the other hand, were a bit lackluster. She could manage, but she would consider herself slightly below average in comparison to her classmates. She did, however, excel in archery, and her knife skills were a force to be reckoned with. She attributed this to the many hours she'd spent in The Crow's Nest, playing bullseye with the throwing knives her father had gifted her for her nineteenth birthday. Her bow skills, she had gained from hands-on experience while hunting with her father. They had only gone out when supplies were running low and had been careful to use every bit of the animal they could. They were not trophy hunters and had had their fair share of run-ins with poachers over the last few years.

Enara had offered to tutor her in combat outside school hours, but Soren firmly believed four p.m. to bedtime was reserved for relaxation. Enara would shake her head as Soren stuffed her face in a book on the porch and sprint away to train on her own. Soren would often watch her, though, looking up from the pages in awe of the talent she possessed. She was ruthless.

Soren's father had kept trying to design a sparring dummy that could withstand more than a week of Enara's abuse, to no avail. Soren knew that a large part of Enara's skill came from her father drilling it into her since she had been old enough to swing her fists. She would often show up at Soren's house, bruised and hungry. She wouldn't be allowed to eat if she lost a skirmish which, until the later years, was more often than not. Soren would always pack a little extra in her lunch to share with her at school. Enara had refused the offerings for weeks until she lost three fights in a row. The poor girl had been wasting away, her skin stretched over her protruding bones like an animal hide laying out to dry.

They had tried to get her help, but Altair Montgrove was well-loved in Vreburn and was part of the council, making him near untouchable. He was a charmer and would brush it off as "kids being kids." Enara would sneak away at night to sleep in the woods behind her house when he drank so she wouldn't run the risk of him coming into her room to pick a fight. Her skin had grown tough over the years, and she could take most of the abuse with a straight face, but that only seemed to anger him more.

The worst part was he treated her brothers like gods. Rayden and Hawke had never felt his wrath or tasted the tang of blood on their lips. They had never had to hear their own bones crack or had to lie about where a black eye had come from. Enara never understood what she had done to deserve to be treated the way that she was by her father. She knew that her mother had given birth to a son before her, but he had died shortly after conception, and her father had never gotten over the loss.

Her mother loved her, but not enough to try to get between her and her father. When he drank, she would sneak away to her room, ignoring the screams that escaped Enara's lips. She felt sorry for her mother in a way. She knew she would never leave him, and after years and years of torture, Enara had finally had enough.

She'd arrived on Soren's doorstep one night, covered in blood. Her eyebrow had been split, and her arm had been bent in an unnatural position.

"Please don't make me go back," she'd begged, and Soren's father had not asked what had happened. He had simply taken her in, cleaned her up, creating a splint for her arm, and tucked her into Soren's bed while Soren had cozied up on the floor.

"You will never go back there again. If he steps foot on my property, I will not hesitate to kill him, and no one will find his body," he'd said, his voice like ice. "I am a professional, after all." Being an archeologist did come with extensive knowledge of where to hide a body.

Soren's father had never known the extent of Enara's treatment until that day. Honestly, neither had she. He would have done something sooner if he had and had scolded himself for not seeing the signs, considering his childhood had been much the same.

In his anger, he had gone to The Crow's Nest one night and had beaten her father within an inch of his life. Tarak had not been a violent man, but he hadn't been a small one, either. The scars from his past had strengthened his resolve.

The next day, Enara's brothers had dropped off her belongings in silence. Everyone in town had pretty much steered clear from them after that, apart from Baz, his moms, and a few others who had seen Altair's charismatic façade slip.

Soren didn't mind, though. She liked their secluded little corner of the earth. It was quiet here. Peaceful. She only wished that Enara hadn't had to suffer to make it happen.

She didn't talk about it much, and when she did, she would shut down for days, going for runs in the middle of the night to blow off steam and annihilating the newest practice dummy. She was a force to be reckoned with, and Soren was constantly amazed by her.

She looked back and forth between her friends in appreciation. "I would be lucky to have you both by my side. I love you guys."

"We love you, too, Sor," they said in unison.

With that, the trio cleaned up the rest of their spoiled dinner and got to packing. They savored those last few mundane moments together, joking in the dimly lit kitchen. They snacked on potato crisps and indulged in a few too many beverages before wobbling up the stairs to Enara's bedroom. They snuggled into her king-sized bed, giggling from the drink.

Enara and Baz dozed off in minutes, while Soren lay awake, begging sleep to come. All she received in return was a little voice warning her from the back of her mind.

Tomorrow, everything is going to change.

CHAPTER
THREE

As the golden light crested the dusty sill of the bedroom's second-floor window, Enara shifted in her sleep. She mumbled something about her father, her body twitching.

Baz, awoken by the movement, turned to face her. He took a moment to take in her features. Her burnished brown hair, tied into a mussed braid, shimmered bronze in the morning light. A frown rested on the bow of her lips, her arched brows furrowed in discomfort. He reached out and gently stroked her cheek until the tension dissipated.

She had shared some of her family history with him, yet she had avoided going into detail. He understood. Why would anyone want to relive the things she had survived? He often felt guilty that he was blessed with such supportive parents, while Enara was cursed with a demon for a father. The world was a broken place, but he hoped he could make her corner of it a little bit brighter.

He pulled the blanket up over her shoulders, covering the thin, white scars that marked her skin like cracks in a ceramic vase. Letting out a yawn, he then relaxed back into the folds of the comforter, closing his eyes.

His satisfaction was short-lived when Soren ran in, belting out a crisp, "Good morning, humans!" He hadn't even realized she wasn't still in the bed with them.

His cheeks reddened. "Maker, woman, you could give a guy a heart attack," he said, rubbing his neck.

"I will actually unalive both of you."

Soren and Baz shared a laugh as Enara sat up, groaning. Her hair was a tangled mess, and the bags under her eyes made it look like she had gone ten rounds in the sparring ring.

"What are you staring at?" she growled.

"Maker, someone woke up on the wrong side of the bed."

"Yeah, lady, you're in need of some serious TLC," Soren said sympathetically, handing her her favorite mug.

"Tell me about it. How long have you been up?"

"About an hour. I watched the sunrise out back. Couldn't fall back asleep."

"Yeah, I was dreaming about Dad again. I feel like garbage." Enara sighed into her coffee.

"Well, I feel full of vim, vigor, and vitality!" Baz chirped, jumping out of bed with a flourish.

"I hate you," Enara said, using her free hand to whip a pillow in his direction, narrowly missing his head.

"Hey!" he exclaimed, returning fire.

She batted it away, hiding her smile. She could never stay mad at him. He was like a golden retriever—full of energy and fiercely loyal. He was the exact opposite of her. She was all shades of black and gray next to his kaleidoscope of color. She thought back to the day they had met. The memory would always be one she kept close to her heart.

Enara had been indifferent in school. It was an escape from her home life, but she had always felt like the odd man out. The girls envied her because she had a brilliant mind and natural beauty. The boys steered clear out of fear her brothers would get involved. It was well known around school that if any guy showed interest in Enara, Rayden and Hawke would change their minds in a painfully efficient manner, no doubt following instructions given to them by their father in an attempt to keep her isolated.

Aside from the social aspect, she had excelled at pretty much everything, apart from creative arts. She would try to follow the lesson briefs, but her creations had always turned into something monstrous, so she had dropped the class. The instructor had said to create what you knew, and she had only known pain. The last thing she needed was to call more unwanted attention to herself. She was bullied enough outside of being a high school outcast.

On one particularly harrowing day, she had sat out in the courtyard, using the trunk of a large fir tree to block out the wind. Autumn had been digging in her roots early that year. She hadn't wanted to sulk around the hallways without Soren and had forgotten her jacket at home.

Her best friend had been invited to join her father on his most recent dig outside a small city in Braexmirth. They had invited her to join, but she'd declined, knowing her father would never allow it. So, she had sat there, shivering, going over her notes for her upcoming foreign languages exam, when Baz had strolled over, whistling an old folk tune.

He stopped when he saw her and said, "Hey, do you want my jacket? It's getting a bit chilly out here?"

Enara remembered thinking how odd it was that someone who didn't know her from a hole in the ground would just offer her their coat.

"Um … no, I'm okay. I'll be going back in soon."

"No problem. Do you want me to walk you?" he asked with a boyish grin, making his eyes glint in the afternoon sun.

"I don't even know you," she responded flatly. She tended to always have her guard up around the male population.

"Oh shit, I'm sorry! The name's Baz, short for Baztien. Last name's Greymark. I just transferred here a couple of weeks ago." He extended his hand to her, and she shook it firmly, noting the flecks of gold that peppered his almond-colored eyes.

"I'm Enara Montgrove," she replied curtly, "and I should get going before our handshake causes you a black eye."

"Are you threatening me, Miss Montgrove?" he asked, a devilish smile forming on his narrow lips.

"Ask any of your classmates; I am a danger to your health," she deadpanned.

"That's okay. I don't plan on making it past thirty, anyway." He shrugged, holding out his arm.

Enara shook off her surprise and linked her arm with his, her heart thawing a little. *It will be nice*, she thought, *to have more than one friend.*

She glanced up at him, feeling his warmth through his jacket. "Your funeral."

THE MORNING WENT BY QUICKLY AS THEY PACKED THE REST OF
the essentials into their respective rucksacks. Soren didn't have
much of an appetite, but Baz and Enara settled for scrambled eggs and a few orange slices. She watched them eat while
downing her third mug of coffee, having a feeling these quiet
moments would soon be few and far between.

Once they finished tidying up, they stepped out onto the
front porch, breathing in the scent of the earth.

"Well, this is it, I guess." Soren hesitated, taking one last
look at their home. "Anyone have anything insightful to say?"

"Onward!" Baz exclaimed, hopping down the two
front steps.

The girls rolled their eyes and followed the silly bastard
down the trail to town.

They stopped in the center of Vreburn's marketplace at
a local equestrian dealer to acquire a more efficient means
of transport. After haggling for over an hour, Soren handed
over two items from her father's collection. The crystallized
skull and miniature third-century statue were solid pieces and
would fetch a good amount of gold at auction.

Soren knew they were getting ripped off, but they couldn't
spare the time. She reluctantly let the merchant take them,
walking away with three sturdy horses in return.

Baz claimed the palomino filly for himself. "We were
meant to be. She is just as pretty as I am," he said proudly.

Enara pretended to hurl as the Arabian mare walked right
up and nuzzled her cheek. "Well, looks like you're the chosen one."

Soren chuckled as she reached up to put the bridle on the Friesian stallion. He reared back on his hind legs, snorting angrily.

"Whoa, whoa, boy." Soren put her arms up, trying to calm him. "It's okay, we're not going to hurt you. See?" She pulled a carrot from her rucksack, a peace offering.

He whinnied and paced back and forth, looking skeptical.

Soren sat on the ground in frustration, blowing the hair from her eyes.

Tentatively, the stallion approached her again, stretching its neck down to nibble at the carrot resting in her lap. As he did, their eyes locked, and something clicked into place. He seemed to sigh and bowed his head to hers.

She was momentarily taken aback. With a nervous breath, she leaned forward to meet him. They stayed like that for a moment, Baz and Enara staring in awe. After another minute, the onyx stud lifted his head and stood back, allowing Soren to push herself off the ground. She gently brushed his mane with her fingers, the fawn of his eyes blinking back at her.

"Shall we try this again?" she asked, holding up the bridle.

He blinked in response, and she placed the leather over his ears and let him take the mouthpiece in his own time. She stroked his muzzle. His coat was like velvet, making the skin of her hand look pale in comparison.

Soren was naturally tanned, thanks to her father, who had been born in Vakari, known for their rich brown skin and flowing black hair. She considered herself lightly toasted as the genes from her mother's side added a lightness to her skin. She had been born with brown hair but would often use pigment to dye it different colors. Her preferred style was a deep indigo, as she wore it now, though it would fade soon. She loved that it matched the color of the starry midnight sky.

She was never good at being feminine. Lining her eyes with charcoal and painting her cheeks with rose powder was never her strong suit. She couldn't style her hair beyond simple braids or a high ponytail. Then again, she never really needed to. Her talents lay elsewhere. She was nearly unmatched at the archery range, and her talent for throwing knives often helped her win bets with her former classmates. She had also taken out a knee or two playing soccer in the courtyards with the boys. She preferred to live her life with scrapes on her knees and a cold drink in her hand, cussing like she was being paid for it.

The unfortunate result of her behavior was that it had landed her in the outcast circle. She didn't mind, though. She had Enara, and Baz provided the comedic relief they both desperately needed. It had been the three of them against the world for four years now, though none of them knew how true that would be until now.

Soren was terrified. She would never admit it out loud, but she was. It took everything in her not to fall into a cataton-ic state from the panic building in her bones.

She finished putting the saddle on her noble steed then looked over to her friends. They were in a heated disagree-ment about who was better at equestrian studies. Soren muf-fled a laugh.

"Come on, you two; we still have to stop by your place." She nodded toward Baz.

This was the moment he had been dreading. Even though they had spoken about him going off on his own, his mothers were fiercely protective of him. They had adopted him when he'd been six, shortly after he had arrived in Ilastead. The fisherman traveling toward Saipea, who had found him, had said that it was a miracle he'd survived.

The storm that had killed his parents had taken out more than a few ships that day. The fisherman had been sent out to clean up the wreckage when he'd come across Baz floating on the broken vessel. He was the only survivor out of all the ships that had been sunk by Mother Nature's wrath. To this day, Baz avoided large bodies of water for fear of drowning.

He steeled himself, brushing his hair out of his eyes. "Let's get this over with then."

They trotted up to a small stone cottage a half mile down from the market square, tethering their horses to the wooden post. It was a quaint home, but it burst with joy and laughter. They had spent many nights here with Baz and his parents, enjoying all the amazing meals that Laraline would whip up. She was an amazing cook and taught ancient history at Voxridge.

Baz's other mother, Alondra, owned the apothecary in town and had developed the herbal medication that Soren used to combat her panic disorder. They were a lovely couple. Soren had always looked up to them. She would admire the way they walked hand-in-hand, unabashed, around the square. *That is how true love should be.* They paid no mind to those who gawked and screwed up their faces in disgust. Not everyone approved of their relationship, but they never cared. They loved each other, and that was all they needed.

Tarak had cared for them like sisters, and they would often try to set him up with the eligible ladies in town. He would always respond to their attempts by saying, "Soren is the only woman I need telling me what to do," to which they would all laugh.

Much like Soren, Baz, and Enara, the three parents had stuck together. Laraline and Alondra had stood by Tarak in the wake of his attack on Altair, happy that the man had finally gotten what he deserved. They had been horrified when they'd found out how he had been treating Enara. The six of them were a family, maybe not by blood, but in all the ways that mattered.

The three braced themselves and entered Baz's home. His mothers were cozied up on the couch; Alondra reading a book while Laraline massaged her feet.

When Baz walked in, Alondra placed her book on the side table and slipped her feet from her wife's hands, placing them into her fur slippers.

Laraline spoke first. "Hey, sweetheart, we were wondering if you were going to be home for dinner. Will you two be joining us?" she asked, looking at the girls.

"Um ... no, thank you," Soren stammered.

"We won't be around come nightfall," Enara finished, playing with the strap of her rucksack.

"Oh, no problem," she replied. "Are you two going to the show at the tavern tonight? We heard there was a folk group from Stelonbriar coming in to perform. We debated on going, but it was a long day, and Aly wanted to get off her feet." She smiled at her wife, who stuck her tongue out in response.

"Yeah, about that ..." Baz said, looking sheepish. "She means *we* won't be in town come nightfall."

"What exactly do you mean?" Alondra asked, rising from her spot on the sofa, her green eyes flashing in the firelight.

"Well, it's a long story," he started, "but the girls are going on a quest and require my protection." He puffed out his chest.

Enara smacked him on the back of the head. "The only thing we need protection from is your overinflated ego."

Baz cringed and shrugged.

"What he means to say," Soren stepped in, "is that my father left a very important task for me, and Baz has volunteered to join."

"Oh really?" Alondra said. "And, what exactly does this task entail?"

"Well …" Soren launched into a whole play-by-play of the last day and a half, the words rushing out of her mouth like water from a fountain. "And I can't promise he will return in one piece, but we need him. I promise we will protect him to the best of our abilities," she finished, holding in a breath.

His mothers shared a knowing look, entwining their fingers together. They knew their son, who loved fiercely and without question. He would go to the ends of the earth for his family.

Alondra spoke for the both of them, looking Baz straight in the eyes. "Are you sure you want to do this?"

"Yes, she would do the same for me," he said, all humor removed from his voice.

"Well then, you're going to need some help," Laraline said, her blonde hair waving back and forth as she sauntered out of the room.

Enara and Soren looked at Baz, eyebrows raised in question. He shrugged, unsure of what she meant, while Alondra stood there stoically.

Laraline returned a moment later, carrying a large, narrow crate, and laid it on the dining table.

"This," she said, cracking open the top with a kitchen knife, "was your grandfather's." She set the lid to the side, and the trio leaned in to see what the box contained, eyes glistening.

Alondra stood beside her wife. "We were saving it for when you got married, but it will probably be of more use to you now." Only adding to their confusion, Alondra reached in with both hands and pulled out a pointed object covered in a dusty sheet. She unraveled it, shaking off the dust to reveal the hilt of a longsword and its leather sheath.

"Holy shit," Baz said, eyes as wide as dinner plates.

"Mind your tongue." Alondra smacked his shoulder.

"I remember this from the photo at his funeral. Wasn't he gifted this or something?"

"Yes, it was a gift from Lord Krikseth for his service in the Battle of Braexmirth." She smiled, offering it to him. "Now it's yours."

Baz's adoptive grandfather had served in the Draestellion infantry during Braexmirth's separation from Patrivah. Braexmirth's army had not been strong enough on its own with Patrivah paying off Boa-Ren to use his forces.

Draestel would not sit back and let their allies be ravaged by senseless war, so they had sent in their troops to assist. The Draestellion army had attacked Boa-Ren's soldiers from behind, and they had fled. Without their ally, Patrivah had backed off, knowing the odds were no longer in their favor.

Baz's grandfather had been the one to kill the Xian Dao troop leader, gaining him personal favor with the mining lord. When the battlefields had cleared, he'd invited Greymark Senior to dine with him in the Braexmirth's capital. It was there he had been gifted the sword.

When he had passed away, the sword fell to Laraline, and since she was against violence of any kind, she had put it in storage for a time when it would be needed.

"I can't take this," Baz said, his face falling as he backed away.

Lara rounded the table and put her arms on either side of her son's face. "Sweetheart, you are strong and kind. You are selfless and a protector of those who cannot protect themselves. You are more than deserving. He wanted you to have this. Please …" She took it from her wife's hands and offered it to her son. "Just promise you'll use it well and make your way home to us when all this is done." Her eyes brimmed with tears.

Baz reached out with shaking hands and took the sword from her grasp. "I'll make you proud, Mothers." With one swift movement, he unsheathed the sword, pointing it upward and admiring the metalwork.

Enara and Soren gaped at its beauty.

The weapon was honed to perfection and glinted dangerously under the light of the dying flames. The hilt was inlaid with obsidian, as dark as the deepest depths of the ocean. Two translucent pieces jutted out on each side, resembling the wings of a dragonfly. The blade itself was made of an unfamiliar metal. It shone silvery blue with a pearlescent undertone. It was magnificent. Even the sheath was made of the finest leather.

Baz couldn't help the smile that spread across his face. The metalsmiths in Olecastor were said to be unmatched, and now he knew why.

"I don't know how to thank you guys. This is the best gift you could have given me, apart from the day you took me in as your own," he choked out. Then he put the sword down on the table and pulled his moms in for a hug. "I love you guys."

"We love you, too, sweetheart. Just get home safe to us, okay? Write us when you can," Lara said, squeezing him hard.

"Hey, you two," Alondra said, gesturing to the girls, who were both crying silent tears, "get in here."

The five of them stood there, holding each other, no one wanting to break away first. Each of them knew there was a real possibility that this could be the last time they saw each other. So, they stayed there, breathing each other in, laughing and crying, and hoping and loving until the fire's final embers burned out.

CHAPTER
FOUR

Celandine looked out over the edge of Anistera, observing the world below. The ivory tower that she occupied sat at the edge of the world and was where she went when she wanted to be alone.

She could see Entheas from here. The tiny world was a blue and green orb, shining amongst the stars. It was her father's most treasured creation, and it was easy to understand why. Humans were funny little things, and she was forever fascinated by them. She often wondered what it must be like to live as one of them and have a will of your own. She longed to live in a world free from the responsibilities of her position within the Celestial realm.

She leaned back on the settee and stretched out her long legs, brushing out the tangles in her golden hair with her fingers. Then she closed her eyes and daydreamed about the days she'd spent in Entheas.

Celestials were able to visit from time to time but could never stay more than twenty-four hours. Their bodies were not designed to survive beyond the gates of Anistera, and the provinces of Entheas were no exception. Celandine would spend those fleeting moments amongst the mortals, relishing in the urgency in which they lived their lives. They were beautiful and flawed in so many wondrous ways. They could be ruthless and hateful beyond measure, waging wars and killing without conscience. But they could also be unyielding in their faith. They cherished every moment given to them, no matter how small. And, above all … above all, they loved.

It was not that Celestials did not grow to care for one another. It was just different, as they were all designed to be self-sufficient. They would connect and build relationships to keep their population up, but since they lived endlessly, it was not common practice to form a physical bond. They were timeless, living for centuries, and spent their time traveling to the other worlds that her father had created. They did not age, or want, or lust, or need, or love. They were capable, but given their long lives, such things became tedious.

For ages now, mated pairs were hand-picked by her father, and the process was never questioned. Mated pairs were endlessly happy. The only downfall being that their life force waned when they lost their mate. It was the only way a Celestial could meet their end, apart from losing their grace or dying in battle.

The entirety of Anistera owed their lives to the great Architect. He was the creator of all things. No one knew how long he had wielded the power of the Oculus, only that he was the reason for their creation. He could have continued to populate Anistera with the power he possessed, but he enjoyed experimenting. That was how Entheas had come into being. Living in a world based on perfection, with beings that were unendingly loyal to him, had gotten boring. Her father had given the humans the gift of free will and had designed a world with a harsher climate to see how they would adapt and overcome. He loved his children, but every Celestial knew that Entheas was by far his most favored creation.

Every chance she got, Celandine would visit the human world, basking in their lands like a wildflower soaking up the first rains of spring. It gave her new life and hope for what was to come. She often wished she could extend her stay, but to linger in the human world would cost Celandine her grace. It was said to be the most excruciating pain a Celestial could experience. She would become a shadow of herself, and her motivation to live would seep out of her human form, as blood would from a wound. They were not created to survive in an imperfect world. A day-long visit would require a month in Anistera to replenish their energies before they could return.

Every thirty days, she would float down to the realm below, using her powers to grant miracles and spread joy. She never interfered with free will, only helped things along that were already meant to be. Every now and then, she would save a life that was about to be unjustly cut short.

The humans she did encounter knew she was not one of them, but seeing as she was not a danger to them, they did not fret. The connections she made grew over the years, and it warmed a part of her chest she had not felt since she had first been made.

She had visited Entheas once every month for the last eight centuries, and the humans had since named her Saint Celandine, the ageless beauty who granted wishes to those she deemed worthy. She was never one to place importance on titles, but this one meant much to her. It made her feel like she belonged with them.

Longing to join them, she had even asked her father to use his powers to make it possible, but it was not meant to be. He was stern when he'd told her, "The Oculus grants your mother and I the power to create, and to destroy, but we do not hold the power to change. To do so would create disastrous results for us all. I am sorry, my sweet Celandine."

She had half a mind to go against her father's wishes and stay in Entheas past her Celestial body's allotted timeframe, but the burial hall was a stark reminder of what the quest for freedom granted you. So, for now, short-lived moments in the human world would have to suffice.

Celandine steeled herself and rose from the settee, her waist-length hair flowing free from tangles. "Until next time, my sweet mortals." With one final glance at the world below, she turned and descended the steps, her footfalls pattering on the stone.

Her father had requested a meeting, and she was happy to oblige.

As she crossed the terrace leading to the Hall of Creation, she squared her shoulders and schooled her features into a mask of compliance.

"My dearest Celandine," her father boomed from the end of the room.

"Father," she replied, bowing when she reached him. She brushed her fingertips over his sandaled feet and grazed her forehead, a sign of respect. "You summoned me?" She was impatient, wanting to skip the pleasantries.

"Come. Join me in the assignment chamber."

Celandine followed close on his heels as he entered the official office of the Architect. He went by his formal title when the occasion called for it, but he preferred to be referred to as Father.

He was not their father in the physical sense. However, he had created the first of the Celestials in his image. Even those conceived from mated pairs had a little piece of him in them. It would be more accurate to call him Great Father, as it was more in the ceremonial sense. Regardless of the circumstances, they owed their entire existence to him.

Though they liked to speculate, no one knew who had come first—the power of creation or the creator himself. The only being who might have known the answer would have been his mate, Aurora. However, she had passed many decades ago, and the Architect had never been the same since. Without his partner, the power of the Oculus had gone cold, and his strength had begun to wane.

The artifact could only be used when the blood from two mates was placed inside. Her father had yet to choose a successor, though she had her suspicions. Once a heir was chosen, the Oculus would fall to them, lying in wait until a new mating bond was formed.

Celandine clasped her hands together, awaiting her father's instructions.

"As you know, without Aurora by my side, I am fading. It is time I name an heir so that the power of the Oculus can be passed on."

She waited in silence for him to continue, unsure of where her place was in all this.

"I have chosen to name Adriel as next in line to be Architect once I am gone."

Celandine scoffed.

"You disagree with my choice?" he asked, his tone stern.

"Of course not, Father …"

"But?"

"He's just so …"

He raised his eyebrows. "So?"

"So arrogant. I would hate for you to boost his ego any higher. He is already the commander of Anistera's armies. I worry that naming him as the next Architect Regent would overinflate his already large head."

He let out a soft laugh. "My child, I understand your concerns, but you need to trust that I am making the best decision for us all."

"Of course, Father."

Adriel was striking—there was no denying that—but he was narcissistic, and his icy-blue eyes were cold and calculating. He had torn down other worlds with no sympathy and lived for barking orders. He had earned a nickname among the ranks. They called him the Raven King, on account of his hair. It was pitch black and buzzed on the sides, the top jutting up like tiny talons ready to strike. He was excessively tall, towering half a head above all others. Celandine would have found him attractive, if their encounters hadn't required him to open his mouth.

"Forgive me, Father, but I fail to see what part I play in your decision."

"As you know, the Oculus will only work properly with mated blood."

She nodded, stiffening. She had a feeling of where he was going with this and was not sure she was ready to hear it.

"I was hoping that you would agree to pair with him."

She clutched her chest as if he had struck her, the air rushing out of her lungs. "Father, I—"

"I would not ask it of you if there was a better match."

"He's vile."

The Architect shook his head, disappointed. "He needs guidance. I am entrusting you with this."

Celandine calmed herself for his sake. "As you wish, Father." She looked down with a resigned expression.

Her father reached forward and tilted her chin up to face him. "There must be balance in all things. It is my hope that, over time, you will learn to care for each other."

"Unlikely," she whispered under her breath.

He looked into her eyes, waiting.

"I will do my duty to Anistera."

"That's my girl."

She turned to leave when he called out to her.

"And Celandine?"

"Yes, Father?"

"Do try, would you?"

"Yes, Father." She nodded then left the room.

ADRIEL LOOKED UP THROUGH HIS LONG EYELASHES AT HIS MAKer picking the dust from the office's shelves out of his fingernails. His father had just told him he was to be named Architect Regent, to which he should have been elated. After a few hundred millennia, the old god had finally decided it was time to pass the torch. *And who better to decree as his successor than his oldest and strongest creation?* Adriel was frustrated at the caveat his father had imposed upon his coronation, however. Adriel was to choose a consort.

"No one being should possess the infinite power of creation alone. You must find a counterpart who will keep you honest, as Aurora did for me. Then and only then will you be able to acquire the power of the Oculus."

He understood the necessity but loathed the idea of being latched to another indefinitely.

"Father, is there no way around the mating? I should not be required to do something so beneath me."

"You know as well as I that the Oculus only works with the power of two. My instructions are final."

Adriel rolled his eyes. He hated when his father went all Architect on him.

"Adriel, my son, this is a decision that needs to be made with the utmost care. The partner you choose will be bonded to you for life. You will have to be equals in all things."

Equals? I have no equal.

"Yes, Father, I understand."

"Might I make a suggestion?"

"You are the Maker of all things; I would expect no less."

"I thought you might want to consider Celandine. I know you haven't seen each other much since you became commander, but I believe her warm soul might help cast the shadows from your eyes."

Adriel straightened his spine. "I'll take your suggestion under advisement. Now, may I be excused? I must check on my forces. They just returned from Ealuroth."

"You may."

He walked out of the hall, his overcoat trailing behind him. His boots clacked angrily as he mulled over his father's suggestion. *Celandine.* He flared his nostrils in annoyance. She was a know-it-all. All legs and no curves. The idea of being bound to her for the rest of his days left a sour taste in his mouth.

Pushing open the intricate wooden doors, he gazed across the promenade. For a moment, he let himself imagine what it would feel like to see all of Anistera gathered to celebrate his ascension. His eyes shone bright with triumph. He would soon be the master of all creation.

LATER THAT EVENING, THE ANNOUNCEMENT WAS MADE TO A smaller group of attendees, most of which were his early creations, coming into being shortly after Adriel.

The commander stood proud at the entrance to the hall, armor glinting like polished glass. A devilish smile hid his satisfaction. *Soon, I will rule you all.*

After making a small speech, he descended the steps, chin held high for all to see. A few of his comrades rushed in to shake his hand and congratulate him on his upcoming inauguration. Adriel soaked up the attention like a dry sponge. The power of the Oculus was so close he could practically taste it. All he had to do was win the affection of Lady Celandine. *I do enjoy a challenge.*

He sauntered home, trying to drum up ways to woo Celandine as he hopped in the shower. He stood under the warm water, letting it beat against the muscles of his back. He almost felt sorry for the habitants of Entheas. *How do they function without electricity and plumbing?*

He washed himself with a luffa, the suds smelling of citrus and sandalwood. The steam fogged up the mirror, blurring his reflection. He shut off the water and hopped out, wrapping a towel around his waist. It felt good to wash off the sweat of the day.

Though his father had designed him to be in impeccable shape, he still went to the training grounds every day. He needed his troops to see that they were required to work for everything that they received.

He lived in the war master's quarters in the training hall, and his suite was the largest in Anistera, apart from the Architect's. It would be different for him to live in another part of the realm, but the perks outweighed the possible discomfort.

He changed into his dress whites then headed to the central part of the training center to meet with his second-in-command. General Corvus stood at attention, awaiting his orders.

"Commander." He saluted.

Adriel's mouth curved as he raised his hand, saluting in return. "At ease, Soldier." His smooth voice dripped with authority. "How did the raids go in Ealuroth?"

"As expected, sir. The locals did not put up much of a fight."

Adriel rubbed his hands together with satisfaction. "Wonderful. I'll have your full report on my desk by the end of the day."

"Yes, sir." General Corvus bowed his head.

"You and your men can take the next week off. Enjoy yourselves."

"Thank you, sir." He saluted again then marched from the room, leaving the commander with his thoughts.

CHAPTER
FIVE

After bidding Baz's parents goodbye, the friends mounted their horses and headed through the market square. They stopped by a stand for some lunch, enjoying the fresh produce that had recently been shipped in from Stelonbriar. Then they hydrated their transportation at the troughs that lined the edge of the square, grabbing some last-minute necessities. They filled their rucks then headed toward the dirt path that led out of the city.

As they reached the town limits of Vreburn, they all took one final look back. Realization set in. They were leaving, and they might never come back.

They had all spent their formative years here and felt like they were walking away from everything they knew. Though Soren had traveled often with her father, she always felt grounded here.

The capital of Draestel was a decent-sized town, but it felt more country than city. Most of the inhabitants' homes speckled the countryside with a few small groupings choosing to live closer to town for convenience.

Soren was happy that her father had chosen to live out of town. It made sense for Alondra and Laraline to stay close to the market, as it allowed for less travel time to the apothecary, but the Nightsongs preferred their secluded property. Soren never minded that it was a few miles journey to town when they needed something, and Enara was more than happy to put distance between her and her father.

"Last chance, you two. Are you sure you want to do this?" Soren mused.

"Did you not see the sword?" Baz stroked the leather sheath affectionately. "I need an excuse to use it."

"You are such a man-child." Enara rolled her eyes. "Soren, for the last time, yes. We are with you till the end, lady."

"Yeah, you're stuck with us."

Soren's heart fluttered in appreciation, and she blinked the mist from her eyes. She never knew what she had done to deserve friends like them, but she was forever grateful that they were by her side.

They rode on in silence for most of the afternoon, Baz humming quietly in the background, with the faint buzzing sound of bees collecting the last bits of nectar before the frost came in. It was the beginning of autumn, and they were fortunate that it was not as rainy as it usually was this time of year. Bordering the Emerald Narrows meant that their town got more precipitation than the more central parts of Draestel.

Soren loved the rain. On nights when it stormed, she would climb out her window and sit under the roof's edge to watch the lightning put on a show. It gave her an adrenaline rush, feeling the electricity flow through her veins as the thunderclaps shook the house beneath her.

Enara always thought she was crazy. Storms made her uncomfortable, and she was not a particular fan of sudden, loud noises. It brought up too many bad memories.

Though their opinions differed in that regard, they did both love to go tree-shaking. After a big storm, they would go out into the trees, grabbing the trunks of the smaller ones, making their own rain. The droplets would slide off the leaves in a gentle shower, and they would dance around and laugh as the water soaked their clothes. They would do this for hours until the chill of the rain filled their bones. Then they would run inside, shivering, and plop down in front of the fireplace, drinking hot cocoa with looks of contentment on their faces.

"Hey, do you guys remember the storm season a couple years back?"

"How could I forget?" Baz's eyes glazed over, his thoughts trailing back. The rains had raised the water level so high that the Boreal River had started to overflow. Baz had volunteered to join the crews building up sandbanks to stop the few homes that lined it from being damaged.

"Did those guys ever pay for that boy's death?" Enara asked.

"I'm actually not sure," Soren replied.

Baz winced. "I feel so sorry for his father."

The night before the crews had gone out, one of the councilmen's sons had gone to check out the river with his friends. They had been drinking, and he had slipped down a steep edge, falling into the churning water. It was three days before his friends had fessed up. By the time they had issued the search, there was nothing left to be found.

Soren remembered the look on Baz's face when they had officially announced his death six weeks later. She could see the heartbreak in his eyes, knowing that if it weren't for that kindly fisherman, that could have been him.

"They never should have been out there." Enara shook her head in disbelief.

"Hey, it's nothing we haven't done before. We were just smarter about it."

"I don't want to talk about it anymore," Baz said, stopping his horse abruptly and jumping down. The Palomino whinnied in surprise, and he reached up to calm her. "It's okay, Ellie. Shh … girl." Her name was Eleanor, but Baz preferred Ellie.

She relaxed into his touch, and then he led her to a nearby tree.

"I guess we should give them a bit of a break," Enara said, following suit. She trussed up her horse next to his, giving it a quick pat, then sat down on the side of the road, opening her rucksack. "Want some?" she asked, holding up some deer jerky.

Baz grabbed a piece without saying anything, making her frown.

"Thanks. I needed a snack," Soren said, taking two. Then she walked over to Baz, feeling bad for bringing it up.

"Hey, I'm sorry."

His head dropped, and he sighed. "It's okay. It's just hard to think about sometimes."

"I shouldn't have said anything."

"It's fine. I just miss my mom and dad. I can't even remember what their voices sounded like." He pulled a twig off a nearby tree, tearing off the pine needles one by one.

Soren awkwardly shifted her weight from one foot to the other. She wasn't sure what to say. She had never been good at helping others deal with grief. She could barely deal with her own.

Enara came up from behind, grabbing Baz's hand. He dropped the twig, looking up at her.

"They would be proud of you, you know."

He stared into her eyes, the sadness in his melting away, and took in a calming breath. "Got any more of that jerky?"

They continued their journey, the road stretching out ahead of them, looking more foreboding. The weight of the task ahead bared down on each of them like a tidal wave. They were resting in a low tide, just waiting for the wall of water to rise up and pull them out to sea.

After a few more hours, Baz asked, "Are we there yet?" Dusk was settling on the horizon, casting long shadows across the trail.

"Seriously, Baz, are you five?" Enara groaned.

"We're almost there," Soren interrupted. "The river is just around this bend." Sure enough, about half a mile further, the trail opened up to reveal a softly flowing river. Soren knew this area well, as her father would bring her up this way for hunting trips.

"We can set up camp here," she said, blinking back the tears that had formed in her eyes. Her father had loved this place. "Baz, can you help Enara set up a lean-to? I'm going to do a quick canvas of the area and see if I can rustle us up a hot meal."

"Can do, El-Capitan," Baz replied, pulling a hatchet from his rucksack.

"Hey, pretty boy, I'm going to get a fire going first. I'll join you in a minute," Enara said, twirling the flint in her hand.

"Sounds good. I'll clear out a spot."

They got to work setting everything up while Soren dropped her pack and disappeared into the trees. Once she was out of earshot, she let out a rough breath. The cold ocean of grief lingered at the edge of her heart, threatening to plunge her under.

She had so many fond memories of this place. She had caught her first fish here, felled her first doe, had learned how to make the best snares. After a long day's hunt, her father and she would curl up by the warm fire and sing folk songs, savoring every last bite of their well-earned meal.

As an academic, Tarak had been a surprisingly talented hunter and had taught her to respect the animals. "You must appreciate the creature that feeds you," he'd said. "We hunt out of necessity, not sport. We do not enjoy the kill. We must remember that we are of this earth, too. When we die, we will become the earth that feeds them. Take only what you need and nothing more."

She wiped away a droplet that had escaped her tear duct, her spine going stiff when she heard a branch shift overhead. She looked up to see a raven peering down at her. Its beady eyes were miniature black holes. It was like no raven she had seen before, as its feathers were creamy and smooth, like fresh milk. It seemed to tilt its head, assessing her. Then, with a swift flap of its wings, it was gone.

Soren only had a moment to wipe the shock off her face when the crunch of dried leaves from her right captured her attention.

There, just a hundred yards away, stood a doe. She was a beautiful little thing. *She can't be more than two years old.* She hated when they were young, but they needed to maintain their strength.

She double-checked that there was no fawn in sight then lifted her bow. In one fluid movement, she notched an arrow, took aim, and let it fly. It was over quickly. The arrow embedded broadside, allowing the animal to bleed out in seconds. It did not suffer.

Soren jogged over, throwing her bow across her back and pulled out her hunting knife. She made quick work of the field dressing and cut off any other non-essentials for the wolves to find.

She was small but had always been strong for her size, easily carrying the doe back to camp and dropping it by the fire with a huff.

"Soups on!" she said triumphantly, grinning from ear to ear.

"Shit, Soren, looks like we're eating good tonight!" Baz cheered.

"Hey, can I get a hand with these branches?" Enara muffled through the thicket.

"*Oops*, sorry. Coming! Soren brought us a whole deer for dinner!"

"Thank the Maker. I'm starving."

The trio roasted the meat over the fire, Soren taking care to dry out the leftovers to pack for later. Then they sat back, satiated, rubbing their full bellies.

Enara had pulled off her worn leather boots to let her feet breathe. It was getting dark now, the sun playing hide and seek with the warrior on the moon.

"I see why your dad brought you out here, Soren," Enara said softly, poking the fire with a long branch. "It's peaceful."

She looked into the distance, caging her tears. "Yeah, it is."

"We should make this a regular thing," Baz said, "after all this is over."

They all felt the weight of his words. *After.* It was the whisper of a promise that none of them could keep. There were so many questions and little to no answers. A map and a poem from a dead man were not much to go on, and they knew that whoever had taken his life would be coming for them, too. It was only a matter of time.

"Well"—Enara stretched, grabbing her boots—"I think we should turn in for the night. It's still another two-days ride to Eldrin and, as you saw this morning, I am in desperate need of some beauty sleep."

"You said it, not me." Baz chuckled, earning him a playful shove. He flashed Enara a winning smile. "I call little spoon!" Jumping up from his place by the fire, he dove toward their makeshift shelter.

"Maker, help me." Enara stifled a laugh and crawled in after him.

"I'll be right behind you guys. I just want to spread the embers out a bit."

Once she knew they were no longer at risk for starting a forest fire, she padded into the brush for a much-needed bathroom break. After she finished, she visited the horses, giving them each a few bedtime carrots and stroking their manes. "Get some rest. We have a long day tomorrow."

They whinnied in response, nuzzling one another.

Soren smiled at the sight then glanced up to the sky. It was a cloudless night, and the stars winked at her playfully.

"Soren? You coming?" Enara beckoned.

"Yeah, coming." She took one last look upward, wondering what secrets the stars carried and if they might whisper them in her dreams.

SOREN SAT UP, A SHEEN OF SWEAT LICKING HER SKIN. SHE WAS breathing hard, and it took a moment to slow her heart rate. It was still dark. She must have only been out for a few hours. She could make out the silhouettes of her friends, still heavily under the dream fairy's spell. She got up, quietly slipping out from the layer of furs and relishing the cool breeze on her hot skin.

The moon hung brightly in the sky, and the world was quiet. She could hear the faint rush of the river nearby and the rustle of leaves as the wind wrapped her arms around them. The embers had faded to black, but the smell of the fire lingered on her clothes.

She reached for her canteen to splash water on her face when a distant voice whispered to her.

"Hello, little bird." It sounded like the caress of silk on bare skin.

She whipped around, her breathing ragged, her eyes trying to find purchase in the shadows. She reached for her bow, coming up empty. *Shit.* It was still in the lean-to.

"Who's there?" Her voice was laced with fear.

"Don't worry, little bird; I won't hurt you," it crooned.

"Show yourself, or I swear I'll choke the life out of you with my bare hands," she seethed.

"Promises, promises." The voice was an invitation coming from behind her.

She spun again, turning face-first into a man's chest. It was bare and shone alabaster in the moonlight. Smooth and as fine as porcelain, it was cool to the touch, and Soren could feel the muscles tensing under her fingertips.

She took in shallow breaths and tilted her head up to assess this strange man. Before she could see his face, however, everything went black and she sat up in the tent, accidentally hitting Baz in the face with a rogue elbow.

"What the hell, Sor!" he cried out, holding his nose, "I think you made my nose bleed."

Enara shot up, sucking in a breath. "What's happening? Is everyone okay?" Sleep clouded her vision.

"Yeah, it's fine. Soren just tried to take me out in my sleep."

"I am so sorry. Bad dream. Here, let me look." She lifted his hand away, assessing the damage. It was a little red, but nothing a good breakfast wouldn't fix. "I think you'll live," she joked, mussing his coppery hair.

"Gee, thanks." But he smiled, rolling up off his makeshift bed and throwing on his white cotton tunic.

"I guess it's as good a time as any to get on the road, then," Enara grumbled, pulling her fitted trousers on.

Soren nodded. "I'll muster up some breakfast."

After they refueled and saddled up the horses, the friends continued on, following the path on the other side of the river.

The next two days went by in much the same manner—travel, eat, rest, repeat. Each night, Soren lay her head down, wondering if the stranger would return in her dreams. Much to her disappointment, he did not appear again. However, she could feel his presence was important somehow. If only she could figure out who he was.

She was lost in thought when the horses came to an abrupt halt at a small cabin on the edge of the adjoining river. They were still half a days' ride from Eldrin and were ready to take a break from being on horseback. They would need to continue their journey on the river rather than traveling beside it. The horses would not make the trek when the river narrowed to the cliff's edge farther down.

Soren did not want to say goodbye to their four-legged friends. She had grown rather attached to them over the last few days.

She took a moment to nuzzle them all, giving an extra thanks to her dark-haired companion. She sent a little prayer to the Maker that they would meet again and handed the reins over to the wrinkled man who owned the cabin. His skin was a hard leather from too many hours in the sun, but his eyes were kind.

"I will properly care for them until you return, miss." He patted her hand. "I have a stable up the path there that I will hold them in for safekeeping until you return my boat."

She grasped his hand. "Thank you. And please, take this as payment. We do not know how long our journey will take." She extended her hand, holding out a few pieces of silver.

He closed her fist around it. "Keep it." He smiled and pointed down to the docks. "Take any canoe you like. We will be waiting here for your safe return." With that, he walked away, all three horses trotting happily after him.

The three friends smirked at each other then loaded the necessities into the largest canoe available. After scarfing down the rest of the fresh produce and some dried meat, they hopped aboard.

It was only a couple hours upriver to Eldrin, so they took shifts rowing, chatting casually to pass the time. The afternoon sun warmed their skin while a light breeze skimmed across the river's surface. The trees lining the water's edge provided enough shade that they did not need to worry about getting sunburned.

It was afternoon, and the trio had regained much of their energy. The canoe required little effort to navigate, almost as if it knew the path.

The river narrowed, and the tree line became dense as their excursion led them upstream to the entrance of the trade city. A dock jutted out up ahead on the right-hand side, a uniformed man standing at the edge, holding his arm out for them to stop. Not that the action was necessary, as there was a heavy wall of vines and foliage blocking their path. Baz figured the stance made him feel good about himself and hid the smirk on his face.

"What is your business in Eldrin?" the guard asked, puffing out his chest.

"We seek business with the Oracle," Soren said, stone-faced.

The guard looked back and forth between them. Then, with a resigned sigh, he pulled on the wooden lever adhered to the side of the dock, motioning them through. "Welcome to The Tree City."

CHAPTER
SIX

Celandine assessed herself one last time in the mirror of the dressing room, admiring her reflection. She was not one to boast about herself, but she was grateful to the Architect for gifting her such beauty. Her sharp features and flowing blonde hair caught much attention during her days in Entheas. She had grown into her body well and had many admirers. She appreciated their intentions, but her existence was so much more than her good looks.

Her blue-green eyes looked back at her with a grim expression. Celestials were all made relatively equal, apart from Adriel, but she always felt that she had been given a little something extra. She had deduced that her father had made her this way for a reason, and the feeling was disconcerting.

She had been summoned to a meeting with Adriel tonight. The commander of Anistera's armies had always rubbed her the wrong way. Celandine felt there was something off about him—the way he looked at others like he was better than them, holding his head a little too high. She never understood why they had an army in the first place, since they had no need for one, not really. Now and then, they would be dispatched to disperse discontent amongst certain worlds but, for the most part, they were used as scouts.

The Architect thrived on hearing stories from the other places he had created. He was quite eccentric. She truly loved him above all things and had only agreed to this match for his benefit. Besides, the need to obey would have forced her hand, even if she had tried to refuse.

When they had been created, her father had not intended for them to obey his every whim in the literal sense. The power of the Oculus was finicky, and you had to create everything with specific intent. He had only wanted them to obey when he needed help to keep peace on Anistera, but the effects had been amplified. The result was that the Celestials thrived on his every word. They had the freedom to act on their own accord, but if Father requested something, they all agreed without question.

Over the years, Celandine had adjusted her mindset to match the rest of theirs by just going along with his wishes. He was a kind patriarch and, apart from the odd request here and there, he didn't ask for much.

She wondered idly if Adriel would inherit the power over them that their father had. The idea made her skin crawl. She loathed to think what he would do if he was given the chance to use them as puppets.

She set aside her concerns. As Father had said, he would not have asked this of her if it weren't meant to be. Adriel could not be all bad if he was fated to be her mate. She had to give him credit where it was due. He was respected among his ranks and adored by the majority of the realm.

Celandine understood why Father had chosen her—she was his opposite. He had created them to balance one another. His first and second creations were destined to wield the power of creation together. Her, the glowing ember; him, the icy shadow.

She stood from the chaise and smoothed her gown. She had gone more to the formal side this evening to make a good impression. The rich, emerald fabric clung to her in all the right places, and her heels were crafted from the finest strands of gold. The opal belt accentuated her small waist and glinted beautifully in the realm of light.

A light breeze fluttered across her bare collarbones, and she shivered. Letting out a final breath, she relaxed her features and walked out to meet her fate.

Adriel's mouth gaped open when she entered the room. This was not the female he remembered when they had first been made. She was immaculately designed. Every surface was hand-crafted to perfection.

He would have to thank his father later. He never would have thought them a match before, but now …

She is stunning.

Her gown showed just enough that it left him wanting more, his fingers itching at the thought. Celestials were not designed to want as humans did but were still gifted the ability to enjoy each other on a physical level, if they so chose. He was not disappointed at the idea of enjoying her body for the rest of his days. He practically salivated at the thought, raking her with his eyes.

"Adriel." She curtsied formally, extending her hand.

He kissed it gently, bowing in return. "Lady Celandine." He looked up, his smile radiating. "I am pleased you could join me."

"Yes, well, Father insisted."

"That may be so, but I appreciate it all the same." He gestured toward the dais, and she breezed past him, her hips swaying sensuously. He stifled a growl of appreciation as she sat down on the lounge.

"Now, no need for formalities. Father asked. I have come. What now?" Her response was unexpected, and he coughed to cover his bewilderment.

"As you know, I have been named to take Father's place as the Architect when he steps down—"

"Yes, I attended the announcement." Her face was a calm mask.

"And if you know our histories, I am sure you can guess why he has asked you to join me here tonight."

She nodded as she gazed across the violet sky. Twilight was sneaking up on them quickly, and the above would darken soon.

"Father has assigned me as your mate," she said plainly.

"Ah, he told you."

"Even if he hadn't, it didn't take much to put the pieces together. We are his first and second; it only makes sense that he designed us as a pair." She looked down at her hands, deep in thought.

"Are you disappointed?" he huffed, crossing his arms.

"Would it matter if I was?" She felt no need to stifle her honesty.

He glowered. "You should be grateful that you were chosen. I could have had my pick of any being in this realm."

She shifted to face him, her turquoise eyes boring into his. "I am here to fulfill my duties to our father, nothing more."

His eyes narrowed in annoyance. "And how do you expect to create a strong mating bond with that kind of attitude?" His voice had sharpened to a knife's edge.

"Well, I've heard that fondness comes with time," she said, standing. "Maybe in another millennia or two, we could have a hope of establishing something."

His nostrils flared as he leaned forward, his breath hot on her face. "I will have you," he snarled.

"There he is," she said, stone-faced. "I was wondering when you would show your true face." Standing abruptly, she turned to leave.

He caught her wrist, a sickening smile twisting his features. "You have no idea, my sweet Celandine, of the plans I have for you and I."

She pulled her wrist away, challenging him. "And I cannot wait to sabotage them all." She smiled sweetly. "Until we meet again." She walked away without a single look back.

Adriel paced back and forth, willing his anger to dissipate. She was not what he had expected. She would not bend to his will so easily. He would have to change his approach if he wanted to attain the power of the Oculus.

Well, my darling Celandine ... challenge accepted.

Knowing that the Architect only had so much time left, Celandine forced herself to hide her disdain for Adriel. They continued to meet twice weekly for the next few months, and she found herself finding his presence easier to tolerate. Apart from his outburst at their first meeting, he was nothing but a true gentleman. His features began to soften, and his narcissistic tendencies began to fade to distant memory. Much to her surprise, she found herself at ease in his presence.

She could not deny that her father had crafted him beautifully. He had full lips and a strong jaw. His icy eyes lit up when he spoke of things he enjoyed. He was incredibly intelligent and spoke eloquently when he put his ego aside. Slowly, she began to feel a small spark flicker between them.

Their relationship grew slowly over time and, eventually, she looked forward to their meetings.

Every year on the anniversary of the Architect's mating with Aurora, he would throw a ball in her honor. The Hall of Creation was decorated in her favorite tones of green, blue, and purple, and everyone would dress in grandiose attire. When Adriel had formally asked Celandine to attend with him, she was happy to oblige.

When she caught sight of him across the ballroom, she understood why he was called the King of Ravens. He wore a black-on-black, slim-cut tuxedo that complemented his muscle tone, and his onyx hair was slicked back. He stood tall and proud, flashing his opulent smile at passersby. He glided through the crowd effortlessly, as if he were floating across the marble. His gaze fell on hers, and the room went quiet.

"You shine brighter than all of Anistera tonight." He eyed her dress, appreciating how the skirts glowed in the light of the chandeliers that hung from the high roof.

Her cheeks warmed as she thanked him. "You look handsome, as well."

He held out his hand. "May I have this dance?"

Excitement bloomed in her chest as she accepted and allowed him to pull her to the center of the room.

All eyes were on them as he spun her effortlessly around the dance floor. They gaped in awe as he dipped her, the fabric of her dress shimmering. The iridescent ballgown flowed to the floor, the layers of tulle covered in soft sheets of organza. The light blue matched the irises in Adriel's eyes. Thin straps of tiny rhinestones hung from her shoulders, the floral beading spreading down the front of her dress to the waistline. Her midriff was unlined, and the crystals sparkled like dewdrops on her fair skin. Adriel's pulse quickened when he realized how thin the material was between his hand and the small of her back.

The other pairs in the room broke their stares and joined them, the dance floor turning into a flurry of movement and color.

"Thank you for joining me tonight," Adriel said as they swayed to the angelic music, and Celandine couldn't help but feel her chest warm as he spoke.

"Thank you for asking me. It has been"—she paused, looking for the right word—"illuminating."

His eyebrow lifted, and a smirk played on his lips.

She looked away. "I just mean, I have enjoyed our time together lately."

"As have I."

"Could we step out for some fresh air?" She was breathing quickly. The room suddenly felt stifling.

"Absolutely."

She took his arm, and he led her to the balcony that faced the back gardens. They stood facing the grounds, both not knowing where to start.

Adriel cleared his throat, breaking the silence. "I believe I owe you an apology." He sighed. "I know I behaved inappropriately during our first meeting. I am used to getting what I want, and when you challenged that, I reacted immaturely. I hope I have shown you that I am not the spoiled brat you thought me to be." Finished, he let out a strained breath and brushed his hand nervously through his hair.

"I must admit, when Father first assigned me to you, I was less than excited."

He laughed apprehensively. "I hope I have done enough to rectify the situation."

Celandine was taken aback. Even polite as he had been recently, he always seemed to have his guard up, so it warmed her to see him show his more vulnerable side.

She turned to face him, placing her hand on his. "I realize now that I may have acted hastily, as well. You always seemed so cold in my previous observations, and I wanted to protect myself."

"I'm sorry that's what you thought of me. I'm afraid being a commander made me get in my head. I always have to be focused and stern when I am giving the troops orders. It became a part of me, you know. I can never be seen as weak."

"I don't think you're weak," she said, brushing her thumb over his knuckles.

No one had ever said that to him before.

Not knowing how to respond, he lifted his hand, offering it to her. "Ready to head back?"

She nodded. "Happily."

DUSK HAD FALLEN, AND THE LAVENDER SKY CAST A FAINT GLOW over the promenade. The pair had decided to escape the noise and take a stroll around the grounds, out front of the hall. They had spent much of the evening whirling around the dance floor and needed a moment to catch their breaths.

Adriel was a formidable lead, and Celandine had found herself blushing on more than one occasion when he would squeeze her waist or pull her close against his chest. He smelled heavenly, like fresh linen and mint leaves. Her father would be pleased with the attraction forming between them.

They walked arm-in-arm, discussing the night's events, the taste of sweet nectar still coating their tongues. The electricity surrounding them was palpable, and time seemed to slow down.

"Shall we rest our dancing feet?" Adriel gestured to a bench that sat below a large willow tree.

"Only if you massage them for me." Her eyes twinkled in the moonlight.

"If you promise to return the favor." He winked as he sat down, pulling her with him. He took her hand in his.

"I never had intentions of hurting you," he said, tucking a loose wisp of hair behind her ear. "I'm afraid that my responsibilities have hardened me over the years. I only hope that, with time, you will forgive my actions."

She laughed softly, the sound lifting his heart. "I already have," she said, reaching out to cup his cheek, lifting his eyes to hers. He leaned into her touch, covering her hand with his.

"I want you to be mine," he said fiercely.

"And if I refuse?"

"We both know Father wouldn't let you."

Tension filled the air, and Celandine bit her lip in frustration.

"I want you to be mine," he repeated, "but on your own terms."

She looked up at him, her chest rising and falling with shallow breaths.

"And if I say yes?" she asked, her voice quiet.

"Then I will care for you until time itself ceases to exist."

Her heart stuttered. She looked into his eyes, getting lost in the snow-capped mountains that lay there. Her breathing turned shallow, and she leaned into him.

"Yes." The word was barely a whisper.

He moved closer, inches from her face. "I want to hear you say it." His voice was thick and raspy.

"Yes, I will be yours."

And he closed the distance between them.

The brush of their lips was soft at first, almost as if he were asking permission, and she answered by pressing her body into his. He let out a groan and deepened the kiss, lifting her onto his lap. He held her firmly, planting soft kisses all over her face and neck, making her giggle, before returning to her mouth. The kiss turned feverish then, and his hand slid up the back of her neck and into her hair, gripping her tighter. She sighed between breaths and began to rock back and forth on his lap, teasing.

"If you continue doing that, I will have you laid bare by the time the rest of the guests retire for the evening," he growled, his composure slipping.

She covered her mouth, blushing. She had forgotten herself. "I'm sorry," she said, clambering off his lap and straightening her dress. "It would seem the nectar has bested me tonight."

He stood up and wrapped his arms around her, pulling her close. "Do not apologize. If it were not for appearances, I would have you right here." His voice was urgent.

"I think we should head back. They will be expecting us for the speeches," she said, breaking away from his embrace.

"I suppose you're right … keeping up appearances and all." He sighed dramatically, making her laugh. "Shall we?" he beckoned, extending his arm to her.

"We shall." Wrapping her arm around his, they walked back into the event with knowing grins plastered on their faces. The night's events were their little secret.

After the speeches had finished, they continued to dance the night away, each looking forward to what the next day would bring.

CHAPTER
SEVEN

Three sets of eyes glazed-over as the wall of greenery glided upward to reveal The Tree City. All their senses came alive as they crossed the botanical threshold into Eldrin.

Night had fallen on the last leg of their journey, but the city was bustling with life. Bioluminescent moss cast a mischievous glow all around them in shades of indigo, violet, and fuchsia. Fairy lights added some warmth to the mix from where they hung overhead. Music drifted out from the tavern by the trading docks, and the air smelled of tobacco and mixed florals.

"Incredible," Enara sighed in appreciation, voicing what they were all thinking.

Baz was silent for once, his puppy dog eyes trying to absorb everything.

Soren reached out to grab the wooden post as they sailed into an open loading dock. The marina was empty apart from a few small vessels that must have required an overnight stay. In the game of trade, time was money, so staying in one place for too long meant potentially missing out on the next available shipment.

Baz jumped onto the wooden platform as Soren held the canoe steady. He reached out to Enara, pulling her up with ease, as Soren tied a simple knot around the metal cleat and gave it a couple of sharp tugs for good measure. She would hate to wake up without means of transportation. Plus, they still needed it to get the horses back.

"Here." Baz pulled her up to join them. "Now, how do we find this Oracle?" he asked.

They all stepped back, scanning the area to see if anything jumped out at them.

The marina was a sort of semi-circle that hugged the bottom of an enormous sequoia tree. This was the trade center. Soren's father had said it had taken over eighty woodworkers three years to carve out all six stories while still being able to maintain the tree's ability to continue to grow. It had been a labor of love. The people here adored nature, almost as much as they adored a full pocketbook.

The trade center was flanked by more hollowed-out tree shops of various shapes and sizes, and smaller huts made of driftwood and clay filled in any gaps. Signs in bright colors lined the storefronts, beckoning patrons to enter.

Some of the locals lived above their shops, but most resided in the canopy houses where the noise from town was muted. If you strained your eyes, you could see the rope bridges connecting one house to another, the planks swaying high above the forest floor.

They canvased the area, looking for signs of the Oracle, when a small, second-floor shop caught Soren's eye.

"There!" She pointed excitedly at the sign to their left.

"Where?" Baz asked, following the line of her hand and squinting.

"Just up from the apothecary. You see the blue and silver sign with the crescent moon on it?"

"Yeah."

"I'd say that's probably a good place to start."

They began to head in the direction of the shop, their boots thumping on the wood of the dock. Water splashed up from between the boards as a wave drifted into the lagoon.

"After this, we're hitting that tavern," Enara said. "After three days on a horse, and then a river adventure, I am in dire need of a drink."

"Sounds good to me."

"Yeah, I'm down," Soren replied. *I am going to need a double after this.*

Enara shrugged her pack over her shoulder then speed-walked down the dock, the other two trailing behind her. Their pace slowed when they reached the shops as curiosity took over. This place was nothing like the little market they were used to. Anything you could think of was bought and sold here—simple items, such as quills and ink, or more complicated fair, like healing potions and enchanted weapons. Enara was particularly entranced by the bladed staff that was on display in the armory window. *I'll come back for you later.*

The trio paused in front of the makeshift door, looking up at the sign. It was more detailed close-up. The silver paint was flaking off, and Soren peeled off a chunk, admiring the way it glimmered in her hand. There was faded script below the crescent moon.

Do not question if you need to enter.
You already know you will.

She smiled, squaring her shoulders. "This should be interesting," she said as she pushed open the door.

A bell chimed overhead as they entered, the soft tinkling tickling their ears. The space was small and smelled of incense, the smoke so heavy that Soren stifled a cough. The shelves were filled floor to ceiling with all sorts of curious objects and ingredients.

Baz grimaced. "Never thought I would know where to purchase fresh snake tongues." Shivers crawled up his spine.

"Baby." Enara smirked as she came up beside him to take a look.

They walked amongst the shelves, picking up one jar after another, examining their contents.

Soren held a frosted green jar up to the lantern, squinting at the label. *Butterfly wings.* The thought of someone plucking the wings of the majestic creatures upset her.

"Buy two, get one free, if you're interested," an unfamiliar voice broke in from the next room, giving them all a fright.

"Maker, were you trying to scare the shit out of us?" Soren shouted at the curtain, her heart thumping in her chest.

A chuckle drifted from behind the shimmering fabric. "Come, Soren. We have business, you and I."

"How did you—"

"You know who I am," the mysterious voice cut her off.

"Well, yes."

"Then you know the answer. Come now. Tell your friends you will be but a moment."

Soren felt sweat dampen her skin as she looked at her friends, nervously shuffling her feet.

"It's okay, lady. You got this. Your father sent you to her for a reason. You need to find out what that is."

"Yeah, but—"

"Just go. We will be right here."

"Yeah, just yell, and I'll come in swinging!"

Soren's lips quirked, and she hugged them both. "I'll be quick, I promise."

Soren parted the curtain, the fabric gliding through her fingers like water over pebbles in a creek bed. This room was smaller than the last and had better ventilation, she thought, noting the lack of smoke. Apart from a few shelves with countless grimoires and a few jars with rare ingredients, the room held little interest. A window to her left was propped open, and a rectangular skylight gave an unobstructed view of the stars. The slight breeze made the candle flames flicker and cast abstract silhouettes on the walls.

An altar sat in the corner, a book of shadows propped open, the spine cracked from years of use. A blue candle sat alight in an iron holder, and Soren thought she could see a raven's feather and some white powder she didn't recognize. It was hard to tell in the dim light. She was curious as to what the items were used for.

The furniture was sparse. A cushioned bench sat between the shelves, and a small, circular table was planted in the center of the room. It was draped in a black velvet tablecloth, with sturdy armchairs on either side.

Nothing in the room was out of the ordinary, apart from the woman sitting across from her. She had remained silent while Soren took in her surroundings, studying her. When their eyes met, she spoke.

"You've grown into your beauty. I assume your father nurtured your mind just as well." Her voice was omniscient and ethereal, almost as if multiple people were speaking in unison.

Soren shivered. Her presence was intimidating, though she sensed that was not her intent. She felt a familiarity with her and relaxed her shoulders.

"My father is dead," she replied sadly. "He sent me."

"Yes, I was saddened when I heard the news of his passing. He was quite lovely."

"Did you know him well?" Soren asked, tugging on her sleeve.

"He came to me once, after your mother passed. He needed … guidance. You would have been about three at the time."

"That explains why I don't remember. What was he here for?" she pressed.

"He was having a hard time with her passing. It is my belief that he never truly healed from the loss."

"Did he mention anything else while he was here?"

"He did, but I will spare the details. Your mind's eye will show me the answers you seek."

"Let's get started then."

"Of course." She gestured to the empty chair. "Come. Sit."

Soren closed the few steps between them and slipped into the seat.

The Oracle reached her hands across the table, palms open to the sky, her silver eyes flashing in the firelight. "If it makes you more comfortable, you may call me Zamirah. Now, place your hands in mine, and we will begin."

Soren reached across the table, joining their hands and taking notice of the lightness of Zamirah's palms. The Oracle's fingers were cool, and her night-kissed skin was flawless, apart from her seer's marks. The white tattoos were delicate, the fine lines resembling vines curled down from her shoulders to the center of her hands, wrapping a halo around her fingers. A second marking rested like a crown of twigs above her dark brows and framed her sterling eyes. Her ebony hair hung to her waist; some sections braided, others had been relaxed into soft waves, like a waterfall. She was a piece of art, youthful and ageless at the same time.

Soren could feel her heartbeat quicken as their palms touched, faint electricity buzzing beneath her fingertips.

"Now I will begin. Do not let go until you are instructed to."

"I … I won't." The hair on the back of her neck prickled as she waited for the seer to begin.

Zamirah started whispering in the old tongue, and the candles seemed to burn a little brighter. Soren recognized a few of the words from old translations that her father had taught her but could not pull the meaning from the corners of her mind.

The chanting became more urgent as the Oracle rocked back and forth in her chair, her grip tightening around Soren's fingers, making her gasp. An invisible wind whipped around them, somehow having no effect on the candlelight, and the walls groaned. It felt like her fingers were about to shatter. Just before a scream escaped her lips, Zamirah's grip loosened, and she went slack, her head lolling forward.

Soren didn't move, her breathing shallow. She held fast to Zamirah's hands. *She told me not to let go.*

"Hey … you're kind of freaking me ou—"

The Oracle's head shot up, her eyes boring into Soren's. The silver was gone, and all that remained was a blank slate.

Soren's eyes felt like they were being stabbed with a white-hot branding iron, but she could not break the hold. Zamirah seemed to be looking into her soul, pulling out whatever secrets might be hiding inside.

Soren seemed to fall into herself, her eyes unseeing. She wasn't in a void; she was the void, black as a starless sky. Soren floated in the emptiness, not sure where the shadows ended and she began. A soothing voice washed over her.

> *"The son of one is a master of none,*
> *Yet yearns for the power of all.*
> *The blood of the two will hold true,*
> *Bringing the Maker's downfall.*
> *The power of three holds the key,*
> *A sordid tale, to say the least.*
> *The hearts of four, joined forever more,*
> *Only a bird can tame the beast."*

Suddenly, Soren was encased in blinding white light and shot back into her chair, her eyes refocusing. She was covered in sweat, her chest heaving as she sucked in oxygen. Letting go of Zamirah's hands, she struggled to speak between breaths.

"What … the fuck … was that?"

"I apologize for the pain, but tampering with the mind's eye does not come without cost."

"You could have warned me," Soren seethed, glaring up at her.

"I worried you may not let me proceed. I assume the prophecy revealed itself to you."

"It did."

"Good. Our business is finished then." She stood, flattening the crease on her robe.

"Wait—that's it?" Soren asked, flustered, rushing out of her chair.

"I'm afraid I must retire. The soul-awakening takes much of my energy, and I require rest now."

"But I don't know what any of it means," she cried helplessly.

"My dear, I am to relay the prophecies, not interpret them. The answers will come as they are meant to." The woman cupped her cheek, her expression warm. "Take care, my sweet Soren." She turned, walking out a door that Soren hadn't taken notice of, leaving her with her thoughts.

SOREN RETURNED TO HER FRIENDS, WHO WERE WAITING OUTSIDE. "Sorry, lady, the smoke got the best of us. How'd it go?" Enara asked.

"I'm pretty sure she almost killed me, but we got what we came for."

A look of concern flashed over Enara's face. "And?"

"I'll tell you at the tavern. I need a stiff drink to calm my nerves."

"After you, my lady." Baz gestured to the staircase that led to the lower-level shops, trying to lighten the mood.

"Why, thank you, good sir." Soren chuckled as she scooted past him, taking the steps two at a time.

"Hey, do you guys mind if we make a quick pit stop?" Enara asked.

"I thought you wanted an adult beverage first?" Soren sighed.

"Yeah, and I don't want to see you when you're hangry," Baz added.

"Shove it, you two. There's a shiny new toy calling my name, and it would be rude to ignore it." Enara's eyes twinkled as she stopped in front of the armory, gesturing to the window. "Isn't she beautiful?"

THE TRIO LEANED BACK ON THE BENCHES OF THE CORNER BOOTH. The table was littered with pint glasses and bowls with remnants of the chef's special—bison stew.

Baz undid the top button of his trousers. "If I have another bite, I'm going to explode," he groaned.

"That was just what I needed," Soren commented, a satisfied look on her face.

The tavern was cozy but far from elegant. The entire place smelled of stale beer, the floorboards sticky with liquor.

"I can't believe you didn't upgrade your bow. I can practically feel the power radiating from my staff," Enara crooned, stroking the weapon fondly.

Soren had tested out a few of the enchanted bows, finding them to be a bit excessive. She preferred the simplicity of a regular bow versus a charmed one.

"They just didn't speak to me. Plus, I would never give up the one from my father. It's sentimental."

"Okay, fair, but can we all take a moment to appreciate Coraxis." Her eyes beamed.

"Coraxis?" Baz's face was a mask of confusion.

"Yes, Coraxis. Every good weapon needs a name."

"What does that even mean?" Soren asked.

"Corvus Corax is the scientific name for a raven. Seemed fitting."

"Hmm … I didn't know that." Soren sipped her beer.

"You're not the only one of us who is well read." Enara bumped her arm, making the liquid drip down her chin.

Soren gave her a face then used her sleeve to wipe off the spittle.

"I'll have to think of a name for this baby then," Baz said, patting his sword.

The girls chuckled, knowing he would likely name it something ridiculous.

The bladed staff was truly a work of art. The core was made of blackthorn with a silver filigree adorning the end. The metal design continued two-thirds of the way up, adding detail to the raven's head that rested there. The beak was an elongated blade. The metal looked liquid and seemed to be alive. It had been charmed to obey whoever bloodied it first. Enara was only too happy to nick her finger for the cause.

Baz had tried to test the theory before they had gone into the tavern but dropped the staff a moment later, his hand red with heat. "Well, at least you got your money's worth," he'd said as he treated the burn in the marina's dark waters. Once the blade was imbued with the blood of its owner, no other was able to wield the weapon, apart from those who shared the same blood.

Soren had filled them in on the prophecy while they ate, but they had struggled to make any headway. They repeated the ominous words over and over until they had exhausted themselves. After some resistance from Soren, they decided to take a break from riddle-solving and get a good night's sleep. Hopefully, some rest would dredge up some better theories about what it all meant.

They rose from the booth in unison and consulted the barkeep about accommodations on the way out, deciding on a spot closer to the marina. The hostel was quaint, and the couple who owned it seemed nice. They stretched out on their respective cots, making small talk until they dozed off, one by one, the sound of water lapping against the dock lulling them to sleep.

IT WAS WELL PAST MIDNIGHT WHEN SOREN SNUCK OUT OF THE room, wrapping her tunic around her, skin prickling with anticipation. She walked barefoot along the docks, her body following some invisible thread.

The city was quiet, the fairy lights had been snuffed out, and only the glow of the moss remained. Her body led her to the other side of the marina. There, at the end of the dock, stood the mysterious man from her dreams.

His back was to her, a hood covering his hair, and his broad shoulders were draped with a long, dark jacket. Fitted trousers were tucked into shiny leather boots.

She approached slowly, hoping to catch him off guard.

"That's close enough, little bird." His words were a command, but his voice was soft.

"Who are you?" she asked again more urgently than the last time. "How are you here?"

"I'm sure you realize by now that I am not physically here."

"I wasn't sure until now … You're a dream walker, aren't you?" The question came out in a whisper. Dream walkers were uncommon but not unheard of. Their power was usually limited to people they were close to, as they required a personal effect from the dreamer to enter their sleep realm. The skill was hereditary. The first rumors of them dated back to the first age of Entheas.

Soren hadn't guessed it at first. She had no idea who this man was and definitely didn't know him on a personal level. *He must be more powerful in some way.* Some had honed their skills more than others but, to her knowledge, had never done it without a token from the dreamer.

"Clever little bird, your father taught you well, I see."

Soren took a step forward, fury flashing in her eyes. "What do you know of my father? Are you who he warned me about? Wait …" Venom spilled from her tongue, "Did you have something to do with his death?"

The stranger was silent, contemplating his answer.

"Answer me!" she roared.

"My father did," he said, clearly disinterested in her outburst.

Soren pulled a throwing dagger from the garter on her thigh, aimed to kill. "Then I will take you as retribution," and released the blade.

Just before it hit its mark, the stranger vanished in a plume of white smoke, leaving behind a single white feather. Soren growled in frustration, blinking to clear her vision. She knew if you killed a dream walker while they were still in your mind, they would not wake up again.

He was faster than she had expected and, adding to the confusion, she had yet to wake up. Then the realization hit her. *I must have sleepwalked.*

"Shit," she huffed. She reached for her daggers, grumbling when her fingers slipped over an empty slot. She looked out toward the water where a ripple had just settled. *For fuck's sake.* "Well, I'm not getting that back."

She trudged back to the hostel, a chill creeping through the fabric of her blouse.

Enara sat up as she walked in. "Everything okay?"

"Yeah, just needed some fresh air," she replied nonchalantly.

"Okay." She yawned, still half-asleep. "Sweet dreams."

"Yeah … sweet dreams."

CHAPTER EIGHT

Celandine let out a soft sigh as she looked out at the wisteria sky. The sheet from Adriel's bed hung off her waist. Her back was bare, and her skin tingled from the previous evening's activities.

She walked out to the balcony, the linens billowing behind her. It was a lovely morning, as it always was. The Architect had made it that way. This realm was designed to be as close to perfection as possible, its beauty unmatched, weather included.

Each day was like the beginning of spring—warm enough not to require a jacket, with a gentle breeze to quell the heat of the day. Anistera existed past the moon and stars, so the sky was an endless sea of violet. The shade changed to accommodate for a sense of night and day.

The Celestials were the most fortunate of all the beings in the many worlds her father had created, but living amongst such perfection could be stifling. This morning was the first time Celandine had appreciated their perfect little bubble in over a decade.

Her cheeks heated, and she shifted in her seat. The muscles between her legs ached, reminding her of the strenuous activities she had partaken in.

Last night, she had decided to lie with Adriel. It had been a few weeks since the ball, and she was glad to have waited until the nectar's effects had worn off. With a clearer head, she had been able to enjoy him to the fullest extent. It had been a night filled with passion that she would not soon forget.

It had been years since she had taken a partner to bed, but she was not surprised that Adriel's performance had outshone their efforts. She never required physical intimacy and only participated every now and then out of boredom, but it had been different with Adriel.

She had expected it to be enjoyable. After all, he was designed to be the greatest being in every manner. Something had changed yesterday, though, and she could not help but smile when she looked over at him.

He was still asleep, his chest laid bare. She let out a sigh of appreciation. Her mouth watered, and she reminisced about how he had tasted under her tongue.

She thought back to when they had first met and how she had wanted nothing to do with him. Her opinion had completely flipped over the last few months. Now, all she wanted was to have him by her side.

She did not regret her decision to form a bond with him. She had a duty to the realm and her father, but now she was grateful for it. She had come to care for Adriel and now looked forward to the life they would build together.

She could not describe the elation she had felt when their mating bond had clicked into place. They had left a meeting with the Architect, informing him of their progress. Their father had been worse for wear, and his previously dark beard was now speckled with white. His golden skin had gone pale, and there was a darkness under his eyes.

He did not have long left—maybe a year or two—and he wanted to ensure that they were on the right track to follow in his and Aurora's footsteps. Pleased with the direction their relationship was taking, he had offered to vacate the Architect's living quarters early to allow them more privacy.

Her father had had all of his possessions moved by the time they had returned from lunch on the promenade. His collection of items from all his creations remained in the Temple of Worlds, so he hadn't had much to move.

Celandine had gasped when she and Adriel had walked over the threshold to his new quarters. He had shown her around his previous abode a handful of times, which was nothing to scoff at, but the Architect's floor was mesmerizing.

The Hall of Creation had been built into the side of Thelmire Mountain, and the Maker's living area resided on the floor above the entrance hall. Adriel's new home was an immaculately carved cave with window openings along the entire outside wall. The space was shaped like an oval with all the furnishings curved to match. The kitchen island was an immovable piece of rock.

Celandine placed her hands on the cool surface. "I can't believe you get to live here."

"You mean, *we* get to live here," Adriel said, snaking his arm around her waist and pulling her in for a chaste kiss.

She turned away to run her finger along the edge of the cabinet doors, the mahogany warming the cold look of the stone. Across the room, instead of a fireplace, was a living waterfall. The room was seemingly built around it. The natural spring fell from a hole in the roof and continued trickling down the walls, falling through a second hole in the floor. There was a raised blockade about a couple feet high to stop one from falling through. A Celestial would survive the descent, but it would hurt.

They continued their tour around the living quarters, taking in the space. Celandine squeezed Adriel's hand as they walked over to the silk rug. A look passed between them, and she blushed, knowing they were both thinking of the fun they could have on it later. The arched walls on either end of the oblong room separated the bathroom and bedrooms from the main area. From a distance, the effect made the Architect's quarters look like an eye. A fitting composition as the Maker and Oculus went hand-in-hand.

They entered the bedroom, their eyes falling on the large, circular bed that took up most of the space. The atmosphere was heady, and Celandine's chest flushed.

Noticing the rise and fall of her breasts, Adriel's hand stiffened in hers. They were nervous. After their heavy make-out session at the ball, they had experimented with each other on more than a few occasions but had ultimately decided to wait a little longer before doing the deed.

They had an eternity, after all, so there was no reason to rush. That was ... until they saw the recent state of their father. It had ignited a sudden sense of urgency to be connected to one another.

Adriel turned to face Celandine and leaned down to kiss her. "I want you," he said, his voice filling her with heat.

"I need you," she responded between kisses.

He grazed his teeth along her jawline. "Then you shall have me," he growled, returning to her lips.

Not wanting to rush the moment, Celandine walked him to the bed and beckoned for him to sit. She gently pulled his shirt over his head and ran her hand along his collarbone, appreciating the way his muscles tensed under her touch. Then she crawled on the bed and kneeled behind him, massaging the knots from his shoulders.

Her eyes took in the lines of his back, and a groan of satisfaction escaped his lips as he relaxed into her hands. Her fingers were soft but strong, and he could feel his muscles loosen as she worked.

A jolt shot straight to his groin as she kissed down the side of his neck, and he spun around to take her mouth. He slipped off her shirt and palmed her breasts, her nipples pebbling. He leaned in to kiss her chest, appreciating the way her heartbeat jumped in response.

They had moved back on the mattress, the remainder of their clothes thrown to the floor, and pressed into each other. He put his hands on her, and she melted under his touch. He did not want to rush either.

He took the time to caress every inch of her body, and she did the same. She brushed her hand through his silky hair as he devoured her. When they kissed again, she could taste the sweetness on her tongue.

He entered her slowly, letting her body adjust to his. She let out a sigh of pleasure as they started moving together.

She looked into the endless ocean of his eyes and felt the mating bond click into place. It was like she was seeing him for the first time.

Her skin sparked, as if a million fireflies were lighting her up from the inside. This was no longer just a merging of bodies, but a merging of souls.

He looked back at her, tears in his eyes. Somehow, she had snuck through a crack in his armor and had pushed into the depths of his heart. He knew at that moment that she was his and they would rule over all the worlds as one.

Afterward, they lay tangled in each other's arms, breathing unsteadily. The bond coursed through them like lifeblood, setting their souls on fire. Neither of them dared to move for fear of breaking the spell.

Their breaths softened, and sleep laid heavy on their eyes.

"I didn't know it could be like this," Celandine said as she pressed a cheek against his chest.

Adriel bent his neck and kissed her forehead, reaching his free arm down to pull the blanket up over their naked bodies.

"It will be like this always," was his response.

Celandine brought herself back to the present. The words Adriel had spoken last night ran through her mind. Looking at him, she had never felt more complete.

Sensing he was awake, she called out to him, "Good morning, sleepyhead."

"Come back to bed," he tempted. His eyes were still closed as he reached out to her.

She grinned and padded over to join him under the covers.

"I want to stay wrapped in these sheets forever," he said, voice still muffled by sleep.

"Now that, we can agree on," she joked as she crawled in, pressing her backside into him.

"I am not going back to sleep, am I?" he asked, grabbing hold of her hip.

"Not a chance."

THREE WEEKS HAD PASSED, AND THE MATES HAD BEEN SENT TO separate wings of the Hall of Creation to prepare for the Changing of Hands ceremony. Mates were not permitted to see each other the day before the ceremony, so Celandine had spent the evening at Luscinia's, filling her in on the last few months with Adriel.

Her friend had been more hesitant when she had heard about them being matched. She had noticed the qualities in Adriel that had cause for concern, as well. After a few glasses of nectar and a little convincing, Celandine got her on board.

"The mating sounds … intense," her friend said after hearing the details of their bonding.

"It was the most beautiful thing I have experienced in my many lifetimes," Celandine responded, her eyes glittering like a thousand polished diamonds.

"Then I am happy for you." Luscinia touched her shoulder, smiling.

Celandine was delighted to have approval from her closest friend. Luscinia was one of the first made, as well, and their friendship had survived for centuries. There was no one else she would have by her side at The Joining tomorrow.

It was set to be the most ostentatious event they had ever attended. Adriel would be granted the Oculus and officially adopt the title of Architect and all that went with it. Following shortly after, the two would complete The Joining and infuse their blood with the Oculus, reigniting its power.

Their father had already prepared the artifact by cleansing it with his own blood and a vial of Aurora's that he had kept since her passing. Now all that was left was for Celandine and Adriel to christen it with theirs, and the transfer of its powers would be complete.

She rested her head on the feather pillow in Luscinia's second room, attempting to get some rest. She let her mind drift to visions of Adriel and relaxed into the mattress. Before she could finish counting the stars in his eyes, she was asleep.

CELANDINE JUMPED OUT OF BED IN A FLURRY OF MOVEMENT. SHE had slept in.

She washed herself at a record pace, not having time to heat the water. The coolness of it jolted her awake. She then ran to Luscinia's room and shook her by the shoulders.

"What?" Luscinia grumbled, trying to drag the covers back over her face.

"Get up. It's almost midday!"

"What?"

"You heard me. Come on!" Celandine yanked off the covers, leaving her friend to scramble out of bed.

She put on her makeup, dotting her eyelids with shades of brown and gold. Luscinia joined her, putting on a simpler mask and donning a dress of her own.

Celandine pulled her gown from the hook and wrestled with the skirts. After a third try, she managed to drag the layers of tulle over her head, nestling the fabric over her curved frame.

Luscinia stood behind her, pulling the corset strings taut. "Suck it in, woman."

"I can barely breathe as it is!" Celandine gasped as her friend held a knee to her back, giving the bounds a last sharp tug before tying them off.

"That's better," Luscinia said, patting Celandine's behind. "Let's go."

THEY ARRIVED JUST IN TIME TO SEE THE FIRST HABITANTS OF Anistera enter the grounds in front of the hall. She tried to breathe as her corset pushed her organs into an uncomfortable position. Luscinia stood beside her by the doors, trying to keep her calm as Adriel walked into the room.

"Slept in, did we?" he asked, smirking.

"It is not funny." Celandine glared at him, the bones of her corset poking into her ribs.

"If you two are finished, we shall proceed." Their father's voice drifted from the end of the hall.

They all straightened their posture and bowed, standing tall when he approached them.

"Father," they all said and, one by one, bent to touch his feet.

"Let us not keep the people waiting," he said.

They followed him outside to meet the others.

THE CHANGING OF HANDS WENT BY SURPRISINGLY FAST. TOO FAST in Celandine's opinion.

As the Architect handed Adriel the Oculus then stood down, she could feel her nerves building, her pulse raced and her throat felt as though it were full of sand. They were about to complete The Joining.

Her father motioned for her to join Adriel in front of the ceremonial table, and she obliged. She gave them each a low bow before standing next to her mate.

Luscinia stood to her right and gave her a nod of encouragement. General Corvus stood to her left, behind Adriel and her father, his stance rigid. *I don't think I have ever seen him relax.* She settled her eyes on the table, not wanting to look at the crowd below.

Inhaling, she willed her chest to rise against the tight fabric of her dress.

"I am ready," she said, wanting to get this part over with.

The ceremony consisted of two parts. The Bloodletting and The Making. The Bloodletting required a mated pair to prick themselves and let their blood meld together in the inner section of the device, tethering its power to them and them alone. The Making was to confirm that the mating bond was legitimate so no one could question their power.

The outer edges of the eye had two small divots that required the users to hold either end. The power could only be used properly when both blooded mates were physically present and touching the Oculus.

To attempt a Making without your mate would cause the magic to take on a mind of its own. Their father had never attempted to use it without Aurora and had warned them during their meetings not to do so, either. They were now partners in all things, Making included.

When the ceremony was completed properly, the artifact would hum and release blinding white light, and when it faded, the creation would appear. The creation of Entheas had been spectacular, to say the least. The light had shone for weeks, and the reveal had been nothing short of breathtaking. Though the Makers were only required to hold on while the idea formed, they still felt their energy being drained as it came to fruition over the course of those days.

"Celandine, are you ready?"

She looked to her father and an understanding passed between them. She had started this journey out of duty to him, and she now understood why he had paired them.

Celandine cleared her head and brought her mind back to the present.

The Bloodletting had already begun, and Adriel looked at her expectantly, placing the knife in her hand. He had already bled into the device. Now it was her turn.

She took the ceremonial dagger and drew a scarlet line across her palm, letting the liquid pool. Her hand shook as she held it over the device, but she calmed when Adriel touched the small of her back in support.

As her blood touched his, the device began to hum, waves of energy drifting off and lapping against the edges of the crowd. The couple reached forward, placing their fingers on the divots, and closed their eyes.

They had decided a few days prior on what they wanted their first creation to be and formed the thought in their minds. They had decided to start with something small and work their way up to larger creations down the road.

All of Anistera was in attendance, and they gasped in awe as a little orb of white light took shape next to Anistera's new leaders. A shadow organized itself inside the orb, and when the light broke, it revealed a winged horse. It was still just a baby and trotted around awkwardly on the table. It spooked as it tripped over the Oculus, letting out a shrill whinny that had Adriel covering his ears.

Celandine reached out to pet him, stopping short to let the creature come to her. She was overcome with joy when the small horse nuzzled her palm and flapped its tiny wings excitedly. When Adriel reached forward too quickly, however, the animal reared up on the table and fell back on its haunches. Celandine stifled her laugh.

"He will warm to you. It is his first day, after all," she said.

"You know I am the only reason you exist," Adriel huffed, disappointed that the creature hadn't immediately warmed to him.

Celandine rubbed his shoulders in an attempt to placate him.

"You are going to be a load of trouble, aren't you?" she stated as she scratched behind its ear.

The creature snorted happily, wobbling before finding its footing. It would be a while before he could fly, so the wings were ornamental for the time being.

"What is to be his name?" an onlooker yelled from the crowd below.

Celandine had almost forgotten that all eyes were on them, and the nerves returned. She looked to Adriel for guidance.

"He was your idea. I think it is only fitting that you name him."

"What if you don't like the name I choose?"

"I will love it because you chose it." He smiled, and she relaxed under his gaze.

She turned to face the crowd, standing tall and sure. "Beings of Anistera, we want to thank you all for attending the ceremonies today. Your loyalty to our father is something we can hope to earn as Adriel takes his place as Architect."

The crowd muttered their agreeance, thousands of faces beaming up at her as she finished her address to them.

"We look forward to creating with you and for you. Please join us in welcoming our first." She presented the miniature horse up to them, cradling him carefully between her hands and taking care not to pinch its wings too tightly. "Everyone, meet Obsidian."

CHAPTER
NINE

Enara was the first to wake as Baz's snores drifted softly from the bunk above her. She was groggy and scrubbed her tired eyes with the backs of her hands. She then dressed quietly and clicked the door shut behind her.

Nightmares of her father had plagued her dreams. She could still hear his voice in her head.

You want to cry? I'll give you something to cry about.

She squeezed her eyes shut, trying to push the memory away. However, the vision fought her, forcing itself to be seen.

She had been nine at the time. Her mother had asked for help with dinner, and she had accidentally burned the cake. It had been her father's birthday, and they had been trying to surprise him.

He had left work early to hit up the tavern and had arrived home in a stupor, just in time to see Enara toss the confection into the fire.

He had stalked over to her, finger pointed in her face. "What the fuck do you think you're doing?"

"I … I'm sorry, Father. I thought I had the time right. I didn't mean—"

"*I don't care about your excuses!*" His voice boomed so loud that it vibrated her eardrum.

She bowed her head in defeat, knowing this was a battle she would not come out of unscathed. When he was like this, he was volatile, and anything she might say would only set him off more.

"You will look at me when I am speaking to you!"

She looked up, obeying his command.

"We do not waste in this house. Did you pay for that with your own money?"

"No, I—"

He struck her across the face so hard she saw stars, and the rings from his fingers left indentations in the flesh of her cheek.

"I did not say you could speak!"

She did not move an inch as he berated her. She fought to keep her hands away from her face as her cheek grew hot. She tried to stop it, but her tears had a mind of their own. They trickled down her face defiantly, and her father's nostrils flared. He saw tears as a sign of weakness and exploded at her.

He grabbed her collar, screaming in her ear, "You want to cry? I'll give you something to cry about." He threw her to the ground, her knees scraping against the worn floorboards.

She watched her mother's back as it disappeared into their bedroom and let out a sob when she heard the door click.

"Stupid, useless girl," he seethed, kicking her in the ribs. She could feel the bones crack and let out a sharp cry.

She curled in on herself, trying to protect her organs from further damage, but he found other areas to assault.

After using his belt to slash at her back, he left her in a broken heap on the floor. She stayed there well into the night, until she was sure her movement would not wake him. Then she crawled to the door, managing to use the handle to drag herself to her feet, and slinked out.

She hobbled into the woods behind her house and curled up in the moss. Every movement stung as the fabric of her shirt grazed over the welts on her back. Breathing was near impossible because every inhale felt like a needle piercing her lungs. She cried until sleep took her and did not move until her father left the following morning.

She had come to find out later that he had lost a rather large bet down at the tavern and had already been in a piss-poor mood when he'd arrived home.

The memory made her scoff. How a few lost pieces of gold warranted the abuse she had received, she would never know.

She tried to shake off the sickening thoughts, but her mind was going on a rampage. She strapped on her boots, deciding that a run might clear her head. She took the wooded path past the trade center and deep into the forest to the residential area and back.

After three laps, her legs were screaming, and she was dripping from head to toe, the bad memories forgotten ... for now. She plopped herself down on the dock, dipping her toes in the cool water, and sat back, enjoying the morning sun. It seemed warmer here than back home.

"Saved your life!" Baz grabbed her shoulders from behind, effectively ending her quest for some peace.

"You asshole!" Enara yelled, turning to look up at him, anger screwing up her features.

"Maker, someone's wound a bit tight this morning." He smirked, poking at her.

"I am not responsible for my actions before my shadow marks mid-morning," she said, not wanting to drum up a conversation about her father. "Now, help me up," she commanded, extending her hand.

Baz reached forward and looked into her eyes just long enough to realize what she was up to, but it was too late.

Enara yanked down while simultaneously thrusting her other hand into his hipbone, knocking him off the dock with a loud splash. She stood up with a haughty look on her face as Baz swam up, sputtering.

"You're lucky … I'm a strong swimmer … or you would have had a lot of explaining to do to Soren," he said between coughs.

"You'll get over it," she replied, reaching forward. "Now, come on. I'm hungry."

Baz placed his hand in hers, pressing the other on the dock, and exclaimed, "Your turn!" Using the leverage, he yanked her into the lagoon with him.

When she surfaced, a look of scorn burned on her face. "I hate you, Baztien Greymark!" she bellowed, splashing at him.

"I love it when you use my full name." He smiled mischievously.

Enara glared, holding onto the edge of the dock. It was covered in dark green algae, creating a slick surface that made her cringe. "You are insufferable."

"Yeah, but I'm still your favorite." He shrugged, paddling up beside her.

Her lips curled just slightly.

"Oh, hold on, you got some seaweed in your hair." He untangled the weed. The rest of her brown locks were plastered to the side of her head, and the tips floated on the surface of the water.

She looked at him, suddenly aware of his proximity. The energy around them seemed to shift. The gold flecks in his eyes sparkled like fairy dust, and his shirt clung to his muscular chest. This moment reminded her of the first day they had spent alone together.

Soren had stayed home to help her father catalogue some recent finds, while Enara and Baz had gone for a swim at Tiveron Falls. They had sat on an overhang, and he had looked at her just like this as the water rushed behind them.

"You look beautiful," he'd said, looking at her intently, and Enara's heart rate had quickened.

"Thank you," she'd replied shyly. She had always found him attractive but had kept him at arm's length out of fear of what her brothers might do.

He had then leaned in to kiss her, his lips brushing hers, but she had turned away and jumped back into the water. It wasn't that she hadn't wanted to kiss him; she just cared about him too much to risk it. They never spoke of it again.

Thinking back now, she wasn't sure why. He hadn't tried for anything more than friendship after that. She had not been upset by it, though. She figured he was just being respectful.

Now, three years later, they continued to ride the line between friends and something more.

Even water-logged, he still smelled of cinnamon and clove. The combination of the two was intoxicating. She inhaled, gathering up all the courage she could muster. Her brothers were miles away, and she decided it was time to throw caution to the wind.

She wrapped her legs around him, draping her free arm around his shoulders.

His expression went from surprised to excited to something else as the heat radiating off his skin sent sparks through her.

"Enara, I—" he started, but she cut him off.

"Maker, do you ever stop talking?" With that, she leaned in to kiss him.

"Guys?" Soren called from a few feet away.

The two scrambled to separate, and then Baz helped Enara lift herself onto the dock, clambering up after her.

Soren scanned their drenched clothes, laughing. "What in the Maker happened here?"

"Don't ask," Enara huffed, trudging past her toward the hostel.

Baz, having no poker face, reddened under Soren's gaze. "Just out for a morning swim, is all," he feigned nonchalance.

"Mmhmm … tell that to the tent you're pitching." Soren chuckled, turning to walk back down the dock.

Baz covered himself, swearing under his breath. "Maker, take me now," he said, trailing after them.

After Baz and Enara had found some more suitable clothing, the three grabbed some granola and fruit from a market stand then headed toward the trade center. The landlords of the hostel had informed them that the top floor was home to a massive library, and they figured it was a good place to start looking for answers.

When they reached the landing, they saw a petite woman with nymph-like features sitting at the small desk. Her back was to the wall separating the library from the entrance, and she smiled when they stepped out of the stairwell. Her yellow hair was adorned with a crown of flowers, and her pointed ears jutted out playfully.

"Good morning, travelers! Welcome!" Her voice was like a happy song.

"Good morning," they replied.

"Could you show us the history of magic section?" Soren asked. "We're … " She hesitated. The fewer people who knew what they were doing, the safer they would be. "We're writing a paper about some artifacts my father found. You may have heard of him … Tarak Nightsong."

"Ah, yes!" she trilled. "He used to visit every so often. He would spend hours by the bay window, reading and perusing the shelves. Though I haven't seen him for quite some time."

"He passed about two months ago."

"Oh …" She quieted. "I'm so sorry."

"It's … it's okay." Soren's eyes misted. "You didn't know." She struggled to hold back tears. The journey was hard enough without her being reminded of his loss every five minutes.

"You wouldn't happen to have records of the books he was reading, do you?" Enara asked, changing the subject.

Soren silently thanked her.

"Of course!" she replied, the happy cadence returning. "We keep extensive records. Many of the texts here are the only existing copies and have been charmed to take the name of each person who touches them."

"So, how do I find the ones he looked at?" Soren questioned.

"Normally, it takes a day to sift through the records, but the books will remember him. Since you share the same blood, a golden tether should approach within a certain distance of the ones that were graced by his touch."

"Perfect. I guess we will just head in, then. Thank you for your help."

"It's my pleasure!"

The trio turned and entered through the large double doors. Their breaths pulled out of their lungs at the sheer beauty of it all.

The library was a masterpiece. Shelves were hand-carved out of the trunk, following the curve of the room in three rows ending with a sitting area in the middle. Above them was a ring of stained-glass windows. All were scenes from nature, reflecting soft rainbows of light around the room.

Soren loved libraries. They always felt like a safe space for her, and she often used reading as a means to escape the outside world. She would seek them out on her travels with her father, but this one was, by far, her favorite.

Enara couldn't tear her eyes away. "This is breathtaking."

"I am not touching anything," Baz said, stuffing his hands into his pockets.

"Probably for the best." Soren snickered as she brushed the spines on a nearby shelf. She gasped when a thin line of gold appeared.

If she hadn't been told about it, she would have mistaken it for a trick of the light, but there it was. It led her to a smaller book on the shelf labeled, *"Celestials Among Us."* She skimmed the pages but found nothing of consequence.

The next two hours went by in much the same manner. Soren walked the shelves, pulling out this book and that until all tethers pointed to the table in the center of the room. Unfortunately for them, her father had spent more time here than they'd realized, and the stacks were quite extensive.

"Nothing." Enara snapped another book shut before slamming it down on a stack to her left as Soren added the last one to their pile.

"Same here," Baz said, adding another to his discard pile.

"I'm sorry, guys. I know this is shitty, but we've already come this far." Soren picked at her fingernails.

"It's okay, Sor. Not like you expected us to read an entire library. I am going to take a quick break, though." Enara stood and trotted out the side door that led to a wraparound balcony covered in reading chairs.

"Not going to join her?" Soren asked, wiggling her brows at Baz.

"Nope, we're not having this conversation," he said, stuffing his face into another book.

"As you wish." She followed suit and cracked open another herself

She must have dozed off, curled up in the armchair, because the next thing she knew, Enara was shaking her awake.

"Soren ... Sor ... get up ... Baz found something."

She shook the cobwebs from her head and sat up, heart racing. "Wha ... what did you find?" Her voice was still rough with sleep.

"So, remember how your father's letter said something about a mind's eye?" Baz asked.

"Mmhmm …"

"So, I thought maybe we should look at it literally. I started looking for references to eyes and came across this." He held out a book on ancient artifacts that Soren remembered finding in a crack on one of the shelves. She hadn't thought anything of it at the time, but now she wondered if it had been hidden there on purpose.

Baz pointed to some handwritten scripture. "Look."

Soren glanced from her friend to the book, trembling. It was her father's writing. It read:

> *To the girl with stars in her eyes,*
> *The Oculus is a magical artifact of unimaginable power.*
> *The device was designed for one purpose—to create. However, with the power to create comes the power to destroy. If it fell into the wrong hands, it could bring destruction to all we hold dear, so I have taken it upon myself to hide it somewhere safe. The Goddess of Halcyon protects it now. In the event of my death, it must be moved. If they found me, I may have betrayed its location.*
> *Remember what I told you in my study. My darling, I have one last poem for you. Take from it what you will.*
>
> *Teardrops rest upon thy chin,*
> *Portraying sorrow deep within.*
> *A sorry sight to thine eyes,*
> *To see the beauty as she cries.*
> *Shoulders shaking as she weeps,*
> *Close to her heart, a rose she keeps.*

The velvet flower scarlet red,
Glistens with the tears she shed.

Love you tons,
T.N.

Soren pushed past the lump of grief that had risen in her throat and tore the page out. The act felt like she was committing a crime. Books were a sacred space for her, but desperate times.

"Sorry," she whispered as she put the book down.

Baz and Enara waited patiently for Soren to speak first.

After taking a moment to calm herself, she bent down to dig the letter and map out of her pack. "I think … *'what I told you in the study'* is referring to these." She waved the papers around. "I think the clues go together." With her finger, she traced the lines of the first poem as she muttered the words over and over again in a hushed voice, eyes shifting between the two poems and the map.

"Can one of you see if the lady at the desk has some quill and ink? I need to work this out on paper."

"Yeah, I got you," Baz said, darting out of the room. He returned in a flash with a quill, a few sheets of parchment, and a jar of jet-black ink, handing them to Soren.

"Thank you." She bent over the table and began scribbling back and forth like a mad woman, circling sections and scratching lines to connect certain items.

When she was finished, she sat back, breathing heavily.

"I believe I have our heading." She pointed to a symbol on the map.

"A mosque?" Enara asked, looking at the smudged shape on the worn parchment.

"Close. A temple. The Temple of Vedas, to be exact."

"And, how exactly did you come to that conclusion?" she questioned, genuinely trying to understand.

"Yeah, I'm trying to make sense of your drawing here, but I'm at a loss," Baz said sheepishly.

"Come take a look," Soren offered. She explained the chaotic scribbles to them, pointing back and forth to different items. She clarified what the lines meant and their connections to the Oculus.

"At first, I didn't understand the correlation between the two poems, but when I read the first one again, it clicked. You see this." She pointed to a line in the poem. "It says, '*A secret story buried deep, Whispered to you in your sleep.*' When I was young and couldn't sleep, my dad would always tell me the same story. The story was called *The Goddess of Halcyon.*"

"That can't be a coincidence," Enara said, leaning forward, a serious look in her eyes.

Soren nodded in agreeance. "Father would tell it to me over and over again, about this powerful being who was as beautiful as she was graceful. He even said they made a statue of her in secret, and that it had been buried under the temple."

"Sounds promising," Baz remarked.

"It has to be her," Soren said. "I remember him saying that the statue held a rose. It always stuck out to me because they are my favorite flower." She stopped to take a breath, her mind trying to catch up with her mouth.

"Okay, it's starting to make sense now. But, how does that tie into the map?" Enara asked.

"That's the best part," Soren said excitedly. "You guys know how my father's family came over from Vakari when he was a child?"

"Yeah, your grandpa was a badass," Baz chimed.

"So, back home, the Vedas are their religious texts but are considered to be 'not of man' or 'superhuman.' I think my dad added this temple to the map himself. I think that's where he hid the Oculus."

"I know how we can test the theory," Enara said, standing. "The trade center's navigation room is on the third floor; they would have every map you could think of, and they must be updated regularly."

"You're a genius!" Soren hugged her then gathered the papers into her backpack, leaving out the map.

They exited the library and gave a quick wave to the clerk, taking the steps two at a time to the third-floor landing.

Soren practically skidded into the navigation center, startling the dark-haired topographer who was sitting behind a large desk.

He pushed his glasses up the bridge of his nose, his tone clipped. "May I help you?"

"Sorry to interrupt, but we were hoping you could tell us what the name of a certain map marking is?"

He sighed. "Make it quick. I am very busy."

Soren unfolded the map, flattening it on the polished desk. "This one here."

"Is this a joke? Did Lark send you? That guy, I swear." He shook his head "I'll wring his neck the next time he tries to play another prank on me."

"I'm sorry. I don't follow," Soren said in confusion.

"Look here," he said, gesturing to one of the many maps that lined the walls. "This is the true map of Entheas, and your little marking is not on it. Now get out."

Soren didn't hear the last part as a wide smile spread across her face. She looked from her map to the wall and had never been happier to see an empty space in her life.

CHAPTER
TEN

It had been a month since The Joining, and Celandine had adjusted well to her new position as the Architect's mate. Adriel had been busy training, so she had decided to take Obsidian for a ride through the mountain valley. The pegasus whinnied happily as they trotted toward the Emerald Pools.

He had grown into a stunning creature, and Celandine had become attached to him. They had designed him to age at an accelerated rate and to stop growing when he reached maturity. In human years, he would have been about six years old and was still adjusting to his condensed training regimen.

The basin anchored the waterfall from their home, and if she squinted hard enough, she could make out the lines of their living room. Her face pinked as she remembered how they had made love on the sofa, the waterfall rippling playfully behind them.

She stepped down from the saddle, taking a plunge into the churning water, needing to cool her hot skin. Then she climbed out, wringing the excess water from her riding gear, and reached up to stroke his mane.

"Good boy, Obie," she crooned.

She waited while he drank, stroking his neck affectionately. He unfurled his wings and stretched them out before curling them back into himself. Celandine did not need to worry about pinching them as they rode since they melded into him when they were not in use. This was by design so that she could bring him to Entheas when she traveled there. After all, a winged horse would be bound to spark questions amongst the mortals. Their world was not devoid of magic, but a charmed weapon was a short cry from a Celestial's familiar.

Obsidian lifted his head when he'd had his fill, and she climbed back in the saddle. They completed a lap around the pool, letting the mist from the waterfall drift over them.

She led Obie to the stable that they had made and removed the reins, pulling the bit from his mouth. He looked sad, his big brown eyes begging her to stay.

"I'm going to find your dad, okay? I'll be back later." She kissed his muzzle then headed in to change out of her wet clothes.

She was feeling bold and decided to slip into some more risky undergarments, throwing on a garter for good measure. She donned a navy-trimmed peasant dress and headed for the training grounds.

It would be midday soon, and she thought she would surprise Adriel at work. They were training outside today, and she loved to watch him work up a sweat. The way his muscles shifted and flexed as he moved made her mouth dry and other places quite the opposite.

She scanned the training grounds, disappointed when she couldn't find the half-naked body she was looking for. There were plenty of bulging pectorals to go around, but none that belonged to her mate. Feeling ridiculous for getting dressed up, she went inside to search for him. *Maybe he is in the war chamber.*

The space was aptly named and held an air of foreboding. She had only been in there once before when Adriel had given her a full tour of the military quarters. The chamber was shadowed in comparison to most of the spaces in Anistera, all walnut and dark granite.

The walls were lined with maps and books with information on all of her father's largest creations. A large, circular table was the centerpiece, papers and ink strew about. There was a distinct lack of chairs. Celandine guessed this was due to the seriousness of making war plans. It would be hard to take a commander seriously if they looked like they were waiting for dinner to be served.

She sauntered up to the door, hoping to find him alone, when she heard voices coming from inside the room.

"I have prepared the ranks, Commander. They will be on standby for the unmaking to settle any unrest."

Celandine stilled herself as her ears perked up.

"Thank you, General Corvus. All your requests will be granted as soon as this is done."

"It will be my honor, Commander, to stand by your side when your plan comes to fruition. I hope you will allow me to continue to serve you after you unmake your father's abomination."

At this, she gasped, not believing what she was hearing. She peered through the crack in the door and could see Adriel leering at a map of Entheas in disgust.

Little did Celandine know that the mortals were no more than playthings to him. During his visits to Entheas, he would sow chaos.

Though the humans had free will, he was cunning and could easily influence their decisions. A push here, a pull there, and he could produce much devastation. And he reveled in it. She had been led to believe that he cared for them as she did.

"Yes, humans are vile creatures, aren't they? I will be glad to be rid of them. Now, leave me. I must be getting home; Celandine will wonder where I've run off to."

"As you wish, Sir."

Celandine backed away, hiding in an alcove as General Corvus exited the room. He was an unfortunate character, and she had always sensed there was something off about him. His nose was pointed like the beak of a bird, his shoulder-length hair tied loosely at the base of his neck. He never said much, and she tried her best to avoid interactions with him.

She held her breath and remained out of sight until his footsteps went silent. She gulped in a few breaths and steadied herself. She didn't have time to lose her head. She had but moments to compose herself, as Adriel would be out any second.

Right on cue, she heard his heavy footfalls head for the door and popped out of the alcove just in time to look like she had just arrived.

"Well, don't you look handsome," she lilted, touching his embroidered overcoat.

"And you, my sweet, look ravishing as always." His eyes filled with desire as he leaned in for a kiss.

She did not hesitate, stroking his ego with her lips before pulling away, looking coy. "There will be more where that came from later," she said, her eyes betraying nothing.

"I can't wait." He smiled hungrily. "But I will. Let's go home." He held out his arm, and she grasped it, using every ounce of self-control she had not to be disgusted by him.

"I'm ready when you are."

Her mind was racing with the revelation from the two-minute conversation she had overheard. *He wants to unmake Entheas. Why?* She forced herself to remain calm as her insides turned to rot.

She looked up at him, thinking of all the ways she could end his life, but he was smart. She would have to take him by surprise.

She had let him into her heart, into her soul. She wanted to crawl out of her skin and light it aflame to erase every touch he had placed upon it.

The mating bond that steadily burned in her veins had gone ice-cold as she forced herself to keep it intact until the opportune moment. There hadn't been a rejected bond in over a century, and it would be unimaginably painful to wretch her soul from his.

In a world where time had always been inconsequential, she suddenly found herself counting the moments and days as they passed. Every second that ticked by was one minute closer to the end of Entheas.

She had come up with a plan, but it was risky. She would have to face Adriel head-on.

Fear gripped her throat, threatening to collapse her esophagus, but she fought it back. She could do this. She had to save them, her beautifully flawed little things.

Adriel presented his plan in only a way a true narcissist could. He tried to convince her that Entheas was dying and they needed to unmake it to make it again. "It will be better for them all. We can give them a second chance." He pretended as if he cared for them when, in reality, he loathed their entire existence.

"Doesn't that defeat the purpose of free will?" Celandine asked, if anything, just to see what lies he would spin next.

She forced herself not to flinch as he touched her face.

"Of course not. We will keep everything else the same, just simply make the world a more fruitful place. They won't even remember that anything changed. Their decisions would still be their own."

She pressed her palm to his, ignoring the shiver of disgust that slithered under the surface. "If it's to better their lives, I am all for it." She smiled through her teeth, her response seeming to ease his mind.

They made a plan to complete the unmaking in two days' time, when Entheas had a lunar eclipse. That way, any residual weirdness they felt could be blamed on the full moon.

They were the longest two days of her existence, and that was saying something, considering her age. She had forced her body under his no less than three times in the short window and had hated every second of it.

The body she had once loved felt foreign and cold. She tried to remove herself from her physical form as much as she could and played her role well. If Adriel sensed anything, he didn't show it.

They stood in the same spot where they had created Obsidian, the people of Anistera waiting patiently below. Everyone had turned up to watch the unmaking, and all eyes were on them.

Their father stood to her side, and a look of understanding passed between them.

She took a deep breath and leaned forward to let her blood fall into the center of the eye. The cool metal warmed as the scarlet liquid marred its surface.

Out of the corner of her eye, she could see a crooked grin take shape on Adriel's lips. She had to act. It was now or never. The fate of Entheas rested on her shoulders.

"Now," Adriel said, his words dripping like ice down the back of her neck, "we remake the world."

As he leaned forward, extending the Oculus to her, she lunged up with the dagger and planted it firmly into his breastbone.

He yelled out, his voice like thunder, "What have you done?" and staggered back, falling to his knees, coughing up blood.

Celandine had to move quickly. She grabbed the Oculus, broke it in two, and ran, leaving Adriel to choke on his own blood.

She didn't know where she was going until she got there. She was gasping for air as she ran into the stable and launched herself onto Obsidian's back. They shot out of the barn and headed toward the gate to Entheas.

Without a saddle, she struggled to grip the reins and dropped a piece of the Oculus as she righted herself. She looked back at the metal glinting in the dirt and let out a cry of frustration. She did not have time to turn back. She tightened her grip on the other piece and kept moving.

The humans knew not of her true existence apart from rumors and stories. She owed them nothing. Nevertheless, she had grown to love these mundane creatures.

She had traveled to many worlds and had visited many planes and realms, but the humans were truly unique. They were flawed in the most perfect way possible, and they deserved to live.

She was willing to face Adriel's wrath for them. Turn on her brothers and sisters if necessary. Her father understood. She could see it in his eyes at the ceremony that he knew what her future held.

She had existed for millennia and had experienced so much. She would go happy knowing she was right where she was supposed to be.

She held tight to Obie's neck, closing her eyes. Gripping the broken half of the Oculus tightly to her chest, they jumped, and she shattered the bond.

CHAPTER ELEVEN

Soren thanked the owner of the apothecary for her help as they gathered some much-needed medical supplies. They had packed her father's back in Vreburn, but it was running low on many of the vital healing aids. The older woman had led them around the store, helping them pick out everything they would need for healing general injuries.

Soren stuffed everything in her pack, the bag bursting at the seams, and tossed it over her shoulder, taking care to not damage her bow in the process.

Baz and Enara had popped over to the east side of the city to acquire a more efficient mode of transport but came up dry. They would be limited to traveling on foot, as they would not require the watercraft that they had arrived in past the edge of the river.

Well, shit. Soren blew her hair from her eyes. "Looks like we're taking the scenic route."

"I also grabbed a new pair of boots with reinforced insoles and a couple of extra firs for each of us," Enara said, looking to the sky.

The solstice was coming, and the chill with it. She wanted to be prepared.

"Thanks, lady, good call."

"Speak for yourself. At least you didn't have to carry it all," Baz whined, his arms straining from the weight.

The girls smirked as they all turned to head back to the hostel, their trusty pack mule following behind them. Hoping for a good night's rest, they all turned in early, agreeing to leave shortly after breakfast.

Morning came all too soon, and they groaned when the light in the room turned golden. They ate mostly in silence and, after a quick bathroom break, were on their way.

They hopped in the canoe and exited the city's living wall through a different channel to the west. They were only able to travel for half a day before having to disembark on a bank at the base of the mountains that bordered Braexmirth.

The province of Braexmirth consisted of a rocky landscape with a few small towns peppered about. Most of the inhabitants were miners and metalworkers, many of whom had honed their skills since childhood.

Any weapon of true caliber, like Baz's sword, was made and sold from Braexmirth's capital, Olecastor. The trade city owed much of its business from Braexmirth's imports, its largest purchaser being Xian-Dao.

Bao-Ren spared no expense, wanting only the best for his imperial armies. This, of course, angered the Patrovians, who had a sizable army of their own.

Soren was thankful that Draestel was a neutral territory and had yet to worry about her home being ravaged by war. She could not imagine the horrible things Baz's birth parents might have seen before they'd fled Xian-Dao.

They pulled the canoe into the bush, covering it with vines and branches, vowing to come back for it later, as they had with their trusty steeds. Then they trudged along the narrow mountain path, the trees becoming more sparse as they went up.

The wind was cool, but it did not compare to the snow-capped peaks of Thorncrest, northeast of here.

When evening began to fall, they agreed to make camp in a small, vacant cave that sat up on a plateau.

"Wow." Baz whistled, looking down from the cliff's edge. "We should tie Soren to a tree tonight in case she decides to sleepwalk."

She rolled her eyes but felt a pang of guilt. She had yet to tell her friends about the dream walker. She wanted to but wasn't sure where to start.

She pushed aside the intrusive thought and went to check out the cave.

Baz suggested they set up a fire near the entrance to ward off animals, so they did just that. They pushed stumps into a semi-circle around the mouth of the cave as the distant clicks of cicadas filled their ears.

Enara stood, folding one of the furs and placing it on her assigned hunk of wood. She then turned, plopping back down with an annoyed grunt. "I already miss those seats in the library. I had half a mind to stuff one of the cushions in my pack," she said, inspecting the blade of her spear before setting it down.

"I think I'll miss the dock the most. The view this morning was beautiful," Baz said, catching Enara's eye.

Her cheeks flushed, and she looked away.

"In a few days, I'm sure I'll be begging for a tavern," Soren added, popping out of the cave entrance. "Their cold cellar was amazing. I wondered if Dad ever had the chance to go there." Her voice dropped. She could feel the panic crawling in her veins, the negative feelings threatening to burst and bleed her dry.

Enara grabbed her hand. "I'm sure he did, Sor. Don't forget he had traveled there on more than one occasion."

The warmth of Enara's fingers pushed back the dread, and Soren calmed.

"Yeah, I guess you're right," she said softly, releasing her friend's hand. Then she pushed her seat closer to the flames, willing the fire to burn through her pores and flush out any anxiety that remained.

"So, what are the travel plans for tomorrow?" Baz asked, shoving a hunk of hardened cheese in his mouth.

"Well, I figure it's about another day and a half to the temple," Soren said, pulling out her pack. She unfolded the close-up map of the area, thankful that they'd had a copy available back in Eldrin. "So, if we rest here tonight, I think we should aim for this point tomorrow." Her finger pressed to a picture of a natural spring north from their current location. The miniature body of water sat about three-quarters of the way between where they were and her father's temple marking. "That leaves us with a short trek to the temple, giving us plenty of time to search around and still leave some daylight to set up camp after," she finished.

"Sounds good to me," Baz replied. He had finished off the cheese and was starting in on the cured meat.

"Do you ever stop eating?" Enara admonished, grabbing the venison from his hand and popping it into her mouth.

"Aw … come on. A guy's gotta eat," he said, reaching for another piece.

Soren joined in, feeling quite famished herself.

The trio relaxed by the fire as night blanketed the sky. When their bellies were good and filled from their picnic-style dinner, Soren whipped out a deck of cards.

They spent the next hour or so playing poker, Baz winning nearly every hand. Soren was about to say fuck it and go all-in when she caught something from the corner of her eye.

She looked past Enara, her eyes searching the darkness in the trees behind the cave. *There.* Sticking out from the edge of a spruce tree, barely noticeable to the untrained eye, was the silhouette of a man.

Not wanting to alert the onlooker, Soren looked at her friends and said, "I'm gonna have to fold, guys. I think I'm going to retire for the night." She stretched, groaning loudly. "Besides, the stars are silent tonight."

They all exchanged a knowing look and readied their weapons.

Before leaving Eldrin, they had come up with the code phrase. They wanted to be able to warn each other if there was danger nearby. If it was daytime, it would have been: "The sun has dimmed since morning."

Enara's grip on Coraxis tightened as Baz nonchalantly pulled out a honing stone to sharpen his sword. Soren stood at the mouth of the cave, out of sight, bowstring taut, an arrow ready to fly.

Everything was quiet for a moment; the only sound was the crackling of the fire when two large bodies fell from the sky and landed squarely behind Baz and Enara.

Hands steady, they whipped around.

Enara took out the legs of her attacker with a low swipe, causing him to land on the ground hard. She swung Coraxis up then slammed it down like an axe to finish the job.

Baz ducked and rolled to the side, toward the edge of the camp, popping to his feet and parrying forward, catching the second in what he thought was an arm. He was shocked to see that when the assailant grunted and backed up a few steps toward the fire, that it was, in fact, a wing. Whatever it was, it was repulsive and inhuman, and it terrified him. Half-man, half-bird, but in the most disturbing way.

He heard a twig snap behind him, but before he could swing his sword around, Soren's arrow flew past him. It nearly grazed his cheek before taking out a third creature.

The three friends stood back to back, waiting for the next wave, but it never came. They assessed the area, all of them dumbfounded.

Soren searched the spot next to the cave where she had seen the first of them and found only a few footprints leading away before they seemed to just disappear. She shook her head to clear it and joined her friends, who were examining the bodies.

The creatures were truly ugly. Their human features were stretched forward in a grotesque manner. Their eyes were black and glossy, set deep in their misshapen skulls. She suppressed a shiver.

"What the hell are these things?" Baz asked, poking one with his boot.

"I have an idea," Enara responded, "but I thought they were a myth."

"You know most myths are based on fact. The details just get skewed over time," Baz said.

Enara nodded then winced when the acrid scent of the creature's bodies drifted into her nostrils.

"Soren, do you remember the story your dad told us about the birdmen?"

"Vaguely. I mean, it was so long ago." Soren looked to Baz. "He used to scare us when we were kids to stop us from sneaking off the property. He would say the birdmen were always watching and that they would carry us away to another land if we misbehaved. They had another name, but I can't remember it … k-something, I think."

"Ke … kestrels. That was it, right?" Enara asked, hazarding a guess.

"Yeah … yeah, that sounds right. Kestrels. Creatures that were half-raven and half-man. Dad said they were created by darkness that bound them in their monstrous state." Soren looked exasperated. *Were there hidden truths in all his stories?*

"Well, it makes sense. Your dad did mention that King of Ravens guy," Enara reminded her.

"Oh yeah, I'd almost forgotten that part," Soren said thoughtfully.

"Either way, I'd rather not have to deal with more of them," Baz said, cleaning off the tip of his blade.

"Agreed," Enara said. "We should take some more precautions. Soren, do you think you could set up a couple snares in the tree line?"

"Yeah, no problem."

"We should probably take shifts sleeping," Baz added.

Enara thought on it for a moment. "Okay, when Soren's done, I'll take the first watch while you two get some rest. At least the cave will give us coverage from above."

"Sounds good to me," Baz said, shoving the last of the bodies over the edge of the cliff.

Enara opened her mouth then closed it.

"What?" He put his hands up, feigning innocence.

"Nothing."

"I wouldn't be able to sleep knowing these creepy things were sitting outside. They might reanimate or something."

Soren laughed.

"Fair enough," Enara replied.

"SOREN ... SOREN ..." ENARA SAID SOFTLY, KNEELING BESIDE her. "Soren, it's your watch."

Soren groaned lightly and got up, shrugging her tunic over her head. She patted her thigh to ensure her knives were still there and pulled her quiver over her shoulder. "Yeah, yeah, I'm going." She rubbed her eyes and strode past Enara to take up her spot by the entrance of the cave.

Dammit, you two. She quickly realized they had skipped over her first watch to let her rest. It was late and dawn was only an hour or so out.

She hated that they looked to her like she was the leader of this whole thing when she felt like she was at the bottom of the barrel. They were both better fighters, by far, and more clever. She was only able to provide answers because her father had been secretly training her for this moment. Even then, they had still helped. She knew they never would have found the second poem if it hadn't been for Baz.

She rubbed her neck, smoothing out the wrinkles of stress that had settled there. *I'm not made for this.*

She wished she could be back home, back to some semblance of normalcy. She wanted to hit up the market or have a roll in the sheets after too many drinks at the tavern. She wanted to kick a guy out of her bed at six a.m. so she could joke with Enara about how many minutes the poor sop had lasted.

She rested her head against the cool stone, listening to the wind rustling through the trees.

Movement in the brush had her push up into a crouch, knife in hand. Adrenaline coursed through her, sharpening her senses.

"Show yourself," she commanded.

"Tsk, tsk, little bird. So demanding." The familiar voice tickled her eardrums as she realized she must have dozed off against the side of the cave. She swore under her breath, praying that nothing would happen to her friends while they slept.

She had to find a way to wake herself up. She didn't want him in her mind any longer.

"You could at least have the balls to show your face if you're going to keep stalking me in my dreams," she spat.

"But, what fun would that be? I'm enjoying our little game of cat and mouse."

Soren squeezed her knife so hard it hurt. Her knuckles turned white as she racked her brain for a way to wake herself up. She tried pricking her finger, gasping when she felt a faint sting. *Shit.*

"I wouldn't do that if I were you," the stranger said, stepping out of the tree line and into the moonlight.

Soren gasped, fear rearing its ugly head when she saw who she was talking to. She had thought it was one of the vile creatures, but she had been mistaken.

As the moonlight shone brighter, she could see the elongated beak was a clay mask. It had obviously been intended to resemble the kestrels, though this design was more … refined.

The man was taller than she'd realized, towering at least a head over her from where he stood a few feet away. His hair was hidden by the hood of his cape, but she caught a glimmer of the sapphires in his eyes.

She crossed her arms. "And why not?"

"Because this isn't a dream. I *am* here."

"Mmhmm," she sneered. "That's just what you want me to think." Her eyes flicked back and forth, looking around for a way to escape this nightmare.

She wished she could dream up a lake that she could jump into to shock herself awake. *Wait a minute.* She looked over to the cliff. *I can jump.*

"I have no reason to mislead you," he said, his voice breaking through her thoughts.

He was oddly formal, and she found it unnerving. *Does he honestly think I'm that stupid?*

"Your parlor tricks aren't going to work on me," she said, her voice laced with ice. Then she flashed him a teasing smile and ran directly for the cliff's edge.

As she launched herself up, she felt a warm hand encircle her wrist. He yanked her backward onto the hard ground, effectively knocking the air from her chest.

Soren coughed, attempting to work some oxygen back into her bloodstream, stilling when the stranger crouched over her.

He grabbed her chin and forced her to meet his masked face. "Do not try that again," he ordered, pushing up from the ground and brushing the dirt from his jacket.

She turned onto her stomach, spotting the dagger she had dropped, and reached for it. She pretended to struggle to get to her knees, gripping the blade. Then she turned, throwing the knife with deadly accuracy … right off the cliff.

Somehow, impossibly, he was gone … again. And to make matters worse, she was down not one but two of her favorite throwing knives.

Not again. She swore up and down the alphabet as her friends came bursting from the cave, weapons in hand.

"Are you okay?" Baz asked, his bare chest bulging in the moonlight, a firm grip on his sword, ready to strike.

Enara ran to her side, words tumbling out of her mouth. "Maker, you scared the shit out of us! What were you doing out here? Did one of them attack you again?"

"Not exactly," she said, looking down and chewing on the inside of her cheek. *I guess it's now or never.* "I have to tell you guys something."

Enara looked at Baz, and then they both looked at Soren, eyebrows raised.

"Go on then." Enara gestured for her to continue.

Soren launched into the shorthand version of her experiences with the dream walker, answering a few questions along the way.

After some deliberation, they came to the conclusion that the stranger must have been the kestrel's leader. Also, he must have needed Soren alive, or he would have let her jump off the cliff. More importantly, they would be back.

They covered their eyes as the sun crested the mountain, lighting the landscape below on fire. They stretched their tired bodies and packed up camp early, knowing they needed to pick up the pace to avoid another run-in with the kestrels. Soren felt a stab of guilt knowing that she'd had a few more hours of sleep than both of them.

With one last look over the ridge, they turned the corner and followed the winding trail up the cliff, stopping only a handful of times to catch their breaths and refuel.

They kept up a grueling pace, hoping that whatever they found in the temple would be able to ward off another attack.

"Thank the Maker I continued my cardio regime after our training ended," Enara commented as they trudged past the spring that they had originally planned to stop at.

"Speak … for … yourself," Baz choked out between breaths. "I do cardio, too, and I am still not made for this shit."

"Thank the Maker my dad and I used to take turns racing up the foothills outside Vreburn, or I would be so screwed right now," Soren said, out of breath.

The three shared a small laugh at their misfortune, trying to keep their spirits up. They pushed on past the three-quarter mark, determined to reach the temple by nightfall.

They had been climbing for over nine hours straight, and all six of their legs were screaming for reprieve. Right when they thought they couldn't take another step, they reached the peak.

There, through the trees, probably six hundred feet away, sat the Temple of Vedas.

They all sighed in relief, collapsing onto the cool ground and sucking down water from their canteens. Finally, they could rest.

Soren felt a warm flicker in her heart, silently thanking her father for guiding them here. She wiped a tear from her eye and smiled. The temple was real, and they had made it.

CHAPTER TWELVE

"No!" Adriel roared as he felt Celandine rip the mating bond from his chest.

He had reached the edge of the gate just in time to watch his mate jump through the archway, Obsidian's tail trailing behind her.

Anger surged through him as he paced back and forth on the rough stone landing. "Stupid girl," he seethed, hacking up blood. The wound in his chest was still fresh, but it did not compare to the hollow place in his soul. He had come to care for her in a way only a mate could, and without her, his power would wane. It was only a matter of time before he would fade, as his father was. He would need to remake himself, or at least try, but without the full power of the Oculus, it was a moot point.

He growled in frustration, looking down at his chest. He had to hand it to her, she had struck true. The knife had pierced his breastbone but narrowly missed his heart, nicking a lung in the process. Not a fatal blow, but it had slowed him down enough for her to escape.

He wiped his mouth with his sleeve, his breaths labored as he sat down on a nearby bench. His father had gifted him healing powers, making him close to invincible, but the right blow was inconvenient, nonetheless.

He cringed as he felt his bones snap back into place, the skin on his chest slowly weaving itself back together with invisible thread. He coughed a few more times then sat back, letting the night air fill him up, at a loss for what to do next.

"Sir?" Corvus stood at attention next to the archway.

"What?"

His general shifted with obvious discomfort. "The crowd is restless, sir. They are confused as to what just occurred. I had the ranks settle them, but they will require explanation."

"Fine," he said, standing. He ripped off a strip of fabric from his torn shirt to wipe the last of the blood from his now-healed chest. "Then I will give them one."

Corvus cleared his throat, avoiding his leader's eyes.

"Is there something else?"

"Commander, our father's condition has worsened."

"Go on," he replied, unconcerned.

"Well, you see, sir, when the Changing of Hands ceremony is completed, the Architect is supposed to begin pass on and become one with us all."

"I know how the ceremony works," Adriel snapped.

"Yes, of course, sir. My apologies. But ... with the mating bond shattered, the ceremony is no longer complete. Our father has gone into a sort of comatose state between living and lasting."

The look on Adriel's face was as sharp as a thousand daggers. "Take me to him."

His father lay flat on a glass table in the healing sanctuary, a few disciples at his side, speaking in hushed tones.

Adriel walked in, his face a mask of concern for his Maker.

"Tell me what happened." He faked a break in his voice.

"We are not entirely sure," a female healer to his left spoke, her voice calm but concerned. "It seems that his passing has been halted. His physical form is refusing to release his corporeal one. We cannot be sure how long he will remain like this."

"How will this affect my role as Architect?" he asked with mock innocence.

"Your title is your own, Maker. We serve only you now." Her gaze shifted to his father. "We will keep him comfortable in the meantime."

"I see," he said, placing his hand on his father's. "Who else knows of his current status?"

"Well, everyone," the larger male, who stood near their father's feet, spoke.

Adriel lifted a brow in question.

"He collapsed shortly after Celandine fled. You had already left by the time the event took place, but all of Anistera paid witness."

Adriel hid his annoyance by looking away and slumping his shoulders. "I will inform the attendees of our current situation." He turned to leave, speaking over his shoulder at the disciples, "See to it that no one bothers him. We don't know what could happen in his state."

The female responded, "As your will commands."

ADRIEL COULD HEAR HUNDREDS OF VOICES MAKING MUFFLED comments through the door as he approached, the displeasure on his face clear.

He had walked to the Hall of Creation through the side entrance of the mountain to meet with the crowd. Arriving in the same way he had during The Joining ceremony. Corvus stood at his side, awaiting his next order.

"See to it that you relieve the disciples of their watch over our father this evening. He will not make it through the night." Fire burned in his eyes, his voice was firm. "Do you understand?"

"Understood, Commander."

"If anyone so much as whispers in disagreement, have your men dispose of them."

"Forgive me, sir, but would no one notice them missing?"

Adriel rolled his eyes in annoyance. *Must I do everything myself?*

"Do your best to be discreet. If anyone is suspicious, tell them I required their services for Father's Absolution."

"Of course, sir."

Corvus stepped forward to open the double doors and bowed low as Adriel walked out into the chaos. The crowd quieted as their new Architect stood firmly at the top of the hall's steps.

Adriel cleared his throat and spoke in the most regal manner. "It is my understanding that the events of the last few hours have caused much confusion and distress to you all, but I am here to put your minds at ease." He scanned the crowd, looking determined but empathetic. "Our father is being monitored carefully and would like privacy at this time. We will inform you of any changes to his current state."

"And what of our sister?" a strong female voice shouted from the crowd.

Following the direction of the comment, he recognized Celandine's closer relation, Luscinia.

"It pains my heart to have experienced such betrayal from my beloved. She has committed the highest act of treason. For her crimes, she has been banished to Entheas to live out her final moments before the lasting takes her."

Luscinia looked visibly shaken but did not speak another word.

Good. She better keep her mouth shut, or she will be the first I send my men after. Adriel felt a smug smile tugging on the corners of his lips.

"Rest assured that I plan to carry on our father's legacy and will make every effort to return the Oculus to its former state."

The crowd seemed pleased by this and started to look more relaxed.

"Now, I will ask that you all please return to your places of residence, and we will reach out as deemed necessary. Thank you all for your patience and concern in this matter. Our Maker would be proud."

With that, the crowd began to dissipate, leaving behind a few small groups that were milling about quietly. Adriel could feel waves of resistance flowing off a few of them, but they were forced to obey.

At least Father got one thing right. He had felt the pull he had on them settle in the moment they had completed the Changing of Hands. He had yet to exert his will over any of them … until now, and he reveled in it.

"Corvus," Adriel beckoned, his general always at the ready. "Gather the troops and meet me in the training hall in an hour."

"Yes, sir."

Adriel stalked into the hall, following the mountain trail back towards the healing sanctuary. He walked the empty halls, his footsteps echoing as he went. Then he stopped by his father's bedside. The disciples were nowhere to be seen.

Silently, he slipped Celandine's dagger from where he'd placed it in his belt and twisted it into his father's heart.

HIS MOST LOYAL SOLDIERS PREPARED THEIR FATHER'S BODY FOR the Absolution ceremony, careful to hide any evidence of Adriel's blade. The announcement was made the following morning that their father had not survived the night and they would grieve his passing that evening.

A Celestial's Absolution was not a sad event, but rather a celebration. They would eat, dance, and drink nectar until their bodies heated and their heads tipped back in ecstasy.

Adriel had attended these events countless times over the decades when soldiers had not made it back from a mission. He loathed the whole sacrament.

Celebration, he scoffed. *What is there to celebrate?* The loss of a perfectly good soldier was nothing but a waste in his eyes. This was different, however. This time, there was much for him to celebrate because now there was no one with the power to stop him.

IT WAS THE AFTERNOON FOLLOWING THEIR FATHER'S ABSOLUTION and General Corvus gathered the first battalion troops in the training hall. It was a small group, only twenty-five or so. Each one had proven themselves to be skilled in combat and survival. Most importantly, they had never disobeyed a command.

Even with his newfound power over the people of Anistera, Adriel felt it best that only his most trusted knew his plan.

He stood front and center on the raised landing, a healing table placed in front of him. The broken Oculus sat in the center, perched on a metal stand over a shallow wooden bowl. A thin blade sat menacingly at its side.

"I have gathered you here, the most loyal of all my forces, to assist me in the retrieval of the broken Oculus shard that Lady Celandine stole from us." His eyes bored into each of theirs. "You have all proven yourselves to me, and I would trust no others to complete this task. I have asked much of you over the years, but this task is not for the faint-hearted."

He stood tall, confidence radiating as his voice carried over the room. "As your new Architect, I am going to attempt something no Maker has before."

A few of the soldiers' eyes moved, but they kept their composure, not wanting to upset their commander.

"I intend to use this half of the Oculus to bestow great power unto you all to help me with this task. It will likely be … painful, but you will be rewarded greatly."

The soldiers stood, unblinking.

"As you all know, an extended stay in Entheas would strip you of your grace, rendering you all effectively useless. I, however, have found a solution to this." He waved a hand toward the metal centerpiece. "I intend to use the Oculus to replace your grace with added strength, speed, and the ability to use the sky to aid you in your search."

There were a few mutters of curiosity.

"Now … who will be the first to come forward and be granted this gift?" he finished with a flourish.

"I will," they all chanted in unison, making Adriel's eyebrows perk up.

"Commander"—General Corvus broke away from the others—"allow me the honor of being the first."

"Ah, my most trusted general, please," he said, gesturing to the empty space at his side.

Corvus marched over and stood facing the lines of men, a dignified look on his face.

Adriel scanned their eyes, willing them to have no fear of what was to come. Then he lifted the knife and dragged it deep across his palm, the skin parting as blood seeped through the crack. He lifted his hand and let it coat the Oculus, changing it from sterling to crimson, the excess pooling in the bowl below.

He cleared his head of all else and placed the idea of his creation at the front of his mind, willing it to be, then stood back. He waited impatiently for Corvus to be shrouded in white light.

One minute passed. Then another.

Nothing.

Then, just as the soldiers started to shuffle in place, black smoke engulfed the general. He screamed once in agony, but the sound was quickly drowned out by the dark power that surrounded him.

Adriel stared at the absence of light, keeping his features steady as the smoke fell to the floor and melted away. When he looked to his general after the haze had subsided, his eyes lit up. It had worked.

Corvus stood four inches taller, his body bulging with muscles. His fingers were elongated, sharp talons protruding from the ends, and a pair of jet-black wings sprouted from between his shoulders. He stretched them wide, the light glinting off the jewel tones in the feathers.

His nose had become more pointed, his face angular, and the feathers from his back trailed up his neck, blending with his hair, jutting up toward the sky. His face was pale, and his chest heaved, but he stood proud.

"Commander." He nodded toward Adriel, his black eyes void of feeling.

The soldiers remained silent, awaiting their orders.

"Who's next?" Adriel asked.

They all stepped forward, the movement echoing off the stone walls of the cavernous room.

"I thought so." He beamed, raising the knife once more and letting his lifeblood spill over the broken Oculus. The ranks practically vibrated with excitement.

Once again, black smoke filtered in from the shadows of the room and bellowed over the group. A black void swirled angrily, blocking out all light. Then came the first scream, then another, as their grace was ripped out of their bodies.

The room started shaking. The weapons stands rattled aggressively, dust falling from places unseen. Corvus unfurled a wing and held it over his head to shield his eyes.

Adriel's impatience grew as the moments ticked by when, all of a sudden, the smoke became thicker and more violent.

An invisible wind whipped around them, dangerously throwing loose items about the room. Adriel had to duck to avoid being hit by a stray quiver.

The screams became louder and more insistent, the sound reverberating in their ears. The wind was howling now, and Corvus struggled to stay on his feet as he gripped the table. Then, as if it had never been there, the smoke drifted away, leaving behind a pile of twitching bodies covered in soot.

One by one, the men stood, shaking off the black dust. When the ashes settled, it was revealed that they had not been as fortunate as General Corvus.

The magic had been tainted. Without Celandine's blood and the other half of the Oculus to provide balance, the making had backfired. To use the Oculus in its broken state was rumored to cause untold issues with its magic, but without his mate's blood ... the results were catastrophic.

Though the creatures did have wings, they were a bastardized version of what Adriel had imagined. The wings were much the same as the general's, but the men were now faceless, their features pulled forward in a monstrous caricature of a beak. Their hands and feet were rings of wrinkled skin that bled into long, dirty talons, a trail of feathers protruding from their tailbones.

"Commander," they spoke in unison, the sound as unsettling as nails on a chalkboard. There was a hollowness to their voices that made even Adriel cringe. The sound almost seemed to reverberate from their throat, making it utterly disconcerting.

He gathered himself, thinking he would have to order them away with strict instructions to stay out of sight. *If anyone asks, I will say they were required in another realm. No one will question it.*

When they did not move, he realized they were waiting for a command. He had wanted them to obey his every whim. He was pleased that at least that had been a success.

"Now, be off, all of you. Stay out of sight."

They crossed their fists over their chests, a thump of flesh on leather, and bowed their heads in acknowledgement. Then they exited, walking awkwardly on taloned feet down the halls to the dormitories, their wings tucked in behind them.

The rest of his ranks resided in living quarters outside the training zone, so they would fortunately not be bothered down here.

"Not you," Adriel said, stopping Corvus. The general had been about to head toward the mentor's quarters. "We have work to do."

CHAPTER
THIRTEEN

Soren held the door open as Baz dragged himself through. He dropped his heavy pack with a *thud* and sat on the cool tile, his sword still strapped to his waist.

Enara stumbled in behind him on wobbly legs, muscles protesting from the day's journey.

"How you feeling, champ?" she asked, noting the sweat dripping down the side of his face.

"I am never doing that again," he replied, arching his head up to take in their surroundings.

The entrance was grand. A double door separated the great hall from the outside elements, and torches lined the walls.

Soren jumped when she approached one and it lit itself. In a matter of moments, the entire room was bathed in warm, amber light.

"They must be charmed," she said, turning her gaze to the walls. They were white-trimmed in gold, and red script lined the pillars in a language she did not recognize. It was a center for worship, and she felt out of place amongst the ancient stone.

Once they regained feeling in their legs, they grabbed their weapons and began searching the halls for anything that might be of consequence.

Six hallways in total snaked around different parts of the building, and with each dead end, their frustration grew. After coming up empty in the sixth hallway, they decided to return to the central area to take a break.

Soren crossed her arms, dissatisfied. *I am so fucking over this.* She wanted to tear her hair out. She thought this would be the easy part, and she felt like a failure.

"Well, I'm out of ideas," she said.

"Me, too," Enara agreed, yawning. "I'm so sleep-deprived I can barely think."

"I second that." Baz unclasped his sword and placed it on the ground.

"I can keep watch for a bit if you guys want to get some shut-eye. You two shouldn't have skipped my watch," Soren said, eyeing them.

Enara shrugged. "You needed it."

"I could use a little lie down, if you don't mind," Baz replied, already pulling contents out of his pack to form a pillow.

"Go for it. I got you guys covered."

"Thanks, lady." Enara curled up beside Baz, their backs to each other, and dozed off.

Soren kept her eyes plastered on the heavy doors for almost an hour before stretching her legs. She paced the room while they slept, a million questions running through her mind.

Where could the Oculus be? How did Dad come to possess it? Did he find it on a dig? Where did those creatures come from? Was the guy in the mask the Raven King he spoke of?

She continued lapping the room, her head starting to pound from all the thoughts beating on the side of her skull. Then she turned her gaze upward to appreciate the large, circular skylight, hoping to calm her thoughts. It was embedded in the center of the roof and gave an unobstructed view of the sky.

It was a clear night, and the stars twinkled happily, unscathed by the horrors that lurked below. Her eyes glistened when she spotted her and her father's favorite constellation—Avaris.

He had told her how each side of the constellation was a lover that had been separated by a river of stars. To attempt a crossing would ensure a quick death. The stars were beautiful and bright, but they burned white hot. Noticing their strife, a passing phoenix gave its own feathers to create a bridge. Since phoenixes were impervious to fire, the blazing heat of the stars had no effect on the bridge, thus allowing the couple to be together.

Soren admired the idea of the star-crossed lovers making it through when the odds were stacked against them. She often wondered if it was his favorite because it reminded him of her mother.

A small pang tugged at her heart at the thought. Soren would give anything to have had the chance to get to know her.

Her father had only one photo of her that had survived over the years and had kept it with him always. She'd asked the city watch if she could have it, but they had said they had found no such item on his person.

It had nearly broke her. She had just lost her father and now had no way to look upon her mother's face again.

Her throat tightened at the realization of how alone she really was, the panic in her rising like the tides of the sea.

She breathed in through her nose and out through her mouth, reminding herself that it was not the time to have a mental breakdown. She focused on the five senses, a trick Enara had taught her to stop her anxiety from taking hold.

Find five things you can see, four things you can hear, three things you can feel, two things you can smell, and one thing you can taste. The advice had served her well over the years; though, recently, she had struggled to remember to use it.

She cast her eyes back up to the ceiling, taking in the intricate carvings that surrounded the skylight. One, in particular, stopped her in her tracks.

At first glance, it looked like a continuation of the script, but upon closer inspection, Soren could see it made the outline of an eye. A line from her father's poem flitted into her thoughts. *The spoils will be found below, by the blazing torchlight's glow.*

She mulled over it again, working through it in her mind, when the realization struck her.

She ran over to Baz and Enara, shaking them awake. "Guys … guys, c'mon. I know what we have to do."

They gathered themselves and their weapons, waiting for an explanation.

"Dad alluded to the Oculus being underground. I think we've been looking in the wrong place."

"Makes sense," Baz said. "But how do we get from here"—he pointed to the ground—"to there?"

"That's the best part. So, the bit about the torches confused me at first, but do you remember the north hallway?"

"Which one was that?" Enara asked.

"The one with the image of a staircase. It had that sun blazing above it."

"Yeah, I remember. It did seem a little out of place."

"Exactly, so here's what I'm thinking; we grab one of the torches and see if the heat does anything to change the image. It could lead us to another clue."

Baz shrugged. "Well, it's worth a try."

Enara nodded. "Let's do it."

They each grabbed a torch and headed for the hallway, stopping in front of the carving.

Soren stepped forward, the image looming over her, and started tracing the torch around the wall. She prayed to the Maker, hoping to find something—anything. She was about to give up when the red engraving of the frame began to stutter and spark, causing them to jump back.

The flames had set off a chemical reaction, causing the red pigment to burst. The detonation created an opening where the engraving had been, small pieces of rock littering the floor. When the dust settled, a staircase emerged before them.

"You don't think all the walls are like that, do you?" Baz asked, blowing the debris from his nose.

"You never know," Soren responded, stepping through the rubble.

They pressed forward, the staircase descending into darkness. They had to keep their hands on the stone to prevent themselves from slipping. The wall of blackness was barely pierced by their torchlights.

When they reached the bottom, another set of charmed torches lit up, filling the room with dim light. They hung on pillars lining both sides of the circular room, and at the end stood a large statue of a woman.

She cried silent tears, the water pooling at her feet, and she held but a single rose. It was the woman from her father's poem, but to her surprise, Soren realized that this beautiful, ethereal carving was the exact likeness of her mother.

"Is that—"

"Yup," Soren cut Baz off.

"Oh, Soren, I'm so sorry." Enara placed her hand on the small of her back.

Soren sniffled as she took in the sight of her mother. "Don't be. I never thought I would see her again after Dad."

She took a few steps closer, her face wet with tears. When she was only a few feet away, a thin, gold line materialized in the air. The thread of light leaped from Soren's fingertips, leading to a rectangular plaque that sat below the pool of wa-ter. She stopped momentarily, paralyzed. It was the same type of thread from the library.

Her fingers trembled as she brought the flame of the torch up to read the inscription.

Saint Celandine, Goddess of Halcyon, Year 817

Confusion flickered between them. Before they had time to dwell on it, however, the edge of the plaque lit up like a doorway, and a compartment popped open to reveal a large book. It was titled, *The Secret of Celandine.*

Soren pulled it out and propped it open on the ledge of the fountain. Most of the pages had been chiseled out to create an empty pocket, and in the middle sat a curious metal object. There was no mistaking the item, as they had all painstakingly studied the photograph. This was the Oculus.

As she gazed upon the broken shard of inhuman metal, it felt as though it were speaking to a part of her soul. The name on the plaque scratched at a forgotten memory in her mind's eye.

Celandine. She willed herself to remember. *Dad told me stories about her. He said she came from the sky. They had called her many names throughout the decades—Celestial, Angel, Other, Saint.* The knot of confusion unraveled as a once-forgotten bedtime story floated up from the depths of her long-term memory.

Celandine was a rare beauty. Not only in looks, but she had a truly beautiful soul, as well. She looked down from her perch in the clouds, admiring the humans and their frailty. Every life of theirs was but a blink in her eternity.

Once a month, she would come down to Entheas and grant wishes and miracles to those most in need. Stories of her kindness traveled down through the centuries, and a temple had been created in her honor.

As the years went on and the world began to change, she was forgotten, the memory of her temple's location lost to the sands of time. It was rumored that she was betrothed and no longer worried herself with the human world. Others speculated that she lived among them, wanting to escape her immortality. Many thought her to be dead. In a way, they were all right.

Celandine had been betrothed to the strongest of her kind, designed to be his mate, but he betrayed her. He wanted to destroy the humans because he thought them weak. So, she ran, taking a part of his power with her.

She risked her life to save the humans, and her grace was ripped from her body as she fell to Entheas. She lay broken and dying, but fate had other plans for her.

As if by design, a man lost in the woods came across her broken body and nursed her back to health. Using only what nature provided, he built them a shelter, hunted for food, and foraged for herbs that had healing powers.

It took months for her to regain her strength but, over time, she was able to walk again and learned to heal without the power her grace had provided.

The man had dark hair that flowed to his shoulders, tanned skin, and kind eyes. He was strong and had respect for the living world, much like she did.

Over time, their fondness for each other grew into a close friendship, and then into something more entirely. They fell for each other, their love irrevocable and unyielding.

They built a small home in the same clearing where they'd met. Neither had any family in this world, and after a few years, they decided to make one of their own.

They had a daughter, her namesake that of an owl to represent inner wisdom and transformation. She was proof that two worlds could come together to create something unimaginably beautiful. They lived a happy life together but, without her grace, Celandine's life force faded quicker than an average human. Shortly after giving birth, she passed in her lover's arms in a field under the stars.

Soren slammed the book shut with a cry, eyes watering. She knew what it all meant but was not willing to admit it to herself just yet.

Her heartbeat rang in her temples, and she squeezed her eyes shut, willing the tears away.

A crash from above had them clutching their weapons, steadying their grips.

The kestrels were coming. Soon, they would find the entrance to this level and the Oculus would be lost, its power along with it.

"Come out, come out, little bird," a voice boomed from the deep.

Baz shuffled nervously. "As cool as this place is, I think it's time to go."

Enara gave him an exasperated look. "Seriously? What part of that is helpful?"

"There is no other way out of here," Soren cried in frustration, running her torch along the back walls, hoping to create another opening.

They thought they could buy some time and stacked the ornate wooden chests flanking the staircase in front of the entrance, but it was no use. They were already here.

The kestrels' talons tore into the wood, sending splinters flying in all directions. The chests fell, giving way with a sickening crack, and the winged beasts flooded in.

Soren ran to the statue to shove the sacred book back into the hidden compartment. Then she planted her feet and lifted her bow, arrow already notched. Baz and Enara flanked her, their weapons raised. Then he walked in.

The winged beasts had landed in a semi-circle around their master, effectively blocking the exit.

"Well, shit," Baz huffed under his breath, "this should be fun."

The stranger stood across from her, his mask menacing in the torchlight.

"Hello, little bird," he lulled. His voice was like velvet—dark and seductive. The sound of it caressed her ears, and she had to shake her head to steady herself. This was most certainly not a dream.

"Is there something I can help you with?" Soren spat, venom on her tongue.

"Yes, many of which you would thoroughly enjoy."

Soren scoffed. *If you don't say so yourself.*

"But, for now, all I ask is for you and that trinket," he said, eyeing the statue. "To come with me, and we'll gladly be on our way."

Enara snarled, "Take one step further, and I will gladly remove your tongue from your mouth."

"Maybe we will feed it to a couple of your feathered friends," Baz added.

"Shame, really. I was hoping to do this the easy way. I rather liked this outfit." He smirked as he set his jacket down on an unbroken chest. "Shall we?"

Soren chuckled, pursing her lips. "Yeah, how about you go fuck yourself?" Then she loosed her arrow.

The room exploded into a symphony of sound and movement. The kestrels levitated with a flurry of their wings and dove toward them, teeth glistening.

Baz lunged forward, his sword piercing one of them in the chest. The creature shrieked in agony and fell to the ground, but there was no time to celebrate as two more advanced, taking its place.

Soren felled three in quick succession, her bowstring hot, then slid behind the statue of her mother for cover from the onslaught. She inched around the corner to see Enara fighting off a group of talons with her spear.

Her form was impeccable. She blocked every attack with ease and returned a fatal blow. The creatures raked at her, slashing with their claws, but made no contact. Soren made a mental note to train with her more if they ever made it out of here alive.

Across the sanctuary, the stranger was on a knee, palms to the damp floor. Her arrow was laid out in front of him, fully intact. *Impossible.*

Alarm bells went off in her mind. Her heart hammering. *No one could have stopped that shot.*

She observed him in silence, searching for anything that might explain how the hell he was still standing. He looked serene. Calm amongst the chaos.

She wondered where he had come from.

His eyes shone like sapphires holding a secret, and he seemed otherworldly, out of place amongst the stones. *I wonder what he looks like under that mask*, she mused.

"A little help here!" Baz broke her out of her reverie.

She rejoined the battle, sliding the last dagger out of its sheath. She sprinted toward Baz, who was fighting from the ground, and whipped her knife end over end at the kestrel blocking her path.

The dagger sunk to its hilt in the monster's head and, without skipping a step, Soren wrenched it out and jumped on the back of the one towering over Baz.

It flailed in response, trying to buck her off. Hastily, she slit its throat, and it gurgled, attempting to stop the bleeding with its talons. The black ichor sprayed hot on Baz's face as it fell to the ground at his side.

"Seriously, dude? I'm never going to get this stain out," Baz said, glancing down at his blood-drenched clothes.

Soren shrugged. "Sorry, not sorry."

He wiped his face and grabbed the hand she held out to him, jumping to his feet.

"We aren't out of this yet," Enara asserted from their left.

"Yes, ma'am," Baz joked.

"I told you not to call me that, you—" Enara's eyes widened. "Is that your blood?"

Baz shook his head. "Not mine. Soren gutted one of those freaks on top of me." Baz chuckled, looking down. A flood of red was seeping from a gash above his knee, and shock gathered in his eyes.

"Shit, are you okay?" Soren asked.

"Nothing a little ale and the company of a good woman won't fix," he said, teetering. A few seconds later, he fell to the ground, eyes rolling back in his head. He could mend others, no problem, but the sight of his own blood had always been a cause for issue.

"Forever the optimist," Enara groaned, bending to pull her friend out of the line of fire.

"Get that leg bandaged before he bleeds out. I'll cover you," Soren ordered.

She assessed her surroundings. The kestrels had regrouped and were starting to advance again. The stranger, still kneeling as if in prayer, looked up at her. Soren inhaled, taken aback.

His eyes were locked on her, assessing her every movement. Predatory. Lethal.

She broke from his gaze and let two more arrows fly, taking out the closest attackers. She yelled back to Enara, "How's it going back there?"

The blood had drained from her friend's face. "I made a tourniquet, but he's lost a lot of blood. We need to get him one of the mender potions from my pack."

Soren swore under her breath and took down another rival. In their rush to gain access to the lower level, they had left their packs upstairs.

Enara tucked Baz against the front of the statue, guarding him against the beasts. Soren backed up, joining her so they could fight side by side. The statue of Celandine at their backs watched over their friend.

The kestrels were unrelenting. One of their talons caught Enara across the face before she sliced open its belly. She put her hand to her cheek, her fingers dripping crimson. The creature's guts spilled out, and the stench was so foul it made her heave.

Soren gagged, reaching back to find her quiver empty. *Dagger, it is.*

Enara and her stood firm, retaking their positions in front of Baz.

"We are going to make it out of here, or we are going to die trying," Soren said.

Enara gave her a quick look, the two sharing a smile. If this was to be the end, she was happy that Soren was by her side.

They managed to take down two more kestrels, but the odds were still not in their favor.

Before the bloodshed could continue, the stranger growled from across the room, "Enough!" He stood, his voice rebounding off the slick stone walls.

The volume startled the women long enough for two kestrels to swoop in from above and disarm them.

"Bring her to me," their master ordered.

The kestrel closest to Soren dragged her toward their masked assailant. She fought the monster every step of the way, her nails digging into its cold flesh.

"If you harm her, I will find you, and I will unleash unimaginable pain on you and your entire flock!" Enara seethed, struggling to fight free. Then she shrieked as a kestrel dug its taloned fingers into her shoulders. She bit back tears, fighting against the pain.

The dream walker let out a condescending laugh. "I have more important plans for her. You, on the other hand, are inconsequential to me."

Before she could respond, he flicked his finger in silent command, and Soren watched in horror as the kestrel tossed Enara into the far wall.

"You bastard!" she screamed as her friend's limp body fell to the floor.

He grabbed her chin forcefully, planting his mask inches from her face. "Mind your tongue."

Soren's body vibrated with anger. "Mind yours!" She smashed her forehead into the flat part of his mask above the beak, knocking herself out in the process.

He fell back a step and shook his head, mildly amused.

The mask was not just for show; it was magically fortified. Any force applied to it quickly dissipated through the charmed metal. His father had gifted it to him.

"Little bird," he sighed, moving a stray hair from her bloodied face. "You have no idea what the fates have in store for us."

CHAPTER
FOURTEEN

Soren woke to the flutter of wings, a headache grinding at her temples. She tried to gather her surroundings, but the sunlight scorched her eyes. She hissed as she touched the small gash on her forehead, thanking the Maker that it wouldn't require stitches.

She sat up, bile rising in her throat. The pain in her skull reached a crescendo, and she groaned.

"You are quite a vision in the morning."

"What the fu—" Soren exclaimed, falling off what she realized was a rather large bed.

The stranger let out a small laugh at her expense. "You are a truly graceful creature."

"Screw you," she said, scrubbing the sleep from her eyes. "What do you want with me? Where are my friends?" They were the same questions she had asked on the journey here, but had yet to receive any answers.

"They were indisposed, and I only had accommodations for one guest."

"You're a monster! They could be dead by now!" Soren glowered in his direction, trying to focus her eyes. *I hit my head harder than I thought.*

She could make out the shape of a door at the edge of the room and decided to make a run for it. She scrambled to her feet and reached for the brass knob, but her feeble attempt to escape was cut short.

The stranger caught her mid-stride. He grabbed her wrist with one hand and flattened her to the wooden door with the other.

"Now, now, let's not be hasty."

Her adrenaline spiked, clearing her vision. She looked up at him and gasped when she realized that the mask was gone. The heat from his palm seeping into her chest was a startling contrast to the icy glint in his eyes.

She glared back, refusing to break first, taking in the lines of his face. Her eyebrows lifted when she noticed the white shock of hair peeking out from under his hood.

He relaxed his stance and leaned against the doorframe, a smirk forming on his lips. "Now, isn't this better——"

Soren erupted with a swift knee to the groin, causing him to double over with a grunt. She then grasped the sides of his head and dealt a second sickening blow to his angular face, feeling the bone of his nose snap. She smiled triumphantly.

His hood had fallen, and she noticed that his snowy hair stuck up like frozen daggers.

He recovered quicker than she had expected and lunged forward, grabbing her by the throat.

A look of horror painted Soren's face as he threw her back against the oak door. Her head knocked, and the force sent a twinge of pain through her spine.

"Try that again, little bird, and I might just snap those pretty little wings of yours." Blood dripped into his mouth, and the hatred in his eyes burned her skin.

"Fuck you," she choked out, trying to break free of his grasp.

His grip tightened, and the edges of her vision blurred. She could feel her heartbeat slow under his fingertips and a numbness spread over her body.

"Don't tempt me." His response was a faint whisper grazing the shell of her ear.

The last thing she remembered was the smell of pine needles and sweet grass before her consciousness slipped.

THE ACRID SCENT OF METHEDRINE STUNG HER NOSTRILS AS SHE came to. Soren had only dealt with ammonia once before, and it was safe to say she was not a fan.

Faded footsteps shuffled somewhere behind her, and her eyes widened in panic as she noticed the cuffs around her wrists.

The iron manacles were affixed to a lavish dining table, via a circular pin and chain mechanism that allowed for minimal movement. Testing her limits, she pulled and twisted at her bonds until her wrists were bruised and angry. She let out a resentful cry and traced the vines engraved around the table's edge. Even in her petrified state, she appreciated the craftsmanship.

White oak was rare north of Eldrin, and this piece must have been at least twelve feet in length. Obviously, her captor had money.

She took the time to gather details about the room. Paintings lined the walls, mostly muted landscapes with elegant sconces on either side. A large window to the left allowed in the last light of the day, casting the room in a dull orange glow.

Her gaze shifted up toward the chandelier that hung above the table, and her mouth dropped open. The entire piece was made of deer antlers, intricately woven together like a crown of bones, equal parts haunting and beautiful. She wondered angrily how many innocent animals had been slaughtered to create the macabre piece.

A door groaned across the room, returning Soren to her present circumstances.

The stranger sauntered in with a smug look on his face, taking the seat across from her.

She set her mouth in a hard line, her eyes shooting flames in his direction. Apart from a small bandage across the bridge of his nose, he was entirely unscathed. *What the fuck? I swear I felt his nose break.*

He made a spectacle of rolling up his sleeves and clasping his hands together. Soren rolled her eyes, huffing in annoyance. She might be forced to share a table with him, but she didn't have to be nice about it.

"Now, little bird, let us not forget our manners."

Her eyes narrowed as she spoke through gritted teeth, "Stop calling me that."

"What would you have me call you?"

"My name is Soren, if you must know," she said, mocking his condescending tone.

"I prefer little bird." He gave her a once-over, his cold eyes taking in all the parts of her that were visible over the edge of the table.

Her cheeks lit up under his gaze. She hated that she was unable to turn away. All she could think of was how weak she must look to him.

"And what about you?" she redirected, trying to take his attention off her worn-out body. "Do you have a name, or should I just call you Broody?"

A smile played at his lips, eyes flashing. "It's Rook."

Soren burst out in laughter, her response exaggerated due to lack of sleep.

He sat still as a statue until she calmed herself.

"Seriously? Rook?" She wiped a tear from her eye. "What are you? A chess piece?"

He ignored her question, clenching his hands. The movement made the veins pop out of his muscular forearms. He clicked his tongue, like a snake ready to strike. "It is my understanding that we got off on the wrong foot."

"No shit," she retorted. "How's your face?"

Rook's eyes darkened, and his lips set into a hard line. He clenched his jaw, and Soren could practically hear his teeth grinding.

"You would do well to behave, little bird," he said, trying to control his temper. "I can chain you to worse things than a dining table."

Soren's mouth dropped open, and her composure slipped. She broke eye contact, looking down at her wrists. They were now a grotesque mix of plum and crimson. *Idiot,* she scolded herself for causing the injury.

"Now that we have completed our lesson on table etiquette," he said, relaxing his jaw, "do you think we can get through dinner without another outburst?"

Soren was about to give him a smart reply when she heard the door behind her creak open. Two women in servant's clothing scooted past, placing table settings in front of them both, unfazed by her predicament. Judging by their similar appearance, Soren deduced they must be related.

She had a glimmer of hope when they placed the cutlery down, expecting to get her hands on something of use. The light in her eyes quickly faded, though, when she realized they had given her thin wooden tools. *So much for that.* She blew out a breath, shifting in the cushioned armchair.

The ladies snuck back to where they had come from then returned with two silver trays of the most delicious food Soren had ever seen. She inhaled deeply, her mouth watering. She hadn't had anything to eat in almost twelve hours, and her stomach let out an angry growl in reminder.

"Eat," Rook ordered harshly, startling her.

Embarrassed, she gave him an apprehensive look. "How do I know it's not poisoned?"

He tilted his head, studying her. "You don't. But if I wanted you dead"—he stabbed a piece of meat with his metal fork—"you would be." He popped it into his mouth.

Soren's eyes momentarily locked on the thin line of his lips before shifting her line of sight back to her plate. She knew better than to trust him, but she was starving. After another moment of hesitation, she gave in.

Tentatively, she took a few small nibbles, savoring each bite. It truly was the best food she'd ever eaten. The quail was moist and smelled of fresh herbs and lemon. The potatoes melted in her mouth, the butter and garlic dancing on her tongue. She would have assumed the vegetables were freshly harvested if it weren't for the snow skimming across the large windowpane. *We must have traveled north. Nowhere else has snow this time of year.*

She packed the knowledge away, saving it for later, and continued with her meal.

They ate in silence, and Soren's discomfort grew as the minutes crept by. When she finished, she sat back, fidgeting with her chains.

Wanting to break the silence, she asked, "Why am I here?" She then waited as he finished chewing, avoiding his eyes.

"My father will explain. He is due to arrive shortly." He patted his lips with a napkin then set it down on the table.

"Wow, a heck of a first date." Her voice was laced with sarcasm. "Handcuffs and a meet and greet with the parents. How lucky can a girl get?"

He stiffened at the remark and considered his words. To Soren, it looked as if he were deciding what details he wanted to share.

"I never met my mother." He threw the words out quickly, as if they tasted sour on his tongue. "So, it will just be daddy dearest." He traced the top of his wine glass with his finger, seemingly lost in thought.

"Oh." Soren squirmed awkwardly, not knowing what to say. She knew all too well what it was like to grow up without a mother.

"What's the matter, little bird?" he asked snidely, his mask returning. "Cat got your tongue?"

She rolled her eyes and continued to push the food around on her plate, trying to ignore him.

She heard his chair scrape the floor as he stood but refused to make eye contact. The sound of his footsteps echoed in her direction, and the hairs on the back of her neck stood up.

He leaned close to her ear, sending a shiver down her spine. Then Soren yelped when he spoke again, his breath warm on her rosy cheek.

"I am going to undo the manacles now. Do not test me." He leaned forward and used a small key to loosen the pin that held the chains. Noticing her posture change, he added, "If you try to run, I will hunt your friends down and slit their throats while you watch."

Soren sucked in a ragged breath. *Baz ... Enara ... The temple.*

"You wouldn't dare touch them," she choked out as tears began to form in the corners of her eyes, the hands of guilt threading around her throat. She had been so busy with her current situation that she had temporarily forgotten about them. *I am a terrible friend.*

Her breaths came faster now as her hatred for herself grew. She could feel the panic seeping into her bones like slow-acting poison. Images of them flashed through her mind. The blood dripping from Baz's leg. The sound Enara's body had made when it had hit the wall. It was all too much.

Rook cursed under his breath. She was breathing too quickly, and it would be irresponsible to let her pass out again so soon.

"Maker, pull yourself together." The annoyance in his voice was clear.

He searched for recognition in her eyes and received none. Her gaze flitted about the room, unfocused and erratic. He waved a hand in front of her face and got no response.

"Soren, look at me," he commanded firmly. He kept his voice low, trying to snap her out of it.

At the sound of her name, Soren's eyes flicked over to meet his. However, her labored breaths continued, and her pulse raced, making her lightheaded.

"Stop hyperventilating," he continued, rolling his eyes. "Your friends are alive."

She drew in a shaky breath but could not yet speak. She stared into his too-blue eyes, trying to force the question out. He answered automatically.

"My scouts saw a man and woman leaving the temple a few hours after we vacated the premises. They reported that they were worse for wear but very much alive."

At the admission, her panic broke.

"They are alive?" The words crawled from her throat in a broken sob.

Rook sighed dramatically. "Yes, little bird, they're alive."

Soren cried out in relief, some pigment returning to her face.

He glanced at her, the pain behind her eyes reminiscent of his own.

The panic had depleted what remained of her energy, and she sagged in her chair. Her mind rested somewhere on the verge of sleep, and she almost forgot where she was. Exhaustion lulled her into a false sense of security, but just as her lids drooped, a deafening thunderclap shook the rafters.

The trance was broken, and Soren shook off the remaining tendrils of panic that had wrapped themselves around her throat. She straightened her spine, schooling her features back into one of disgust.

"What the fuck was that?" she demanded, finding her voice again.

"That … would be my father."

CHAPTER
FIFTEEN

Enara's fingers slid across the damp stone, her eyelids fluttering open. She cringed against the pain as it shot through her body. The last thing she remembered was the kestrel lifting her off the ground before everything went black. *How long have I been out?*

She looked around, the torchlight flickering in an invisible breeze, casting a shadow over Baztien's limp body.

"Baz!" she cried, willing her muscles to move. Slowly, she got to her feet and limped over to him, ignoring the ache in her bones. A sigh of relief escaped her lips when she saw the rise and fall of his chest.

She took another glance around. Soren was nowhere to be seen. *I am going to kill that masked bastard!*

She crouched down to inspect Baz's leg. Considering it had been a rushed job, she was impressed with how the bandage had turned out. The heavy fabric had staunched the wound, but it would still require more than basic mending.

Enara touched his face then headed for the staircase in search of more supplies. She dragged her body up, using the wall for support, hissing as the rough stone dragged along the cuts on her shoulders.

Miraculously, their packs had been left untouched. She thanked the Maker and pulled out a healing draught, tucking it into her waistband. Then she took the steps down at a snail's pace, not wanting to risk breaking the vial. They only had a few, and there was no way to replenish their stores anytime soon.

She returned to Baz's side and pulled him into her lap. The potions were not a cure-all, but they provided temporary assistance in cases like this.

She unstoppered the narrow tube with her teeth, spitting the cork aside, and then tipped the contents into his mouth. *Please let this work.*

The seconds felt like hours as she willed his body to accept the elixir. She nearly cried her relief when he started sputtering a few moments later. He coughed as the last of the tasteless liquid trickled down the back of his throat.

"Hey," he said, looking up at her. His eyes were hooded and weary, and his voice was strained.

"Hey back." She blinked the moisture from her eyes and gave him a small smile.

"What happened?"

"They took Soren."

"No," he said, horrified. He sat up slowly to avoid jostling his leg.

"They knocked me out and took her," Enara continued. "Baz, I'm scared. I thought we lost you. You were so still ..." She choked as the last words came out. *I can't lose you.*

She should have said the words out loud, but her pride got the best of her. She needed to be strong for Soren. Now was not the time to get caught up in her feelings.

"Hey," Baz snapped her out of her thoughts. He reached forward to wipe some blood from her cheek. Fortunately, the cut looked worse than it was. The kestrel had only caught her with the tip of its talon. "I'm right here, I'm okay."

She smiled weakly for his benefit, leaning into his hand.

They sat there for a moment, taking in the silence, thanking the powers-that-be that they had survived.

"We should go," Enara said, shifting to help him up. "I don't want to be here in case they come back."

"Agreed," he said as they struggled up the stairs together, grimacing with each movement. They paused in the main room to hydrate and eat something, but their stomachs protested.

The potion was starting to kick in, and Baz was able to walk unassisted, whereas Enara's pain fell to a dull throb. After being tossed like a ragdoll, most would require more time to rest, but she was accustomed to pain.

Anger for her father bloomed in her chest. She let it flourish, the fury helping her to ignore the worst of her injuries.

The pair finally exited the temple, staying close enough to watch for their enemy's return, hoping to do some reconnaissance. They did not make a fire for fear of being seen, so they huddled up on a bed of moss next to each other.

When dawn broke, they stretched, their bodies whining in disagreement. Neither had slept more than an hour or two.

"We should change your dressing," Enara said, eyeing the blood-soaked cloth stuck to his leg.

"Not before I enjoy a sailor's breakfast," Baz said, pulling out a small bottle of rum from the side of his pack.

"Where did you get that?"

"The guy that owned the hostel made it himself. He wanted a taste tester, so I happily obliged. He gave me this as a parting gift." His eyes were bright with humor.

"Of course he did. Well, go on then, you're going to need another swig or two from the looks of that bandage."

He conceded and took a large gulp, the amber liquid leaving a trail of fire in its wake. Then he leaned back against a tree and braced himself. *This is going to suck.*

Enara tried her best to be gentle, but there was so much blood, and the layers took more effort to peel off the farther down she got. Baz hissed and swore as she went, his discomfort obvious. After he finished the contents of the bottle, he tossed it in the woods, tears pricking the corners of his eyes.

"Fuck!" he yelled as Enara detached the last part of the cloth from his skin, her eyes widening. He followed her line of sight, face scrunching in confusion as he assessed the damage.

The wound was almost bone-deep and about five inches long. The potion had cinched the main artery and some of the skin back together so he was no longer at risk of bleeding to death, but something was disturbingly wrong.

The blood was thick and black, the veins surrounding the gash dark and almost pulsing, obviously infected.

"I thought healing tonics warded off poison?" he questioned, his voice wavering.

"I thought so, too, but those creatures … they were something else. Maybe the potions don't work the same on the injuries they inflict."

"What do we do?"

Enara racked her brain, searching for an answer. "We can't leave you like this, but I don't think any mender will be able to help. I have an idea, but I can't guarantee it will work, either …" She trailed off.

"Well, let's hear it." Baz was willing to try anything if it meant he could live long enough to see his mothers again.

Enara blew out a breath. "It's a long shot, but I think we need to try the Pools of Patrivah. It's two days' travel from here. The waters are said to heal all things—mortal and magical injuries alike."

"What if I don't last that long?" he voiced the question that Enara was already considering.

"You have to," she whispered as she dabbed a wet cloth around his wound.

He flinched in response, the cold fabric sending shockwaves of fire through his veins. The poison seemed to reject any efforts to be cleansed, and the harder they tried, the more pain it caused.

Baz took a second potion as she redressed his leg, wishing he could wipe the sadness from her eyes.

"Enara, your shoulder," he said, realizing that she, too, was infected.

She tore the sleeves from her shirt, taking notice of the angry black lines trailing from where the kestrel's talons had dug in. *Maker, dammit.* Mercifully, the graze on her face remained unafflicted, the cut was not deep enough for the infection to take hold.

Baz took the cloth from her hand, wiping away what he could. He winced as she bit back a cry then applied a few smaller bandages. He put extra padding on top and helped her slip the pack over her shoulders.

"Is that okay?" he asked, worry plain on his face.

"It hurts, but it's manageable."

They divvied up the items from Soren's bag to share the load. Then Enara readjusted the pack slightly as Baz pressed into the ground with his bad leg. He cringed but forced himself to stand tall and took a few tentative steps. The more pressure he put on it, the more the poison seemed to take hold, so he would have to tread lightly.

Enara grabbed a large branch and hacked off the smaller pieces to create a walking stick.

"Try this," she said, handing it to him.

He grabbed it, using it as a crutch and walked a small circle around the trees. He gave Enara a wave of triumph before lumbering back to her.

"Ready when you are," he said, a little bit of his pep returning.

They walked in silence, taking it one mile at a time, the boost of energy short-lived. Progress was slow, and they had to take more breaks than they would have liked to rest their tired bodies.

Baz downed another potion in the early afternoon, noticing that the infection had spread. The ichor had bled down his leg, and his ankle was black and angry.

"How are you feeling?" she asked.

He dropped the hem of his pants, not wanting to worry her. "I've been better, but I won't complain about the company," he said, winking.

By nightfall, they had finally reached the ferry. The crossing was at the end of a merchant trail that they'd taken from the base of the mountain.

Enara bribed the captain to allow them passage with an expensive-looking compass.

"Wasn't that a fake?" Baz asked, raising his brows.

She shrugged. "He doesn't need to know that."

They settled in on a low wooden bench, knowing the crossing would take most of the night. Both sent prayers to the Maker that they would get there in time.

"Hey, you two, we've arrived," came a gruff voice from above.

Enara turned to see the captain gesturing to the mass of land before them. Relief flooded through her, and she thanked their lucky stars. *Patrivah, we made it.*

"Baz, get up. We have to go—" She stopped when she took in the state of him. He was sweating, and his hair was stuck to his forehead.

"Yeah, I'm coming," he groaned.

He attempted to stand, but his leg gave out, so Enara helped him along as they disembarked. She was feeling a little worse for wear but pushed through it.

Before continuing, she gave him the last healing potion. She watched as he drained the contents, concern knotting in her stomach. *It just needs to work long enough for us to reach the pools.*

The elixir barely made a difference at this point, and Enara gasped when she saw the black lines sticking out from the neck of his collar.

"Why didn't you tell me it was this bad?" she cried in frustration.

"I didn't want you to worry." He coughed hard then spat on the ground.

They both cringed as black stained the dirt. They were running out of time.

"We need to leave. Now." Enara grabbed his arm, dragging him off the beach, ignoring the pain burning in her own body.

The pools sat approximately three miles away, atop a small ridge that overlooked the Obsidian Sea. They made it up the first half of the climb, but their pace was sluggish.

The poison was polluting Baz's bloodstream, as well as her own, and his skin was pale. He hadn't spoken in a while and worry was taking a hold of Enara's heart.

They had about one mile to go when they rounded a sharp corner and came to an abrupt stop as Enara nearly bounced face-first off an armored body that blocked the path. She struggled to maintain her composure, the poison starting to mess with her mind. She looked up at the man, her eyes filled with desperation.

"The pools are reserved for Patrovian royals only. No outsiders," he said with authority.

"Please, my friend, he's been poisoned. We came all this way from the Braexmirth Mountains."

"I am sorry, but I have my orders." His stance was firm.

She narrowed her eyes, fury gathering inside of her like flames in a forest fire. "Everyone has a price. Name yours."

He looked her up and down. Even covered in blood and grime, she was stunning.

"I'll have you."

She turned her nose up in disgust. *Pig.* "How about I give you this instead?" She held out her palm to reveal a large sapphire from Tarak's collection.

His eyes widened greedily. Patrovians were known to have a weakness for fine jewels, and their obsession with wealth tended to cloud their judgment.

"Now, where did a girl like you acquire a gem like that?"

"That is of no consequence to you. Take it or leave it."

He eyed her with suspicion but snatched up the stone and stepped aside to let them pass.

They trudged on.

Enara looked back to see him stroking the jewel like a pet cat. *Greedy bastard.*

"Are we there yet?" Baz asked, his voice momentarily returning. "I don't think I can make it much further."

"I got you. Come on," she said, tucking herself under his arm, carrying most of his weight.

They made it about a hundred yards before Baz collapsed into the dirt, pulling Enara down with him. She landed hard on her free hand and swore as pain shot up her wrist.

"Not now!" Her voice cracked as she strained to roll him over.

His face was covered in earth, and a few small scratches marred his olive skin. His eyes were cloudy, and the groans that escaped his mouth sounded like a wounded animal. If she did nothing, he would die here.

She threw their packs aside, knowing they would be of no use if they were dead. Then she pulled the leather belt from his trousers and used it to strap his arms together. Kneeling, she threw them over her head and shuffled him up her back before adjusted his body so his head rested on the side of her neck, his legs laying limp at her hips. She attached her belt to the one holding his arms to keep him from slipping off her back. Then, taking a deep breath, she stood, her legs shaking with the effort.

One excruciating step at a time, she made her way up to the pools. It felt as though someone was holding a hot poker to the indents in her shoulders, and her calves screamed. Every part of her body had been pushed past its limits, and she fell to the ground, her muscles giving out. Her knees hit the dirt, sending a shockwave through her nerves.

She undid the knot that bound them together, tears streaming down her face. She screamed in frustration, the sound guttural and heartbreaking.

She could see the pools glittering in the distance, steam radiating off the smooth surface. They were so close.

Baz's eyelids had fallen shut, and there was barely a breath escaping his mouth. He had moments left. *No, I will not lose you!*

She wiped the tears from her face and grabbed hold of his wrists, his skin cold and clammy. With every last ounce of strength she had left, she dragged him toward the simmering water.

Her throat was raw from sucking in haggard breaths, and she let out one last grunt as she hauled him to the edge of the pool.

She jumped down and pulled him into the water with her, untying his hands.

When nothing happened, she let out a sob. "You can't go. I need you." The tears returned as a final breath escaped his mouth. Her lips trembled as tears fell from her face.

She stared at his unmoving chest, and something inside her broke. Grief racked her limbs, and her sobs turned to wails as she looked down at his floating body.

"I love you, you know. I should have told you … I should have let you in." She cried harder, her tears melding into the azure of the pool.

Distracted by her heartache she barely noticed that the small cuts and bruises along her fair skin had begun to heal.

"May we meet again," she said, leaning down to kiss him.

"Wait," a croak escaped his lips, and the shock of it nearly made her fall back into the water. "If you kiss me, I want to be alive to feel it," he finished.

"Baz!" she cried, wiping the snot from her face. She pulled his body to hers, relieved.

"Ow, still broken over here," he said, cringing.

"Sorry." She released him, her tears turning to ones of happiness.

He rotated to get his sea legs under him and stood, testing his mobility. "It's stiff, but it doesn't hurt."

"Hop up on the ledge," Enara said, needing to see for herself.

He did as he was told and hoisted himself up, water dripping from his clothes.

Enara waded over, the water level falling just below her chest. The fabric of her shirt clung to her curves as she unwound the bandage from his leg. She was shocked at what she saw.

His veins no longer showed any traces of infection, and the wound had healed, leaving behind a white scar.

He grinned at her, the blood returning to his face, and she smiled back.

She rested her hands on his knees, sighing with relief. After a moment, she reached up and pulled him back into the warmth of the water, embracing him.

"I thought I lost you," she whimpered out.

"You can never lose me," he said, as if the Maker himself had willed it so.

She looked up at him, her hazel eyes still wet with tears, memorizing every inch of his face. Then she ran a hand through his thick bronze hair.

"I love you, too, you know," he said, happiness plain on his face.

She blushed, looking away. "You weren't supposed to hear that."

He touched the side of her face, turning her back toward him, and lifted his other hand to match. "Yeah, well, I've never been very good at doing what I'm told," he said then kissed her.

It wasn't a clash of teeth and lips, as she'd expected, but more akin to a slow-burning fire. His lips were soft as they pressed against hers and her arms curled around his waist. It was the sweetest of kisses, sending sparks through her fingertips and down to her toes. It was a kiss that felt like home.

After a moment, they parted, smiling sheepishly at each other, and then Baz splashed her playfully. "Took you long enough."

"Oh, shove it," she replied, splashing him back.

"So, what is there to eat around here?" he asked, changing the subject.

"About that …" The packs were still a ways down the hill. "Fancy a morning walk?"

After retrieving their bags, they decided to saunter back up and take advantage of their access to the healing pools. They figured it would be unlikely that the higher-ranking Patrovians would be joining them anytime soon.

Stripping off their grimy garments, they waded into the water. Their blood heated, though it was in no part caused by the temperature of the pool. It was nothing neither of them hadn't seen before, but they both felt suddenly shy.

They wrung out their sodden clothes, leaving them to dry in the late morning sun. Then, after some hesitation, they tentatively took turns washing each other, careful to avoid certain areas.

They stole a few more kisses, breathing each other in. The sensation sent a tingle up Enara's spine. Neither tried to push for more. Instead, they just held each other.

They had spent years pining after one another and, while they had craved physical contact, they craved emotional connection most of all.

Once their fingertips were good and wrinkled, they jumped out, using the furs as makeshift clothes while theirs dried.

They set up a minimalist camp and had lunch, taking a few well-deserved hours of rest.

"We have to find her," Enara said, her cheek pressed against his chest, tracing his bicep with a finger.

"We will." Confidence filled his voice. "Patrovians may be pretentious bastards, but hunting for the world's lost treasures requires a skillset we need."

"And what would that be?" Enara asked.

"The skills that only trackers possess," he replied. "Many of them travel here for work. I'm sure we can render services from one of them to find Soren."

"Well, look at that." She smirked. "Someone did pay attention in Provincial History class."

"You always look surprised," he said, pulling her up to meet his lips. "For the record, I have many hidden talents."

She laughed and shoved off him, grabbing their bags. They headed back toward the gate, the guard giving them the stink eye as they passed.

They paid no mind to his bad attitude as they headed for Edras Mora, Patrivah's capital, with their fingers entwined and their hearts full.

CHAPTER
SIXTEEN

Soren's heart beat faster than a hummingbirds, and a nervous sweat settled on her brow. Her fear was now amplified by the arrival of a new threat—Rook's father.

Rook stood next to her, stiff as a board. His demeanor set off a small spark in Soren's mind. *He seems nervous.* This piqued her curiosity. The idea that he would be scared of anyone seemed outlandish to her, given how they had met.

In their few interactions, he had exuded lethal confidence. Not cocky, but cool, calm, and collected, as if he knew every outcome would turn out in his favor.

She already held so much hatred for the man and could only imagine that his father would be ten times worse. He would have to be to create a monster like Rook.

She could hear heavy footfalls coming down the hall, and her arms prickled. Her breathing went shallow, and her hair stood on end.

She assumed this would be anything but a cordial encounter and braced herself for what was about to come. She rested her bruised hands on the table, awaiting the inevitable, her face betraying none of the fear she felt inside.

Rook's face had gone cold. There was not a single speck of emotion on his porcelain features, and his eyes had gone as dark as the abyss. He stood beside her, his stance rigid, hands clasped behind his back. His chest twitched infinitesimally as the handle where he had entered clicked and the door swung open.

Soren blinked twice, sucking in a breath as she took in the considerable man before her. He was one of the most attractive things she had ever laid her eyes on, which took her by surprise. His hair was jet-black and buzzed on the sides, and his glacial eyes matched that of his son's.

He was tall. Taller than anyone she had met. He had to be at least six-foot-seven, if she had to guess. His skin glowed unnaturally, as if the stars themselves rested beneath. She wondered if the light would spill out if she nicked him with her blade.

His body was chiseled in all the right ways, with large arms powerful enough to crush a man's skull without a second thought. Every muscle seemed to be forged of steel, and she could see the ligaments straining through his shirt as he moved.

Her eyes lifted back up to his face, and she narrowed her gaze when she noticed him smirking.

"I don't blame you for staring, child. Mortals aren't used to seeing such beauty."

"If you don't say so yourself," Soren retorted, her voice laced with bitterness.

The words were barely out of her mouth when her chin was pulled sideways. Rook's hand tightened on her jaw hard enough to leave a bruise as he talked down to her.

"You will speak when spoken to." His words were as sharp as the kestrels talons.

Glaring up at him, she rubbed her face, a bad taste forming in her mouth. She could feel tears welling in her eyes, but she forced the dam of her mind to hold them in.

"I see he is teaching you some respect. Good."

"Of course, Father," he answered for her. "Please, sit down. I'll have the servants bring out another chair."

"We will go to the sitting room."

"As you wish, Father." His responses were automatic, like they had been schooled into him over the years. Respect and obey. Do not question.

Soren kept silent as Rook lifted her from the table and whispered in her ear, "Do not provoke him."

Soren sneered at him, and he squeezed her wrist to convey how serious he was.

He led her down the hall, an iron grip on her arm, and his father at her back. She didn't bother to fight. She would wait for a more opportune moment. There was no way for her to take out both of them in such a small space.

Rook opened a door to her left and forced her through. As she expected, the sitting room was just as lavishly furnished as the dining area.

The fireplace was the centerpiece, the flames already lit and burning brightly against the marble. It was cream-colored with silver streaks jutting across it like lightning bolts.

The walls were a green that matched the darkest parts of the forest, and the entire room was trimmed in white.

Rook gestured for her to sit on the tufted sofa, and she obliged, if only to see where this next interaction would take them.

The sofa was the color of a purple hyacinth and soft to the touch. She imagined that, in another time, she would curl up there with a book in hand, the fire warming her skin. In this instance, it felt as welcoming as a snake den. That was what they were—snakes. Pretty to look at, but ready to strike as soon as you got too close. Their venom would numb you into submission, and then they would eat you alive.

She watched them closely as they took their places across from her, their seats of choice two brown leather armchairs. Soren would have to be on her guard at all times.

His father spoke first.

"I assume Rook has yet to explain why you are here."

"We haven't had much time to conversate with me being abducted and all." She leaned back, feigning disinterest, not wanting to play along with their games.

"He did what he had to do. But no matter; I don't need to waste my time on trivial matters."

Soren raised an eyebrow.

"You see, I have been arranging for you two to meet for quite some time."

Because that doesn't sound stalker-ish.

Soren pressed her lips together and stifled a laugh. "What type of arrangement are you referring to?"

"One that will end happily for all of us," he stated plainly, as if they were discussing a marriage deal and she was the blushing bride.

"I find that unlikely." She could see his patience thinning as the words came out of her mouth.

He continued, ignoring her outburst, "I'm sure you have figured out by now who your mother really is."

"It's impossible."

"Is it?" His teeth flashed in the firelight.

Rook looked back and forth between them, letting out a slow breath.

Her face dropped as the thought solidified itself in her mind. *In all the stories Father told me about her, he never said the name of the man she fell for. Could it have been him?* She did not want to think it was true, but her heart told her otherwise.

"And if I was?"

"Then you know that trinket you discovered is of great importance."

"Obviously, or you wouldn't have tracked me down."

"Do you know how it works?" His eyes glinted dangerously, and something about it sent warning bells off in Soren's mind.

"I've heard stories."

"And what do the stories say?" he asked, a grin curling at the edges of his mouth. He was enjoying this game.

"That she was from another realm and was betrayed by a crazy ex-boyfriend."

He stiffened at that.

Soren smiled inwardly. *He thinks he can best me. I'd like to see him try.*

"I would hardly say that," he finally continued. "My actions simply allowed her to join the world she so longed to be with." As he finished, a knowing look spread across his face. He waited while the gears turned in Soren's brain.

Rook said nothing.

"You—" Soren stared at him, putting the pieces together. *The dark hair. The eyes. The Oculus.*

"Wait." She covered her mouth. "No." Her eyes widened in horror as she realized who sat across from her. "You're Adriel."

"Yes, stupid child," he sneered as Soren slumped back into the cushions in shock.

Her mind was struggling to keep up with all the information, and she felt like she was on the verge of a psychotic break. Until the anger kicked in.

"You're the reason my mother is dead." Her voice was flat, but an inferno blazed to life inside of her. "And you killed my father." She fought to stay seated as anger surged through her body. She vibrated with the effort. She wanted to take the fire poker and stab it through his pretty face but knew she wouldn't make it two steps before being restrained.

"He got in the way," Adriel said.

Flames flickered in her eyes, but she swallowed her rage. *How dare he?* He made it seem like killing her father was a minor inconvenience, as simple as removing a splinter from under his fingernail.

"He got in the way … and you murdered him," she said again. It was a statement rather than a question.

She could taste the anger on her lips and pressed them together to keep it from spilling out. She would be of no use to Baz and Enara if she were dead.

"The details are inconsequential, but if you are looking to place blame, I would start with your mother."

That was the last straw.

"Don't you dare say a word about my mother!" she snapped at him, baring her teeth.

Rook, who had remained silent during their exchange, got to his feet. "Father, can we be finished with this?" He seemed strained. "Let's just take her blood and get it over with."

"I was not finished." Adriel stood, his voice lowered in warning.

Rook looked exasperated. "You said you needed her and the Oculus; I have provided both."

Soren was caught by surprise when a sharp crack broke through the air as Adriel's fist connected with Rook's face. His son grabbed his cheek, tasting iron on his tongue, and did not speak again.

"Forgive the interruption," Adriel went on as if he hadn't just assaulted his son. "Shall we continue?"

Soren did not speak for fear of receiving the same treatment.

"So, let's get to why I brought you here."

Tension vibrated in Rook's arms, and the room was uncomfortably silent.

"I'm listening," she said quietly.

"Your stories tell you that I betrayed your mother when, in fact, she was the one who betrayed me."

"I find that unlikely," Soren muttered under her breath.

"Keep silent, girl, or I will silence you myself."

She quieted, allowing him to continue, wanting to avoid injury so she could keep her wits about her. She was already one blow to the head away from becoming a permanent member of a madhouse.

When she said nothing, he crooned, "Good, you can follow orders. As I was saying … it was your mother who betrayed me. She stabbed me and ran, breaking the Oculus in the process. She fled to your world on that irritating horse of hers, leaving me to choke on my own blood."

Good.

Soren maintained eye contact as she played with the buttons of the sofa, unable to keep her hands still. Her eyes flashed to Rook who was staring unblinkingly at the fire. The flames licked the sides of the hearth, and she could see that his cheek had turned red.

"Before I could receive an explanation, she fled to your world, destroying our mating bond in the process. It was … excruciating."

Go, Mom.

Adriel's steely eyes had gone distant, focusing inward on the memory. "I sent my ranks to search for her, and the horse, but they were never found. I assumed they both died."

Soren had to ask, "I thought Celestials couldn't die."

His nostrils flared in annoyance, but he considered her statement before continuing. "Your texts regarding our realm are fairly accurate. However, they fail to mention that we can barely last a day in your world. Our bodies were not designed to survive here long-term. As for the horse, his life force was connected to hers, so he would have died along with her."

"Based on that logic, Celandine couldn't be my mother then," Soren said, trying to find a loophole. *Maybe they have the wrong girl.* "She wouldn't have survived long enough to carry a child."

"That is what I believed, as well. I called off the search after a few days, refocusing my efforts on finding the Oculus." Adriel placed his hand on the fire's mantle, seemingly unbothered by the heat. "I continued to visit monthly, searching for the Oculus to bring its power back to my people. It had been five years since her fall when I found out about you."

What's so special about me?

"Your mother had already passed on. How she survived as long as she did, I will never know. She was one of the first made, and she always had a particular proclivity for the people of Entheas. My guess is Father used part of whatever was in her to create this world. Whatever it was, she must have passed it on to you, explaining why she faded so quickly after your birth."

Soren's throat tightened. She could feel the loss of her mother all over again. *It's my fault she's gone.* The intrusive thought pushed its way into her mind before she could stop it. Her features showed nothing, but inside, the grief was tearing her to shreds.

"Your father hid the Oculus and raised you on his own."

"Then, why didn't you just kill him, if you wanted it so badly? Why wait?"

"I assumed she hid it from the world before they met."

Soren thought on this for a moment. "So, how do I factor into all of this?"

"Through blood," Rook contributed. He had been so silent that she had almost forgotten he was there—stoic as a statue and barely breathing.

Anger for his son forgotten, Adriel nodded. "The full extent of the Oculus's power can only be harnessed with the blood of two mates. Otherwise, the magic is tainted."

Soren tilted her head in confusion. "Still not following."

"Father and Celandine were mated, and you share her blood. It is the only way to complete the binding ritual."

Her head turned to Rook, who was staring past her, out the window. She could see something was bothering him, but she couldn't decipher what.

Soren couldn't help but let out a laugh at how ridiculous it all sounded. Looking at Adriel, she asked, "So, what? I'm supposed to mate with you because getting it on with my mom wasn't enough? I'll pass, thanks."

She waited for the backlash to come, but it never did. Instead, Adriel smiled, baring his too-perfect, too-white teeth.

"If I had wanted you, girl, I would already have you."

Bile rose in her throat at the thought.

"The Oculus could not be cleansed properly without your mother's blood, so I require yours. It won't take much; only a vial."

She shook her head, exasperated, and threw her arms up in the air. "So, you did all this—hurt my friends, killed my father—for what? A few drops of blood?" She was yelling now.

Rook closed the few steps between them and mouthed, "*Stop*," while forcing her to sit down.

"It is not quite that simple," Adriel continued. "A mating bond is required for the Oculus to work, and since Celandine broke the bond between the two of us, it requires a new one. We can only be mated to one other in our existence, so I have commissioned my son to do it in my stead."

Soren looked to the man who stood beside her, her skin crawling.

"You two"—he looked back and forth between them—"are mated by fate. As you, Rook, are from my bloodline, and Soren of Celandine's, you are the only two who can complete the ritual."

Soren's stomach twisted as the final words exited his mouth. "What are you saying?" she asked, her voice barely a whisper.

"I am saying, my sweet child, that you and my son will remain in this manor until a mating bond is formed. I will return next month to check on your progress. When I once again hold the power of the Oculus, you will be released back to your mundane life."

"And if I refuse?"

"I will kill everyone you have ever known, starting with that chirpy boy. Baz, was it?"

Soren sat up, the heat in her eyes returning. "How did you—"

She stopped as he held up a hand, gesturing for her to remain silent.

"I have eyes everywhere. Do not test me, girl. You will find my polite manner is but a nicety not afforded to all." His voice was so cold it made her ears want to fold in on themselves.

He turned his gaze to Rook. "Now, I will take my leave. Do not fail me, boy."

"I won't let you down, Father."

With that, Adriel walked out of the room, taking all the hope Soren had with him.

"Well, that was rather illuminating," Rook said, breaking the uncomfortable silence.

"Is this a joke?" Soren teetered on the edge of sanity, not sure how much more she could take.

"I assure you my father is not one for humor." He shifted his weight, tension filling his shoulders.

"If you even think of touching me, I will castrate you."

"Don't tempt me with a good time, little bird." His eyes sharpened. "I'm ready for round two, if you are." The cunning viper had returned.

As much as Soren wanted to fight, her body was still weak from overexerting herself.

"I'm not going to fight you," she said, placing her hands in her lap. *Not tonight, anyway.*

"Good, then I'll show you to your room." He held out a hand to help her up.

She ignored it, standing on her own. Small acts of defiance were the only way for her to assert herself at the moment.

"If you didn't know about the mating, why would you have a room prepared?" she asked, noticing the redness on his cheek had already begun to fade.

"I did not know you would be here long-term but was requested to keep you alive and well—sleep being one of those requirements."

She did not respond, her contempt for him rising along with the acid in her throat.

She followed behind him like a shadow, slinking down the hall while staring at the back of his head, debating how many ways she could bash his skull in while he slept. The thought made her smile. She also considered making a run for it, but the ever-present sound of wings reminded her that they were not alone on the property. Though the manor was left to the two of them, with the exception of a couple servants, she didn't want to waste her energy fighting the kestrels in a failed escape attempt. She would bide her time and save her energy for the real enemy.

Rook stopped in front of a door that sat at the end of the hallway. Then he stood aside to let her in.

It was a bedroom, much like the one she had woken up in that morning. On the right sat a hand-carved wooden bed, its spindles glistening in the moonlight. There was a door to the left that led to a terrace with garish floor-to-ceiling curtains held together on either side with golden tassels.

Almost as if reading her mind, he said, "Don't bother trying to jump off the balcony. My winged friends are perched just outside, and they do not sleep." He leaned against the doorframe, his arms crossed over his chest.

"I wouldn't dream of it." Soren rolled her eyes. She then glanced around, noting the bathing room to the left of the bed. Everything was jewel-toned, much like the sitting room, with brass accents scattered about. She hated how cold everything felt compared to her home back in Vreburn and shivered.

"I had the staff bring up hot water for you to wash up. I won't have you skulking around the manor looking like a gutter rat."

She had almost forgotten he was there. It unnerved her how quiet he was. She would never hear him coming if he decided to sneak up on her.

"Don't do me any favors." She turned to look directly into his eyes, making her intentions known. "You are vile and cruel, and I will not hesitate to put you down like the beast you are." Her tone was caustic, and the words dripped like vitriol from her lips.

He straightened, and his eyes darkened. Shadows pooled at his feet like starving nestlings. "Better a beast in a castle," he seethed, "than a bird in a cage." That said, he stepped back, slamming the door behind him.

Soren heard a shifting of metal as the lock clicked into place, followed by silence.

She glared at the door as she stomped around the room. *Asshole.* She rifled through the drawers, looking for anything useful. All she found were a few simple dresses that were close to her size and some sleeping gowns.

"Fuck!" she yelled in frustration.

She walked into the lavatory, the tile cold beneath her feet. *What happened to my boots?* she thought then realized she was in a different outfit from the one in the temple and suddenly felt violated. The idea of Rook touching her unconscious body made her furious, and she felt the need to scrub off several layers of skin.

She did just that as she washed herself until the bathwater went cold then slipped into one of the sleeping gowns. It was a soft blue and made of the most luxurious fabric that had ever graced her skin. She hated that she loved the feel of it.

She wished she could travel back in time and curl up with Baz and Enara as she had only a few days ago. In her home, in her bed, before all this, before her father had died.

The room suddenly felt too big, the walls swallowing her and suffocating her at the same time.

Her tears fell freely now that she was away from prying eyes. She crawled into the bed, pulling the blankets over herself, and let it all out. Her whole body shook as she let her emotions take over.

She grieved her father, she grieved her friends, praying they were all right, and she grieved herself. She screamed and sobbed, her short breaths barely enough to sustain her rapidly beating heart. She cried until the tears stopped flowing, exhaustion falling over her like a weighted blanket. With one last shuddering breath, she drifted off into a sleep-like death, dreaming of a white raven with blue eyes.

215

CHAPTER SEVENTEEN

The butterflies in her ribcage danced as Enara felt Baz's thumb run over her knuckles. They walked the main road into a small town that was settled into the hillside north of the healing pools. It was less a town than a single street that held but a few quant shops. The tiny houses blended into the landscape flawlessly, their roofs covered in greenery. Enara suspected that if you observed it from above, it would seem as though no one resided there at all.

They stepped into a nearby linen shop, on a mission to find some more intact clothing than their own.

The shopkeeper welcomed them with a smile. His white hair stuck out in all directions, and he had age lines around his eyes.

"Anything I can help you find?"

"Just looking, thanks," Enara replied.

She wasn't sure why he had offered, considering there were only a few racks and shelves in the whole establishment, but she appreciated the courtesy.

She settled on a simple navy shirt and a brown vest. Her trousers had seen better days, but they did not need replacing just yet. Enara wanted to be frugal. They were starting to run low on funds, and she only had two items left that could be considered trade worthy.

Her heart-shaped mouth turned up in a grin as she watched Baz peruse the shelves along the back wall. She laughed when he pulled too hard on a stack of trousers and the whole lot of them crashed to the floor. He apologized to the shopkeeper as he helped pick them up, leaving aside a pair in his size.

They tried on the clothes, and Baz stared in admiration as Enara assessed herself in the mirror.

"What are you smiling about over there?" she asked, catching his eye.

"Nothing. Just happy."

Her cheeks reddened as she tightened the laces on the vest, pleased with the way it cinched her waist.

After Baz switched out the pants for another size, they went on their way.

As they were leaving town, they overheard a couple squabbling in the streets.

"If you move any slower, the markets will have closed by the time we reach Amerus," someone complained.

"I'm coming, woman," the man grumbled as he marched out of their home, arms full.

She grabbed one of the baskets from his hands and placed it in the cart before turning back to their house to grab the last of their product from the doorway.

Enara took the opportunity to speak to the woman.

"Hey, sorry to bother you. Did you say you were going to Amerus?"

"Yes, I did. Sorry, I don't mean to be rude, but we are in quite a hurry," she replied, bending to pick up the last two crates and struggling under the weight.

"I can get those for you, if you like," Baz offered, holding out his arms.

"Thank you," the woman replied, allowing him to take the load. With her arms free, she assessed them and raised an eyebrow at Enara. "You are not from these parts, are you?"

"No, ma'am. We are from Vreburn."

"Well, that's quite the ways. What brings you out here?"

"Shopping. I've always wanted to see Edras Mora," Enara replied, trying to pretend she cared about such things.

The woman smirked. "You're a terrible liar." She paused, looking back and forth between the two of them. "But you seem nice. We go as far as Amerus. You can find your way to Edras Mora from there. If you cause any trouble, we won't hesitate to leave you on the side of the road."

"We won't be of any trouble, I assure you," Enara responded. "Thank you."

"Did you go picking up strays again, Nora?" The man eyed his wife.

"We won't be any trouble, sir," Baz said. "We can pay you, no problem."

The man looked offended by the offer. "We don't need your money. Get in."

Baz loaded the crates into the back but hesitated to climb up.

"Forgive my husband. He gets cranky when he forgets to eat breakfast. Hop in. We're already running late."

THEY ARRIVED IN AMERUS JUST IN TIME FOR THE DINNER RUSH. They helped the couple unload what they discovered was port wine.

"They must have quite the distillery hidden in their basement to make all this," Enara said as they helped unload the cart.

"I'd say," Baz replied, the bottles clanking as he grabbed the last crate.

It was the least they could do, considering the free ride. Their feet had enjoyed the much-needed break, and they felt more rested than they had in days.

Emotionally, however, Enara was struggling. She had mentally beat herself up the whole ride there for not expressing her feelings sooner. Emotion had so often been beaten out of her that she struggled to voice it. She knew the blame was not on her, yet she felt guilty, nonetheless.

This could have happened so much sooner if I hadn't been so scared. She tried not to dwell on the negative thought as they waved goodbye to their new friends.

"You okay?" Baz asked, noticing that her mind seemed far away.

"Oh, yeah, I'm good," she lied, not meeting his eyes. "Just worried about Soren."

"And here I thought you were second-guessing all your life decisions."

"Well, there's that, too."

He laughed, the sound tickling her ears. Just a few hours ago, he had been moments from death. Now here they were, all stitched up and on the road to the richest city in Entheas.

Edras Mora was hard to miss, its castle towered over the town below, and its gold spindles cast arcs of light across the land. They reached the outskirts of the city just as the moon crested the horizon.

They meandered around the side streets, stealing glances at the castle that sat above it all. Palm trees sprung up in little bunches along the base of the stone pillars, obviously dug up and replanted from the beach.

The grout between the white bricks seemed to be mixed with gold flecks that sparkled in the moonlight. Enara furrowed her brows. What a waste, she thought, when people were starving near her homeland.

Though Draestel shared a borderline with the farmlands of Stelonbriar, Patrivah hoarded much of their resources, leaving the poorer provinces to fight over scraps. They demanded the best produce and cattle and were willing to pay their weight in gold for it.

Estelar was well off enough. Being a hub for trade allowed for farming exports to come in from the east, but they had tariffs that their home province could not afford.

Maker, I hate rich people.

"*Ow!*" Baz exclaimed, extracting his hand from her death grip.

"Sorry," she apologized. "I was just thinking how the Patrovians wouldn't last one week back home. Maker forbid they don't enjoy a damn feast every night."

"Don't forget we have to play nice. The trackers will already know we're not locals. It won't be easy to convince one of them to help us."

She took a deep breath. "Fine, but I'm not above stealing something for ourselves, if necessary. We're going to need more coin soon."

"I have a remedy for that."

She raised an eyebrow as he took her hand, leading the way.

Baz pulled her down the side streets, each ring leading closer to the edge of the castle. It was getting late, and most of the shops had closed up for the evening. The inhabitants turned up their noses as they walked by, obviously disapproving of their outfits.

"Assholes," Enara muttered under her breath. "How are we going to find a tracker here? You didn't say where we are going, and these people don't look like they have ever traveled farther than the city walls."

"I bet you're right, but every place like this has its dirty little secrets. We just have to look beyond the glamour to find theirs." He yanked her around another sharp corner.

"How do you know where we're going? It's not like you've been here before," Enara complained.

"I haven't, but some things are the same in every town."

"Like what?" she asked.

Her forehead knocked into his shoulder when he came to an abrupt stop in front of a jewel shop. *Weird hours*, Enara thought, surprised it was still open.

"Maker, give a girl some warning," she said, rubbing her head.

"We're here," he said matter-of-factly.

"Did the excessive blood loss do something to your brain?" she asked, peering up at him.

"You see that symbol on the wall there?"

"Yeah, it's a made-up symbol. So?"

"It's the marker of an underground gambling ring," he said, a mischievous grin filling his face. "Look at it more closely."

Enara blinked, staring at the wall. Her breath hitched when she realized what he meant. The image was multiple shapes layered on top of each other to look abstract, but now she could make out each one separately—a diamond, a heart, a club, and a spade. *Clever boy.*

"So, what now?" she asked.

"Now we take these suckers for everything they got."

KNOWING THEY WOULD NEVER PASS AS LOCALS IN THEIR CURRENT outfits, they made a detour. The couple applied a five-finger discount as they walked in and out of a few shops that were still open, taking only what they needed.

After donning some charcoal makeup from a street vendor and tacking on some gaudy crystal earrings, Enara could almost pass for a Patrovian. Almost. Her stolen gown was beautiful, but it didn't quite suit her.

This will have to do.

Baz walked out of the tailors across the way, having traded a chunk of raw jade from the gemstone shop for a major upgrade to his tunic and trousers. Enara would have walked right by him had she not been paying attention.

"You clean up nicely," she said, playing with his collar.

"As do you," he complimented, donning a fake accent.

"Thank you, dearest," she replied, mimicking him.

He extended his arm, and they walked into the jewelry shop together, heads held high. When they got to the counter, Baz spoke first; the comedian replaced by a cool, confident Patrovian.

"My lady and I were looking to purchase a table, wondering if you could point us in the right direction."

She smiled, her white teeth flashing. "What kind of budget are we looking at?" she asked, leaning over the counter and giving him an open view of her extensive cleavage.

"Sky's the limit."

She smiled wider and straightened. "Right this way."

As they followed, Enara tugged on his shoulder and whispered in his ear, "So what? You have a secret gambling addiction?" she asked, frustrated that she had never seen this side of him. He had always been good at card games, but this was another level.

"More of a pastime. How do you think I paid for school? I told my moms I got a scholarship when I found out how much the fees cost."

"Oh."

"Yeah," he said, unfazed by the accusation. He understood her lack of trust in men and didn't blame her for being bothered by the newfound information.

The merchant lady brought them into the back alley where she bent over, way too obviously for Enara's liking, to knock on a cellar door.

"Hey, Xander, I got some fresh meat for ya."

The cellar creaked open to reveal a large man, his hair tied back into a ponytail, features stony.

"Where did you find these two?" he asked, looking past them to the woman.

"What can I say? They just walked right in."

A look passed between them that did not escape Enara. Obviously, they thought her and Baz were easy pickings. *Not today*, she thought. Baz might have played his way through school, but little did he know that she was a card shark, as well, given she had only used the skill when she'd needed to help out Soren and her father.

The room was filled with smoke billowing out from cigars and wooden pipes held by patrons lining the room. To the right was a sitting area with leather chairs. A group of trades-men sat in there, holding expensive crystal glasses, rambling on about shipment prices. To the left was a stage. A woman in a shimmery gown was singing a sultry Patrovian tune, as couples sat at the few tables around her, swaying to the music.

The center of the room housed four tables where patrons were playing Joker's Gambit. As they walked around, watching the games, they noticed the table closest had the lowest buy-in and the table at the back, by the bar, held the highest.

"That's the one," Baz said, heading toward the bar.

"I'm playing, too," Enara stated.

"You can't."

She furrowed her brow, taken aback.

He let out a soft laugh. "I don't doubt your skills. Only that, in a place like this, it would look suspicious if two strang-ers walked in and cleaned them out."

"Fair point." She deflated, disappointed she wouldn't get in on a piece of the action. *Next time.*

They each grabbed a drink, waiting for a spot to open up. Sure enough, a young man stood up, cursing the dealer. The poor soul got a mouthful before the guy left.

"My father will hear about this," he threatened, walking away empty-handed.

Baz sat down, and Enara rested her hands on his shoulders.

"What'll this get me?" he asked, setting a jewelled bracelet on the table. He had grabbed it on their way out of the upstairs shop.

"Well, sir," the dealer said, "that'll cover the buy-in and one rack of silvers."

"Perfect. Rack 'em up," Baz said, relaxing into his seat.

The dealer doled out the chips, and Baz tipped him for his troubles.

He won and lost in about equal measure, the winnings always a small amount more, as he was trying to remain under the radar. *Smart.* She could tell he was counting because she was, too. The adrenaline gave her a rush.

"Do any of you fine men know where a guy could get a tracker nowadays?" Baz asked, pushing past the small talk. "I have some family heirlooms stashed away on the islands and could use some help retrieving them." He looked around the table.

"You can't find them anymore," the man to his left replied. "The king considers them property of the state. Any tracker caught doing a job not sanctioned by the crown will be tried for treason."

And Enara had thought that the guard had been a greedy bastard.

"Shame," Baz said, returning to the game, pretending to be unfazed by the disappointing news.

He played out the next few hands the same as he had started then upped the ante a bit near the end. They needed more funds for the rest of their journey.

"Better get out while I'm ahead," he said, gathering up his chips. "It was nice meeting you all."

The couple exchanged their chips then sat down to have another drink. They were trying to figure out what their next step was when Enara noticed the bartender was listening in on their conversation.

"We should go."

They walked past the guard, Xander, arm-in-arm, pretending to be tipsy. Baz tossed him a couple of chips that he had kept in hopes Xander would forget about them. Then they started down the alleyway to where it crossed at the main road when a voice from behind startled them.

"You two give up awfully easily."

They turned to see the dealer flipping an ace between his fingers, a toothpick poking out of his mouth. His dark eyes looked like they held a secret, and he had an air of mystery about him.

"You mentioned you are in need of a tracker," he said, his teeth flashing from between full lips. "It just so happens that I am the best in these parts." He walked over to them, his tall boots clacking on the cobblestones. His dealer tunic had been replaced with a tight shirt and black leather surcoat with embroidered cuffs.

"*You're* a tracker?" Enara asked skeptically.

"Jai Ashwood at your service," he said with a flourished bow.

"You're kidding? *You're* Jai Ashwood?" Baz exclaimed, "The same Jai Ashwood who tracked down the king's daughter a couple years back?"

"One and the same."

"I heard about that. A few guys were talking about it at the pub when I was out with Soren. You're younger than I expected," Enara said.

"Beauty before age, I always say."

Enara narrowed her eyes in suspicion. "How do we know that you're … well, you?"

"If you remember the story, you'll remember that I took an arrow to the shoulder getting her out of there." He pulled down the collar of his shirt to reveal a nasty scar.

"Good enough for me," Baz said. "Come grab a drink with us, and we can discuss your price."

"Works for me." Jai shrugged, and then the trio headed to a nearby alehouse.

"So, I've gathered that you're not my typical wealthy clientele," he said, fingering his glass of water.

"No," Enara answered. "We're from Vreburn. Our friend was kidnapped, and we need you to find her."

Jai ran his hand through his dark brown hair, considering their offer. Then he shook his head. "I'm out of the people-finding business. Too risky and not enough payout."

"What if we told you that the payout was more valuable than a mountain of gold?" Baz tempted.

"Well then"—he leaned forward—"I would say you have my attention."

Over the next hour, they explained what they had gone through so that Jai would understand the gist of it, leaving out a few key points. Soren had something of great value, and someone had kidnapped her to find it. This alone was enough for Jai to hop on board.

"What can I say? I'm a sucker for an adventure."

"So, when do we leave?" Enara asked, impatient to get on the road.

"I just have some business to take care of before I head out of the city. If you tell anyone about this, I will deny it. I am well known around these parts, and the king will believe me over some strangers from Draestel."

"We won't say anything," Baz promised as they parted ways.

"Thank you." Enara shook his hand. "It means a lot that you're willing to help us."

"I'm not doing it for you," he said, pulling his hand away. "I do everything for me and only for me. Best we get that straight before we disembark. I'll see you two at dawn." He then walked off, his jacket waving behind him.

"He's lovely," Enara quipped as they went in search of accommodations.

They stopped at the hiding spot where they had stored their packs and weapons, not wanting to be seen as travelers. Then they settled on a large inn by the square where they had agreed to meet Jai in the morning.

The room itself was lacking. The double bed took up most of the space with a circular wash basin and a table in the corner. Enara took advantage of this feature and wiped the makeup from her face, glad to have a moment to herself while Baz grabbed them dinner with some of his winnings.

She touched her hands to her mouth, remembering how it had felt to have his lips pressed against hers.

"I like you better this way." Baz walked in, arms full of all different kinds of fare.

"What do you mean?"

"Without all the makeup and crazy jewelry. You don't need any of that," he said, setting the food down on the small table.

"Thanks." Her cheeks warmed as she changed the subject. "What did you do? Buy out the whole tavern? We're never going to be able to finish all that."

"Speak for yourself," he said, his mouth already stuffed with a drumstick.

She chuckled, grabbing some roasted potatoes as she sat on the bed, munching away.

They spent the hour snacking and talking about their card-hustling skills, trying to keep their spirits up.

"I'm worried about her," Enara whispered as they crawled into bed, facing each other.

"I am, too. But you know what we can do to help her right now?"

"What?"

"Get a good night's sleep," he said, tickling her sides to lighten the mood.

"Stop." She giggled, wriggling in his arms. She tried to return the favor, but he pinned her wrists to the pillow on either side of her head. Enara stopped fighting as her body warmed and the mood seemed to shift.

Her chest rose and fell as her breathing slowed and her heart rate quickened, a fact that did not go unnoticed by Baz's speckled eyes. His gaze traveled from her eyes to her throat to her breasts. They were inches from grazing his shirt, begging to be touched.

Without hesitation, he kissed her, and he did not hold back. This time, he took what he wanted, and Enara was more than willing to give it to him.

His grip on her hands tightened as he shifted the rest of his body over hers, pressing her into the mattress. He kissed and nipped at her neck, releasing one of her hands so he could cup her breast. She sighed in appreciation, tangling her hand in his hair.

Suddenly, he reared back, pulling off his shirt before starting to fumble with her dress, his hands shaking.

"Let me," she said, pulling him down to kiss him while she unclasped the corset and tossed it aside, baring her chest to him.

He trailed kisses between her breasts and took her nipple into his mouth. She arched her back in response.

Heat was starting to build below as she reached down to undo his pants. He backed up to rip them off, nearly falling off the bed. A laugh escaped her lips as she drank in the sight of him, appreciating the way his abs flexed with every breath.

"Where were we?" he asked as his hand slipped up her thigh, grazing her undergarments. Fortunately, her wearing a dress provided easy access to what he wanted most.

He teased the bundle of nerves there before pulling the garment aside and inserting a finger into her warmth. He took his time stroking, hitting just the right spot, knowing he wouldn't last long. He wanted her to enjoy this first.

The heat built low in her belly, and she looked at him, panting, "Baz, I want you. Now." She reached for his undergarments.

It took every bit of self-restraint he had to say, "Not before you let go first." His movements were faster now, more insistent.

Her hips rose up to meet his hand as he kissed her and she sighed into his mouth. The heat was an inferno now, and she whimpered his name as she came apart on his hand, her muscles clenching deliciously.

"I will have you now," she said, pulling him down onto the bed and flipping over so she was on top. She unsheathed him, throwing his undergarments to the side then lined him up with her opening. Slowly, she lowered herself onto him, moaning as he filled her, relishing in the ecstasy of it all.

She lifted and dropped down again, and a satisfied growl escaped Baztien's mouth. She swayed back and forth, taking her pleasure as he held onto her hips.

"I want you closer," he said, sitting up and pulling her torso to him. He tucked her legs on either side of his hips so she was rocking in his lap.

She kissed him feverishly now, their bare chests pressed together as they stoked the flames below.

Enara called out his name as she climaxed, stars in her eyes, and Baz followed her to the moon shortly after. Then she gently moved off him, stretching out on her side of the bed and stroking the V-shape below his navel.

"That tickles," he said, his voice still gravelly.

"Well, now you know how it feels." She giggled, enjoying the post-tumble bliss.

There was so much left to do. Her worry for Soren creeped up from the back of her mind, but she pushed it away. She was allowed this. She was allowed this moment of happiness.

"Come here," Baz said, kissing her forehead. "I promise we will find her. Now, let's get some sleep."

And so they did, and for the first time that Enara could remember, she slept peacefully, the sanctuary of Baz's arms keeping her demons at bay.

CHAPTER EIGHTEEN

Soren held the cool cloth over her puffy eyes then wrung it out into the wash basin. She looked in the mirror, scowling at her reflection.

She was thin. The weeks of grief and travel had done a number on her body. Her tanned skin was mottled with wounds from the fight with the kestrels; bruises mostly and a couple of scratches here and there. The leather patches had protected her more than she'd thought.

She changed into one of the peasant dresses, hanging the nightgown on a hook next to her bath towel. She then tied her hair up using a strip of fabric she always kept around her wrist. When they had been young, Soren and Enara had wanted friendship bracelets, so Soren had given Enara one of her leather cuffs in exchange for a strip of fabric from her dress. Enara had said that the trade was unfair, but Soren hadn't cared. She had been old enough to understand why her friend hadn't had nice things.

As she pulled her hair up into a high ponytail, she was happy to at least have a part of Enara with her. She wondered how she and Baz were doing but did not linger on the thought. Worrying about them would only cause her more pain, and she needed to keep her panic at bay if she had any hope of escaping.

She walked to the door, knowing it was unlocked, as she had heard the latch click shortly after she had awoken. Not wanting to run into Rook, she had waited a solid twenty minutes before deciding it was time to explore the manor.

She cracked it open, and when she saw no signs of movement, she slunk out into the empty hallway. *Maybe he's still sleeping.*

She tiptoed down the corridor, passing the doorway to the sitting room, and opened the door to her left. It was another bedroom. It was also virtually colorless and sterile, in mostly muted grays and soft whites with ebony embellishments.

Nothing stood out, apart from a few books on the nightstand. Even the few pictures that hung from the walls were utterly unremarkable.

Wanting to be thorough, she walked toward the bathroom that was through the walk-in closet. She jumped back when she noticed a beak poking out from the entrance and covered her mouth. She whipped around, frantically looking for a place to hide. It was no use. She was going to get caught.

She waited for a minute, and when the birdman did not move, she took the candelabra from the side table and rounded the corner. She let out a sigh of relief when she realized it was Rook's bird mask.

She laughed at herself for getting so worked up. *Idiot.* Then realization smacked her in the face. This was Rook's bedroom.

With newfound motivation, knowing it had to have been a fluke that the door was unlocked, she searched everything more thoroughly. Every drawer. Every shelf. Under the bathroom counter. She even opened the books to make sure they weren't hollow.

"*Ugh!*" she groaned. *How can there not be a single fucking thing in this whole damn room?* The guy was about as interesting as watching clay dry.

She took her time making sure everything looked as it had been then left the room, closing the door behind her. She retreated toward her quarters, heading for the stairway at the end of the hall. She creeped past the door to the dining room in case the servants were setting up for breakfast. When she reached the landing, she returned to her normal gait.

She tugged the handle to her left and found it was locked. *Dammit.* She tried her luck on the opposite side, finding it was open. She searched the room and its neighbor, both of which were sparsely furnished bedrooms. The purpose of which she didn't understand. It was not likely that this guy had visitors and, like he'd said, his creatures didn't sleep.

"*I only have accommodations for one,*" she mocked, replaying her and Rook's conversation. *Lying bastard.*

She headed to the end of the first-floor corridor then paused when she heard something heavy land on the roof. She grimaced. Her skin crawled at the thought of running into another kestrel.

She had kept her curtains shut tight, not wanting to see one peering at her through the folds of the fabric. She would already have nightmares about the perverted creatures, let alone having to see them in the middle of the night, watching her with their beady little eyes.

The door at the end of the hall opened up into a study. She could see a few letters strewn about the desk. Soren read through them but found them to be insignificant. Mostly shipping information for livestock and produce. *That explains the food quality.*

She was about to leave when something flashed in the corner of her eye.

There, on the shelf above the writing desk, was a metal handle. It stuck out just enough for the light to catch it, alerting her to its presence.

She reached up to see what it was, and her eyes lit up when she saw that it was a letter opener. A smile of satisfaction spread across her lips as she twisted it around in her hands. *What an idiot. He might as well have left a dagger on my dresser.*

A slight twinge twisted her heart. She missed her daggers. They had been a gift from her father, and now another little piece of him was gone.

She gave herself a moment then quickly left the room. She had a weapon now, and she intended to use it.

Not wanting to risk losing her only chance at survival, she padded back up to her room and tucked it under her pillow. Just as she finished straightening the bed, a knock came at the door.

Her heart leaped into her throat as she tried to think of something clever to say, but, "Don't come in. I'm naked," was what shot out of her mouth.

"No problem, miss. I just wanted to inform you that breakfast is ready and the master of the house is waiting for you in the dining room … He wanted me to assure you that he would not use the bonds this time."

"Um … okay, I'll be right down," she responded, not knowing what else to say.

Thankful that she had chosen a dress with loose sleeves that hung to her wrists, she grabbed the letter opener and slid it up her forearm, changing her mind about hiding it. The metal was cool against her hot skin.

After checking herself in the mirror to make sure it was well hidden, she headed to the dining room. Once there, she knocked on the door, waiting impatiently, the weapon poking into the soft flesh of her wrist.

"Come in," Rook said, seeming to have calmed himself since she had provoked him last night.

Soren held her arm across her torso, hoping the effect would make her look meek, and opened the door with her non-dominant hand. She walked in, and the scent of fruit and freshly baked bread filled her nose. *Is that bacon?*

Her mouth salivated just thinking about it, but then she mentally scolded herself. *Maker, Soren, you have a job to do.*

Rook was seated at the table, his black shirt draped over his broad shoulders. It was slim enough that she could make out the muscles in his back. He was holding up a sheet of paper, seemingly entranced by what he was reading.

"Come. Sit. Eat," he ordered in a low voice. He couldn't even bother to look at her.

I can do this. She closed the door behind her.

"Sorry, I must have slept in. Getting kidnapped really takes it out of a girl," she said, hoping her casual joke would avoid garnering his attention.

As he shifted in response, she closed the distance between them, sliding the letter opener into her hand. She held the sharp point under his chin, her other arm tightening around his neck.

"Call off your birds, or I'll embed this straight into your thick skull."

He chuckled, completely unfazed. "Did you think I would be so naïve as to leave that lying around by accident? I was curious to see what you would do, given the opportunity. I have to say I'm mildly impressed at the execution, but it was nothing unexpected."

His response caught her off guard, and she loosened her grip just slightly. Before she could steel herself, though, he pushed the chair back, hitting her hard in the ribs. She lost her balance, and the weapon slipped from her fingers, clattering to the floor.

He caught her wrist before her nose smacked the hardwood, wrenching her arm up so she was facing him.

"Well, isn't this a familiar sight?" he said, his face inches from hers. "You never thanked me for saving your life, by the way."

"Forgive me for not saying thank you to my stalker-turned-kidnapper," she replied bitterly as she yanked her wrist free, wincing.

He glared at her before bending to grab the letter opener, spinning it between his fingers. "Now, are we going to have a problem, or are you going to sit down and eat like a good little girl?"

"You're disgusting," she bit out but reached out to pluck an iced muffin from its tray, taking a large bite. She ate aggressively, allowing crumbs to litter the floor.

This is amazing. The lemon and vanilla were a dreamy combination, and her tastebuds lit up.

"Damn, this is good," she said, her mouth full. "Thank your servants for me."

His arm shot out, grabbing her by the chin. "I told you to mind your manners."

Soren smiled, her teeth full of half-masticated food, and spat it directly into his face.

"Are you fucking kidding me?" he roared, wiping the dribble with a cloth napkin. "You childish bitch."

"Hello, beasty," she said, wiping the icing from her lip and sucking it off her finger. "I wondered when you were going to show yourself. I was worried we would have to continue to beat around the bush."

That made his jaw twitch as his facial expression turned glacial.

"You either sit down and eat like a normal human being, or I will lock you in your room and leave you to starve." The fierceness in his voice conveyed that it was not a false threat.

"Then I'll starve," she said, testing him.

"Have it your way then." He dragged her out of the room, and she tripped up the stairs, bashing her shins on the hardwood as his grip tightened around her already injured wrist. She winced but held in the cry that was trying to push past her lips.

He opened the door, throwing her in with surprising strength, and then slammed it shut, turning the lock.

"Fuck you!" Soren screamed. "You stupid, egotistical psychopath!" She slammed her hands and feet against the door, making the wood rattle against the frame.

Her screams were met with nothing but silence.

Rook paced back and forth in the sitting room, resisting the urge to throw his glass against the wall. Hearing Soren shouting profanities from her room, he clenched his fists to avoid going back in there and silencing her.

He lowered himself into the chair, anger brewing in his chest. *I can't believe Father left me in the dark all this time.* It wasn't uncommon for him to be left in the dark, but this? This was too much, even for him. How could his father possibly expect him to feel anything for the vulgar woman he had just dragged, kicking and screaming, across the manor. She was attractive enough, but that did little good for her when her mouth had a mind of its own.

He finished the contents of his glass then slammed it down on the table before dragging his hands through his hair in frustration. Forming any sort of connection with that woman was going to prove impossible, yet he knew the consequences if he were to fail.

There was no love lost between him and his father, but Adriel was not someone you could escape. He had tried once when he had been just shy of seventeen. His father had returned to Anistera the day before, and he had slipped out from under Corvus's watch.

After years of rigorous training under his father's first in command, he had thought he knew the best means of escape. He had been wrong. He hadn't made it three miles before Corvus had dragged him back to the makeshift camp east of the manor. The bastard of a bird had enjoyed punishing him for the indiscretion, too.

He had grown up under Corvus's close watch with his father never checking in for more than an hour when he was in Entheas. All he knew of his mother was that she was a barmaid from Draestel and that he had been conceived from a one-night stand. With Corvus as his only model for behavior, he had grown cold and distant.

His father had used his means and influence over the regular folk to build the manor and all but locked him inside. Rook was allowed to travel, but only when Adriel ordered it so. He had accepted this life. He was his mother's mutt, the general's sparring dummy and, when needed, his father's blade. It was a solitary life, but he preferred it that way. He knew nothing else.

He contemplated refilling his glass but thought better of it. The last thing he needed was to deal with the unendurable woman with a fat head. Instead, he resigned himself to find a way to complete the challenge his father had placed before him. If only he could resist the urge to kill her first.

Soren slumped down to the floor, hands aching from where they had smacked the wood. Her palms were red and angry, and her wrists had turned a deep shade of purple. In an attempt to ease some of the pain, she soaked them in the cool water of the basin.

When she reentered the room, she looked around for something to kill time. *I should have stolen a book instead of that stupid letter opener.*

The room was starting to swallow her up again, so she shoved aside the curtain, cringing as the sun shone directly into her eye sockets. She lifted her hand so she could focus on her surroundings.

The balcony was small, but there was a metal table to her left with a cushioned chair. The frigid air soothed her sore throat. Between last night and this morning, she had screamed herself hoarse.

She cast her eyes down into the courtyard. A thick blanket of snow covered the landscape. The world outside her window felt quiet, serene even. There was not a single footprint disturbing the scene.

As beautiful as it was, the temperature came as quite a shock. It was an adjustment to go from the early fall weather to a wintery prison.

She turned her gaze toward the sky and had the unfortunate experience of making eye contact with two kestrels that were perched on the roof's overhang. She shrank back, not wanting to give them a reason to bother her.

She spent the afternoon scouring every inch of her room, looking for anything that might help her get out of there. To her dismay, there was not a single loose nail or secret hiding place to be found.

Eventually, she gave up and napped on and off. Then she sat around, picking her nails and lounging in the tub until her stomach reminded her that it was well past dinnertime.

I guess he wasn't kidding.

She lay in bed, counting the ceiling tiles to distract herself from her hunger and eventually dozed off.

An hour or so later, a soft knock woke her from her slumber.

She tentatively walked toward the door. "Yes?"

"Miss, I want to apologize on behalf of the master of the house. Please forgive his temper."

"You're kidding, right?"

"Please, miss, you need to eat something. I promise he's not all bad."

She heard the latch unlock and rushed to grab a hold of the handle. "I am not going to subject myself to the presence of that narcissistic prick."

"He's asleep, miss. It is nearly midnight. Please, come out."

"Fine," she said, opening the door and following the servant girl out into the hall. She was barely taller than Soren, with a small frame and honey-blonde hair.

"We must be quiet. I don't want to wake him," the girl said. She couldn't have been more than twenty years old, and Soren wondered how she had ended up here.

She followed in silence as they went down the hall, through the dining room, and into the kitchen. The girl gestured for her to sit on one of the stools that butted up against the counter, and Soren obliged.

"I made some butternut squash soup. You're welcome to have some, or I could whip you up a sandwich." Her voice was comforting and warm, like being wrapped in a cozy blanket. "We don't get visitors often."

"I can't imagine why," Soren replied, and they shared a smile. "The soup sounds great."

Soren stuffed herself with a large bowl and two dinner rolls, thanking the girl for her kindness. "I never got your name, by the way."

"Oh, uh … it's Meena, and the other girl is my sister, Evelyn, but she goes by Evie. She's a couple of years older than me."

"How did you two end up here?" And before she could stop herself, she asked, "How can you even stand him?"

"He's not all bad, really. He found us a few years back. We had escaped a brothel south of here and were seeking shelter." She averted her eyes, as if the memory was painful. "He took us in and offered to let us stay if we earned our keep. I think he was lonely."

"What—with his winning personality?"

Meena pressed her lips together then continued, "When madam's men found us, Rook … well, he took care of them. We owe him our lives."

Soren stared at the girl, pitying her.

"Oh, please don't feel bad for us. We aren't prisoners here," she said. Then her eyes widened as the words escaped her mouth. "Oh, I'm so sorry. I didn't mean—"

"Yeah, well," Soren interrupted, holding up her wrists.

The girl stuttered as she saw how bad they were. "I don't understand. He said he designed them to not hurt. They were only to prevent you from running." The confusion was clear on her face.

"I may have tried to get out of them …" Soren attempted to hide the guilt on her face. *That doesn't change the fact that he has locked me up like some caged animal.*

"Here, let me at least put some salve on them so they don't get infected," Meena said, already rummaging through a nearby cabinet. There seemed to be a whole apothecary of healing supplies in there.

Noticing Soren's interest, she explained, "He tends to get injured during his travels, so we keep the necessities on hand."

Gingerly, she grabbed Soren's hand and began applying the ointment. Soren hissed when it seeped into the parts that she had rubbed raw.

Meena's brows furrowed. "I'm sorry. It will burn for a moment, then I promise it will help them heal." She finished off by wrapping them both in a thin bandage and offered her a mysterious vial.

Soren gave her a skeptical look, not wanting to drink the unfamiliar liquid.

"For the cuts. They will get infected if you leave them," she explained. "Those creatures are a scourge in this world."

"Okay," she said, downing the contents. "Thank you. You didn't need to do all this."

"It was my pleasure, miss. Now, you best get going," she said, ushering her back toward her room.

They stood at the threshold, and Soren thanked her again.

"Don't thank me. Really, I don't mind. But, could I ask you one thing?"

"Shoot."

"Could you give him a chance?"

"You're kidding, right?"

"I'm just saying not everything is as it seems. I'll leave it at that. I have already said too much. He will be furious if he finds out. I must be going."

"Wait," Soren said, reaching for the door.

"I'm sorry." Meena shut it and clicked the lock back into place. "I'll come back tomorrow night if he hasn't gotten over himself by then," she whispered before Soren heard her footsteps retreat down the stairs.

Soren wasn't sure what to think. She had hoped Meena would help her escape, but she obviously had an extreme case of denial. Years of isolation seemed to have molded her into Rook's pawn.

Soren shook her head in disbelief. *There is no way she could have been referring to the fucker from breakfast.*

She walked to the bathroom and scrubbed her face. The bags under her eyes were even darker than the day before. Then she slipped the nightgown back on and crawled into bed, careful not to disturb her bandages.

She tossed and turned, willing sleep to come, and when it finally did, she heard Meena's words hovering on the edge of her mind.

Not everything is as it seems.

CHAPTER
NINETEEN

Enara could feel Baz's arm laced around her midsection. Her body was sore, but in all the right ways. She smiled to herself as she slipped out of bed, reminiscing about last night.

It had been more than she could have imagined, and she felt ridiculous that it had taken such extreme circumstances to get to this point. Realistically, they had both known how the other felt for a long time, yet neither had chosen to act on it. She figured Baz had waited for her to make the first move, knowing her trust in the male population was sorely lacking.

She brushed his hair from his face, kissing his temple.

"Good morning, beautiful," he murmured, voice thick with sleep.

"Good morning yourself, handsome. Come on. It's time to get up. Jai will be waiting for us."

They washed up and dressed briskly, munching on some of the leftovers that had gone cold before donning their rucksacks. They retrieved their weapons from the crack in the wall by the hotel's storm sewer then headed for the market square. They looked around, not being able to spot the tracker's face.

"Where is he?" Baz asked. "The guy specifically said to be here at dawn."

"And here I am," Jai said, sauntering over cooly. "I'm a man of my word, after all. Now, follow me quickly before wandering eyes notice those weapons of yours."

Patrivah prided itself on appearances, and the king did not allow his subjects to openly carry weapons, visitors included. The only ones permitted were guards or royals, and even then it was uncommon.

They shielded their weapons as best they could and followed him down another side street. Jai stood, holding open a rusted iron gate that led into a courtyard littered with large stone sculptures.

Enara sucked in a breath. "Why are we in a cemetery?" she asked, goosebumps forming on her arms.

"No one bothers the dead," he said, walking up to a mausoleum.

Baz raised his eyebrows as he watched Jai, ready to pounce if he tried anything stupid.

The tracker ran his hand along the wall then pushed something. With a soft click, the door popped open. It was dark inside. Jai reached around the corner, pulling out a torch. He dug some flint and steel out of his pocket and scraped them together. Sparks flew, and the torch caught, the animal fat crackling as it burned. The light illuminated the doorway as Jai stepped through.

"You guys coming?" he asked.

Enara shrugged at Baz, and then they followed in after him.

Much to their surprise, the tomb was empty, apart from some dusty bottles of rum, cobwebs, and a narrow staircase.

"Decades ago," Jai's voice cut through the dark, "the old king, King Otis's great-great-grandfather, made tunnel systems all over the province to protect his most precious treasures. They were rumored to have caved in when the hurricanes devastated the island. I came across one by accident one night when I was running from some thugs who wanted to steal my ring."

He flashed the large turquoise stone in their direction. "A gift from the king for saving his daughter. Anyway," he carried on, "I heard about the tunnels when I was a kid and began searching the city. Some of them did collapse, but a few remained standing."

"And the treasure?" Baz asked.

"Have yet to find any. The old buzzard must have had it all moved before the storms hit." He shrugged. "Shame, really."

"So, where does this one come out?" Enara asked, her eyes trying to cut through the shadows out of range of the torchlight.

"This is one of the main arteries that branches off to a few locations, but we are heading to the eastern side of the island. There is an old dock out that way that hasn't been used in years. I have a boat there that I use to get out of the city on jobs like this."

Baz wrapped his arms around himself. "No secret bridges by any chance? I'm not a particular fan of sailing."

"No way around it, I'm afraid. Best prepare your sea legs."

"Dammit," Enara grunted as she tripped over a loose chunk of earth. Baz caught her arm and steadied her.

"Thanks," she said then turned her attention to the back of Jai's head. "How far are the docks from here?"

"About seven hours, give or take. But we're going to pop up in Thesaran to grab some supplies."

"Great," she replied as the darkness began to close in around her.

They continued in silence. The only sounds were that of their footsteps and the pitter-patter of water dripping down the walls. They rounded a corner, and Jai came to a stop, grabbing a cylindrical object from the corner of the wall. It was a metal rod, about six inches long and one inch in diameter. He slid it through a slot in what looked like stone, turning it clockwise.

There was a crack and a whoosh of air as the wall popped open to reveal another staircase. He ushered them up, closing the door behind them.

They were in a worn-down cabana. A couple of hammocks hung from the wall, and there was a washbasin and some shelves filled with non-perishable foods. A chest sat against the wall by a chamber pot. Enara opened it, finding some peasant clothes and a couple of rusty weapons.

"This was a safe house," Jai said, standing by the door. "A place to regroup if the castle was ever under siege."

"Makes sense."

"Doesn't look liked it's been used in a while," Baz commented, plopping onto one of the hammocks. It gave with a crash as the bolts pulled out from the walls. He got tangled in the netting and was flopping around like a beached fish.

Jai and Enara burst out laughing.

"Smooth move," Jai joked, extending his hand. "Yeah, the facilities haven't been used in quite some time."

"I see that," Baz groaned.

The tracker pulled him to his feet then left him to untangle the rest of the net.

Jai strode past Enara and moved the chest aside. The sound of the wood scraping grated against her ears. She watched as he bent down and lifted a couple of loose floorboards. He reached in and pulled out a small wooden box.

"Fake trade documents," he explained, tapping it affectionately with his hand, "in case we get stopped across the pond."

"You've done this a few times, haven't you?" Enara said with suspicion.

"Man's gotta eat," he replied nonchalantly. "Speaking of, best we get lunch out of the way unless you fancy eating with the spiders."

After a quick meal, they returned to the tunnels, backtracking the way they had come to take the fork to the right of the main shaft. Enara swore she saw a few rats scurrying in the direction they were going and cringed.

"How much farther do we got?" Baz asked after a few hours, extending his stride to walk alongside Jai.

"Not too far, maybe about a mile or so. We have to be careful, though; the ground is softer near the docks. You don't want to get stuck down here during high tide."

"What happens at high tide?" Enara's voice drifted from behind them.

"The entrance on the other side fills with water—that's why the ground is soft. It funnels back about two hundred feet before it peters out. If you open the latch at the wrong time, you could drown."

"And you didn't think to share that tidbit before you brought us down here?" Furious, Baz's hair stood on end.

"Would you not have come?"

Silence.

"That's what I thought."

A boom from above stopped them in their tracks. Even being underground, the thunder shook the walls.

"Shit," Jai swore.

"What?" Enara asked.

"Let's hope the storm clouds pass quickly, or we're going to be in trouble. The skies were clear outside the safehouse, but the island seems to have its own weather system."

"What does a rainstorm matter if we're underground?" Baz asked, genuinely confused.

Jai turned and gave him a serious look. His eyebrows created a menacing shadow in the glow of the torchlight. "What do you think happens to the sea when there is a storm?"

"Right." Baz could feel his panic rise as he imagined the tunnel filling with water. He suppressed his nerves and kept moving.

Another boom sounded from above, and dust fell from the low roof.

Jai fixed his eyes on the path ahead. "I recommend we pick up the pace."

"Good idea," Enara said, her stomach twisting into a tight ball of fear.

They started jogging down the tunnel, the torchlight bobbing up and down as they followed the tracker.

Another boom. Then another, the sound building to a frenzied crescendo.

Enara's ears burned, and she could hear the faint sound of rain falling heavily from above.

Baz was breathing raggedly next to her, fighting to keep his composure. He met her eyes, and she could see the terror in them.

"It will be okay," she whispered, squeezing his arm.

Another thunderclap shook the tunnel. Each sound barely ended before another assaulted their ears.

"Guys," Jai said, looking back, "time to run."

They fell into a sprint, following fast on his heels. He was surprisingly nimble, whereas Enara's lungs burned in an effort to keep up. Baz could feel the skin of his scar stretch, but he ignored it and pumped his legs faster. His hand was sweaty, and he struggled to keep hold of Enara, not wanting to lose her in the dark.

The thunder was nearly continuous now, dirt raining down on them, making the already low visibility worse.

"Come on, come on," Jai chanted, willing their bodies to move quicker as the ground began to soften.

Their pace slowed as the mud suctioned at the soles of their boots.

"We're almost there," Jai shouted back to them. "Hurry."

Enara choked on some fallen earth and had to stop for a moment to cough it up. Baz stayed by her side, ready to carry her if needed. She caught her breath, and they resumed running. They struggled to catch up to Jai, who was now about a hundred feet ahead.

He had stopped in front of what looked like a door, but it was hard to tell from where they stood. Their feet sank a couple of inches into the now muddy ground. They caught up to him just as he opened the door.

A flash of lightning illuminated the stairs, and he smiled at them triumphantly. Just as they moved to work their way up, however, a wall of water came crashing into them, flinging their bodies down the corridor. The torch hissed as the flame went out and everything went dark.

"Baz!" Enara screamed, choking on saltwater before she was dragged back under. She tried to grab on to something, but the walls were slick. She twisted in the water, trying to right herself, bobbing up just long enough to suck in a breath.

Baz tried to yell for her but was cut off when Jai's limp body smacked into him, pushing the air from his lungs. They struggled against the current, arms flailing, searching for each other in the blackness.

Enara coughed and sputtered, trying to keep her head up, but was nearly knocked out when the water forced her back into a wall. She saw stars, and her body went slack as the current rushed overhead. The saltwater burned her lungs, and it felt like she had inhaled acid. *I am going to die here.*

Her nostrils burned, and just as she felt like her suffering was coming to an end, a strong hand yanked her upward. She hacked, taking in a shuddering breath. She continued coughing until she started heaving up salt water. When her stomach was emptied, she pushed up into a seated position.

Baz grabbed both sides of her face. "Hey, hey, you're okay." He kissed her cheek.

"Jai?" She choked on the name. Her throat felt as though it had been sliced by razor blades.

"Over here," he said as he felt his way over to Jai's body, pulling Enara with him. "He needs to be resuscitated. You do the compressions, and I'll do the breaths."

She nodded, automatically forgetting that he couldn't see her. Without the torch, the underground tunnel was a black hole. She replied out loud, "Yeah, okay, I'll count them out."

She reached forward, finding the sweet spot on his breastbone, and began to press down, her hands clasped. "One, two, three, four … "

At a count of thirty, Baz pinched Jai's nose and administered two long breaths, using his hand to feel Jai's chest rise.

They repeated this four times until Jai finally turned to the side, gasping for air.

The gurgled sound made Baz wince as he patted him on the back. "There you go, buddy. Get it all out."

Jai sucked in the air like it was the most precious commodity then sat back for a moment as his eyes cleared themselves of the salt. It felt as though someone had scraped them with sandpaper.

"The girl?" he asked.

"Present and accounted for," Enara spoke from his side.

"Good," he said, spitting in the opposite direction. "Now, let's get the fuck out of here."

They had to lock hands to avoid losing each other as Jai felt along the walls to orient himself. The wall that Enara had been pinned against was the last turn they took, so it was relatively easy to find their way back to the door.

They could still hear the storm raging from above as they crawled up the stairs, rushing to escape before another wave took them out.

The steps let out in the middle of the beach. A wooden latch, half-buried in sand, sat a few feet away. Clearly not enough of a barrier to protect the tunnels from the sea's cruel waters.

Baz glared out at the whitecaps, his hands clenched. The rain still poured, but it didn't matter much since they were already soaked.

"Must have been a rogue wave," Jai said, moving a stray hair that had plastered itself to his forehead. "I'm sorry for putting you in harm's way. Please forgive me."

"Hey, man, you couldn't have known," Baz said, clapping him on the shoulder. "Besides, you're the one who came out half-dead."

"Thank you again, by the way," he said, staring off into the distance. "I doubt many other people would have afforded me the same respect."

"We weren't just going to leave you there to die," Enara said, pointlessly wringing out her shirt.

"Others would have." He stared at the water, his mind somewhere else.

"Where to now?" Baz asked.

"The docks are over there." Jai pointed to a mound of sand with two palm trees on it. "Just over the hill."

"Let's get going then," Enara said. "At this rate, I'm going to be waterlogged for months."

They trudged through the wet sand, making their way to the docks, shivering as rain pelted their skin. They settled into the abandoned dock master's shack, waiting for the storm to break. After a half hour or so, the worst of it had subsided and the sun peeked through the clouds. They took turns changing, thanking their lucky stars that they had packed an extra set of clothing. Enara had suggested they do so to avoid being stuck in fur like the heating pool debacle.

They tossed out some of the food that had been ruined and chewed on some cured meat to refuel. Enara looked at the pile of sodden bread that they'd tossed aside, disappointed that it could not be saved.

"We should set sail," Jai said, shrugging his damp jacket back on.

The hard floor provided no comfort. Enara hoped the boat would have better seating.

They clambered down the dock, avoiding the menagerie of broken boards that threatened to steal their legs.

Jai hopped into the dilapidated boat at the end of the dock. "It should be a fairly safe crossing. It's unlikely that another storm will roll in so quickly."

Baz hesitated before hopping aboard, looking out at the open water. An image of his mom being carried away into the churning blackness flashed across his mind. He often blamed himself for their deaths. In his head, they had only left Xian-Dao to keep him safe. If he had never been born, they would still be alive.

"Hey." Enara's voice broke the trance, and he stared into her hazel eyes.

"Hey back." He bent and kissed her before joining Jai on deck. He offered his hand to Enara, and she took it, letting him assist her.

The boat wasn't much, but she was sturdy and Jai seemed to know what he was doing. He untied from the cleats and pushed off the dock. Then he hand-cranked the rudder as Baz and Enara helped with the rowing. Once they were out in the open, Jai raised the canvas and let the wind take them.

Enara snuggled up to Baz as the wind blew past them, running her fingers through his hair. It would have almost been romantic if Baz hadn't been so scared.

When they hit the coast a couple of hours later, he ran onto the sand, praising the crushed rock as if it were a god.

"You okay there, champ?" Jai asked.

Baz gave him the finger, making him chuckle.

"You'll be all right. Come on. We'll set up on the beach tonight."

After laying down their packs and weapons, they started a bonfire to warm the chill from their bones. Fortunately, Estelar was more lenient than the eastern provinces in allowing foreign travel. No border guards had come to bother them, to which Enara was glad. She was exhausted and weary-eyed. She yawned loudly, zoning out as she stared at the flames.

The sun hung low in the sky. Blazing reds and yellows reflected off the surface of the water. The light faded to soft blues and purples before falling beyond the horizon as the stars came out to play.

Enara curled up to Baz on the cool sand, closing her eyes. Jai was already asleep, and she was not far behind him. Baz pulled her closer, and she fell into a dream as the low rumbles of his snores filled the air.

CHAPTER
TWENTY

"Miss?" Meena called from the doorway. "Are you awake?"

"I am now," she grumbled, throwing the blanket off and planting her feet on the cool floor. As she walked over to the door, she wished she had some slippers. "Yeah?"

"The master of the house is out for the day. I figured you might want to walk around." The door clicked, and Soren gave her a cheeky smile.

"Thank the Maker. I thought I was going to have to count the tiles again. And please, call me Soren."

Meena nodded. "Sounds good. I will leave you to get ready."

Soren washed up then headed down to the kitchen. It was almost noon, and her stomach expressed its anger. She was surprised to see Evelyn sitting at the counter while her younger sister finished scrubbing the morning's dishes.

"Come," she said. "Sit." She patted the fabric cushion of the stool next to her. "Meena tells me you're keeping Rook on his toes."

Soren smirked. "Someone needs to put him in his place."

She sat, grabbing an orange from the fruit bowl. She peeled it and popped a slice in her mouth, the juice exploding on her tongue. It was so fresh it might as well have been plucked from the tree that morning.

She didn't want to pry too much, but she had to ask, "I know he saved your lives—Meena told me"—she nodded in the younger girl's direction—"but you can't honestly be okay with him keeping me prisoner here, considering your previous circumstances."

Evelyn straightened at the mention of her past in the brothels, her hands smoothing her skirt. "I may not approve of his methods, but he has treated us with nothing but respect. Though it may not seem like it, he doesn't want any part of this either."

Soren tilted her head, allowing her to continue.

"His father is cruel and unforgiving. Rook does not bode well when he disobeys orders. I know you feel trapped here, and I am sorry for that, but this is just as much his cage as it is yours."

Soren blinked, not knowing how to respond. She hadn't thought of it from his side.

She shook her head. *It's not my fault he has daddy issues.*

"He will earn no sympathy from me," she replied in a curt tone, getting up to toss the orange peel in the garbage. She didn't want to waste her day out of captivity talking about Rook.

"So, what's there to do for fun around here?" she asked, changing the subject.

"Well, there are painting supplies in our quarters, if you are interested," Evelyn said. "I could set something up in the dining room."

Soren hummed. "I'm not much of an artist."

"And there's the library!" Meena perked up, drying her fingers that were well and truly wrinkled from the dishwater.

"It's locked," Evie reminded her. She glanced at Soren. "He is quite protective of his books. Many of them are first editions and could crumble at the slightest touch. He allows us in to dust and polish the floors but never leaves us unsupervised in there."

Noted.

"When he's in a really good mood, he lets us join him by the fireplace," Meena said joyfully, grabbing an apple off the fruit pile and cracking off a bite. "Oh," she said, pointing toward the east side of the house, "there's the billiards room, too."

Soren's eyes lit up. "Show me."

They took her to the billiards room that sat directly below the study, leaving her to her own devices.

The room was warmer than she'd expended. A leather bench sat below a window to her left, letting in some natural light. There was a bar on the back wall where liquids in every shade of amber sat in crystal jars of all shapes and sizes. The oak cupboards were filled with every snack you could think of, including a jar of macadamia nuts. *Fancy,* she thought.

The pool table was a piece of art, the velvet pulled taut over the heavy stone that held it in place. The edges were a dark walnut carved with the same care and skill as the dining table. The pockets were made of the finest leather, and Soren couldn't help but let out a sigh of appreciation. The pool tables at the bar back home paled in comparison.

Cues hung neatly on the far wall, along with all the other pool shark accoutrements. Soren ran her finger along them, appreciating the construction. They had been custom-made.

She pulled one down and ran her hand along the shaft. The carbon handle felt smooth in her hand. She replaced it and grabbed another, moving down the line. She settled on one made of maple that had hints of jade in the handle and set the balls in a triangle on the table.

She helped herself to a glass of what she assumed was whiskey from the smell and chomped down a handful of nuts. She played until her fingers were sore and her head buzzed from the drink.

At around four, Meena walked in, cleaning supplies in hand, and startled when she saw Soren.

"Maker!" She clutched her chest with her free hand. "I thought you had retired back to your room." Her lips turned up at the sight of Soren standing smack-dab in the center of the pool table, the sash from her dress wrapped around her head.

"I'm a pirate. *Argh*," she slurred, waving the cue around on unsteady legs, narrowly missing the ceiling.

"Soren, please get down," Meena said, reaching for her skirts.

Batting the hand away, Soren jumped down, her unsupportive legs causing her to fall to her knees.

"I see you've found the liquor." Meena dropped the cleaning supplies and wrapped her arm around Soren's waist, lifting her. "Let's get you back to your room. He will be home soon, and we will be in a load of trouble if he finds you like this."

"Yerrr noo ffun," she dragged the words out, dropping her head on Meena's shoulder.

The girl turned her nose up at the smell of alcohol on Soren's breath.

Soren leaned into her, allowing her to lead her up to her room. *A nap sounds nice.*

They made it down the hall without much issue.

Soren reached up and poked Meena's face affectionately. "I like you," she said, and the girl chuckled.

"You might not say that when the hangover kicks in."

Meena tried to get her up the staircase. They made it three steps before Soren slipped, causing them both to tumble and land in a heap on the floor.

"Oops." Soren giggled, letting out a loud burp. "Sorry." She covered her mouth.

The sound of a knob twisting behind them made their heads turn.

There, in the doorway, stood Rook. His eyes filled with anger at the sight of them. The muscles of his arms strained the fabric of his shirt as he clenched his fists to contain himself.

"What is she doing out of her room?" he asked, eyes flicking to Meena.

"I ... I'm sorry ... She ... We ... I ..." she stammered, but he held up a hand to cut her off.

"I'll deal with you later." Disappointment was thick on his tongue as waved her off.

She gave Soren an apologetic look then retreated down the hall, no doubt to clean the billiard room.

Rook rubbed his face. He seemed to age as he looked down at her.

She glared up at him. "Thought you were gone fur the day."

"My business finished early. Now get up."

"No," she refused, crossing her arms like a child.

"Fuck," Rook said, grabbing her and throwing her over his shoulder. "Insufferable woman," he muttered under his breath as he climbed the stairs.

She flailed in his arms, beating her hands on his back. "Let me go."

"So you can damage your liver even more? I don't think so." He readjusted his grip, his shoulder digging into her ribs.

She hiccupped as he pushed open the door to her room. "I think I'm gonna be sick," she said as he set her down on her bed.

"For fuck's sake," he growled, walking to the bathroom and returning with the emptied wash basin. "Here." He held it out to her.

Soren grabbed it just in time to fill it with the contents of her stomach. A few pieces of nuts floated amongst the liquid. She set it on the side table, not caring that he'd just seen her puke her guts out. She curled into her pillow and was snoring in seconds.

SOREN WOKE UP, STRETCHING, THE MUSCLES OF HER STOMACH going on strike for the abuse she had put them through. She lifted the blanket and realized she was naked, wondering what the hell had happened. She looked at the side table. The bowl of vomit had been replaced with a tall glass of water and some ginger root. She chugged it down and chewed on the ginger, grateful for whoever had left them there. Then she went to the bathroom and noticed that the wash basin had been cleaned and replaced with fresh water.

She splashed her face and slipped into a dress, the fabric skimming over her, feeling odd without her undergarments.

She sat on the edge of the bed, leaning back against the comforter, eyes fixed on the ceiling when Evelyn walked in.

"You're looking more chipper than I expected," she said, eyebrows raised.

"Years of practice," Soren responded, sitting up.

Evie placed a set of clothes on the bed for her. "Thought you might want these back."

Soren shifted uncomfortably, asking, "Do I want to know why I was naked?"

The woman laughed. "Don't worry; he didn't do anything untoward. You tried to get up and knocked over the basin. You were covered in ... well, you know. He removed your dress so you wouldn't make more of a mess and called for us to help you bathe."

"I am so sorry." Soren reached for her trousers. *Maker, I missed pants.*

"It's fine. Though, you were quite insistent about sleeping in the nude."

"What can I say? Whiskey makes me frisky." Soren waggled her brows.

Evelyn suppressed a smile and rolled her eyes.

"Your dress and undergarments are still in the wash, so I brought you a set of mine, seeing as we're close to the same size."

"Thank you, and I'm sorry you had to deal with … all that."

Evie shrugged. "Everyone has a bit too much drink now and again. I won't hold it against you. Besides, Rook paid us double for our efforts." She winked.

"Oh, good," Soren said, glad they got some form of re-payment.

"And I'll pick up some more clothes for you since you will be here a while."

Soren's face fell, and she picked at her fingernails. "I'm not getting out of here, am I?" she whispered.

The mood turned somber as Evie turned to leave. "Try to make the best of it. When you're ready, come to the dining room. Dinner is waiting. You should eat something."

Soren walked briskly past Rook and sat down opposite him, noticing the restraints had been removed from the table. A few small divots in the wood were the only evidence that they had existed at all.

"Are you going to behave yourself?"

She was about to give him a smart reply back but pressed her lips together when she took in the sight of him. Deep cuts covered his face and arms, and he did not meet her eyes.

"Gifts from my father," he replied to her unspoken question.

"When? Why?" was all she could muster.

"This morning. I told him about our little altercation. This was his response."

"Wait," she said thoughtfully. "I thought he could only come here once a month."

"Yes, but his general can travel to and from Anistera freely. A perk of his transformation. He rather enjoys doling out Father's punishments."

"And the kestrels?"

"They were not so fortunate. Mindless creatures designed to obey, they only follow orders from myself or Corvus. Father's commands trump us both." He sipped his wine.

"I see." She nodded, foregoing the water and sipping the glass of wine at her side.

"Don't you think you've had quite enough for today?"

"What can I say? I'm a sucker for punishment. Cheers." She held up the stem of her glass, waiting for him to respond, and when he did, they both downed the liquid. It was dark and woodsy, with hints of citrus that warmed her throat.

Dinner came and went, the quality the same, if not better than before. She stuffed herself to the brim, paying particular attention to the garlic twists.

She avoided looking at Rook for most of the meal, but she couldn't help sneaking a glance. Impossibly, the bruises had faded, and the deeper markings were thin, already mostly healed.

"Another gift from my father," he spoke, the blue crystal of his eyes meeting hers. "A most efficient type of torture. The injuries caused heal at an accelerated rate, and then they get to repeat the process all over again."

"I'm sorry," she said. The words had slipped out of her mouth before she'd had a chance to stop them.

Sorry? What am I sorry for? How could she feel sorry for him when it was his fault she was stuck here in the first place? He had left her friends broken and bleeding, not to mention his bad attitude and nasty temper.

He looked at her, taken aback by the sentiment, and pushed up from his chair, no longer hungry.

"For what it's worth, I'm sorry, too," he said before leaving Soren to decipher the meaning in silence.

She sat there, trying to will the gears in her brain to function as the shock had effectively halted all processes.

He is sorry, too?

She let the words roll around in her head but struggled to make sense of them. He had gone to so much effort to get her here, but now that she was, he was almost indifferent toward her. She wondered why. Apart from when she was causing issues with her smart mouth, he pretty much left her alone.

He is violent, she thought. *But, was he?*

The other half of her brain betrayed her. *What has he done to me, really?*

Choked me until I passed out.

Stopped the fight from escalating.

Chained me to a table.

The bounds were designed to be painless.

Locked me in my room to starve.

He knows everything that goes on in this estate. He knew the girls would come to you at some point.

The back and forth was giving her a headache as her mind tried to justify his actions.

No. She stopped her racing thoughts by chugging the glass of ice water, wincing when the cold creeped into her head. *He is the enemy, and I need to get out of there.*

The forced thought was halfhearted, and it annoyed her that her resolve was slipping.

She decided to spend the evening pacing the halls of the manor, mentally mapping it out step by step. If the kestrels ever gave her an opening, she would be ready.

The mind map was imperfect since a couple of doors remained locked, but at least she wouldn't hit any dead ends if and when the time came.

She went back to her room and smiled when she noticed a couple of books on her nightstand. She thanked Meena silently and flipped one open, devouring the pages until she passed out.

It was summertime, and the window to her room was open, letting in the sounds of birds twittering their hellos. Her father was out back, watering the irises. She waved to him from the window then padded down to the kitchen and joined her mother at the dining table.

"What's for breakfast?" she asked.

"I thought we might do up some pancakes then pack a picnic to lay out in the yard. It's such a beautiful day."

"Can Enara join us?" she asked.

"Of course, sweetheart."

They finished breakfast then went to town to pick up Enara. They stopped by a few shops to grab some of their favorite finger foods. Smoked gouda was at the top of the list.

Altair waved goodbye to them as they stole Enara away.

"Bring her back in one piece, okay?" he called.

"Love you, Dad," Enara replied.

"I love you, too, my girl."

They set up a large blanket and curled up with their assortment of snacks. Enara and Soren munched away as her parents told them stories of their adventures.

"… and that's how I ended up with this handsome guy," her mom finished, giving her dad a playful shove.

"Well," her father said, hopping to his feet, "I'm going to go get dinner started."

"I'll join you," her mother replied, following him inside. She called back to the girls, "Holler if you need anything."

"Will do," Soren and Enara replied in unison.

After dinner, her parents curled up by the fireplace, and the two girls went out back to look at the stars. They lay together, hand-in-hand, looking up toward the sky.

"You're my best friend, you know," Enara said, squeezing her hand.

"Forever," Soren replied, squeezing back.

They closed their eyes, listening to the crickets, and fell asleep under the stars.

"Quite the dream, little bird."

Soren sat up, heaving. She was still in her backyard, but the windows in her house were dark and Enara was gone. She was no longer eight years old, and Rook lay on the blanket beside her. It was still nighttime, and the moon shone bright over the clearing.

"You just had to ruin it, didn't you?" She wiped a tear from her eye and curled her arms around her legs, resting her head on her knees.

Crying seemed pointless since she knew she was dreaming, but she wished so badly to go back, to have a place where her parents were alive and her friends were safe from the horrors of the world.

Rook sat up, pulling a few pieces of grass from the ground and rolling them between his fingertips.

"Why are you here?" she asked, upset that he saw her crying.

"I prefer your dreams to mine."

Soren was surprised by the admission.

They sat in silence for a moment before she asked, "Are you a dream walker because of your father?"

"No, this is a gift from my mother."

"Who was she?"

"Some barmaid." He shrugged. "I never really met her."

The silence dragged on.

"She seems like a good friend," he eventually said.

"The best. I miss her very much." *And you're the reason she is gone.* She willed herself to voice the thought, but the words never reached her tongue.

"I did not intend to harm them," he replied, reading her mind.

"Baz was bleeding out." Soren's voice was a white-hot flame.

"I instructed the kestrels only to disarm, but it seems my father gave them different orders."

"Your father is a bastard," Soren shot the insult at him, hoping to incite a response.

Instead, he replied, "On that, we can both agree."

She continued to press him, "You said she was inconsequential."

"Because, to me, she is. I need you, not her. But that does not mean I wish her dead." He dropped the grass he had been playing with and leaned back on his forearms, casting his eyes upward.

"You can't keep me here." Her voice was a broken whisper.

"I don't have a choice," he replied before the dream evaporated.

She woke up feeling confused by the night's revelations.

She stretched and clambered off the mattress, splashing water on her face.

She returned to the bed, rifling through a few chapters, when a small envelope was slipped under her door. The paper skittered across the floor, stopping a few feet away from the bedpost.

What the hell?

She opened it, scanning the neat script.

Little Bird,

I was hoping you would join me for a walk in the courtyard. I figured, if you are going to be here for the foreseeable future, I should allow you to stretch your wings. If you choose to accept my invitation, meet me at the main entrance at eleven. If you do not wish to join me, then so be it.

At the bottom, it was signed with a little drawing of a tower.

CHAPTER
TWENTY—ONE

The damp sand caked itself under Jai's fingernails as he dug a hole near the end of the beach and placed the box inside. He had told his companions that it contained fake trade documents. That was a lie.

He brushed himself off and trudged back to their camp, the sand sifting through his socks and between his toes. "Time to get a move on, you two."

The couple unwound from the knot they had contorted themselves into over the course of their slumber and stretched.

"I have sand in places that sand most definitely doesn't belong." Enara shifted uncomfortably.

"Same," Baz replied, shaking a small desert from his hair and facing the tracker. "So, what's our first move?"

"We need to go back to where she was taken. I will track her from there."

"But that's almost three days from here," Enara grumbled.

"No way around it, I'm afraid."

She sat up and retied her plaits, detangling her hair as she went.

Once they had gathered up their belongings, they started the journey back to the temple, heading southwest along the beach.

The first night went relatively smooth as they traveled along the shore to the flatlands that headed toward the base of the mountains. The tip of Braexmirth was barren, and the only inhabitants existed in groupings of no more than four or five families.

Enara admired them. They had next to nothing and still seemed to thrive. They were completely self-sufficient. The trio had been able to trade a few of their med supplies to stay the night in one of the family's stables. The sleep had been restful, thanks to Baz having used some of their now excessive funds to purchase some thin bedrolls. They hadn't used them at the beach, on account that they had been sopping wet. Now that they were dry, Enara lay one down, using some hay as extra padding, and let her mind wander.

As the smell of fodder permeated through the barn, she could hear the sound of the horses shuffling in their stalls. She thought of the ones they'd left with the kind man by the riverside and hoped they would see them again.

Enara had never been great with people, since her experience with them had usually been a negative one. Animals, on the other hand, always brought her comfort. She felt herself gravitate towards them.

When morning broke, she took a moment to say hello to each of the horses before rousing the boys to get back on the road.

The second evening, they set up camp on the same plateau where they had first encountered the kestrels. They decided to take turns on night watch in case any of the beasts returned.

"… and the smell." Baz waved a hand over his nose as he recounted their run-in with the winged creatures to Jai.

"So, these … things are venomous, as well?" the tracker asked.

"Not exactly," Enara answered. "The reaction was more like an infection. We think they are diseased in some way, and it enters our bloodstream when they cut deep enough."

"Sounds fun. And the only way to heal it is by using this?" he asked, holding up a vial of shimmering blue liquid.

"Yep," Baz replied. "As far as we know."

Enara had been clever enough to bottle some of the healing pool's water in case they had another run-in with the kestrels.

The rest of the evening went by with no signs of the enemy returning. It was eerily calm, apart from Baz having the unfortunate experience of running into a bear while using nature's lavatory.

It was quite the sight to see him running into camp, trousers halfway down his legs, with a black bear on his heels. Jai and Enara had scared it off by yelling and waving their hands while Baz got himself together.

"It's a miracle you've made it this far in life," Enara said, humor dancing in her eyes.

"Laugh it up, chuckles," Baz replied, sticking his tongue out at her.

"Happens to the best of us, brother," Jai said, clapping him on the back.

They slept well that night.

By the afternoon of the third day, they had set up camp in the tree line, a hundred or so yards from the temple, keeping their eyes on the sky for trouble. Baz and Enara were thankful that they hadn't had to haul ass the whole way up the steepest part of the mountain this time.

Not wanting to relive the trauma of the kestrel attack, they opted to stand watch from camp as Jai entered the temple. He returned fifteen minutes later and surveyed the area, touching the ground here and there. He grazed the stalks of the trees with his hands, at one point licking something off his finger. Enara made a face, and Baz shrugged.

They stayed out of his way since this was his domain. Besides, they didn't want to disturb the area and make his job harder.

They lost him a couple of times as he bobbed in and out of the tree line.

"They took her north. My guess is toward the hinterlands," he said, walking up to them. He stuffed his hands in his pockets and rocked back and forth on his heels.

"How do you know?" Enara asked.

"Their footprints start a few feet back in the tree line from where they landed. It was hard to tell at first because they came from all sides … but the tracks leading away all face the same direction. There is also this." He held out a leather cuff.

"That's Soren's!" Enara exclaimed, grabbing it and holding it to her chest. "This thing never comes off. She must have undone it when they flew off. Maker, I love that woman."

Enara's heart warmed as she held the leather in her hands. She had the one to match on her left wrist. She was elated to have evidence that her friend was still fighting. *We're coming for you, Sor.*

"So, we have our heading," Baz said. He put his hands on her shoulders and squeezed them affectionately.

She smiled. "We have our heading."

THE HIKE BACK DOWN THE MOUNTAIN WAS UNEVENTFUL. THEY rested when necessary and even took a few short moments to enjoy the views.

When they reached the bottom, Baz stopped to massage his legs. "Thank the Maker. I never want to do that hike again. My legs are beyond sore."

"Yeah, not going to lie; I am happy to be traveling on flatter ground," Enara replied, pulling a twig from her hair.

"If you two are good to keep going, the plan is to follow the river to Vennach and get a quicker means of travel," Jai said. "The town's edge is just a mile or so east at the bottom of the mountain pass."

"I'll do you one better," Baz said, perking up. "We traveled by canoe from Eldrin. It's hidden in the tree line by the river not too far from here."

"Baz, you're a genius," Enara exclaimed, beaming proudly. "I had forgotten about it."

"Yeah, well, I'm known to have a good idea now and again," he replied, waggling his eyebrows in her direction.

Jai adjusted the sword on his belt. "Excellent. That will save us over a day's time. Not to mention birds tend to stay near bodies of water."

They walked the treed path down to the river and dug the canoe out of the underbrush. They bent, inspecting it for any damage it might have sustained in the last week. They were in luck. She was just as they had left her.

They jumped in and started the journey downriver toward Eldrin. If the kestrels' path hadn't changed direction, they would stop for the night there then take the river north, toward Thorncrest, in the morning.

They paused a few times on the way for Jai to jump out and look around for signs of the birdmen. He observed that they were only able to travel a few miles at a time before stopping. He assumed that the handicap had something to do with their wingspans not being in proportion with their body weight. He also found two sets of footprints, one resisting from the looks of the drag marks.

Enara smiled. *That's my girl.*

"It seems she gave them so much trouble that they knocked her out. I found some fungi that is known to produce a drug that incapacitates next to a flat spot over there." He pointed toward the river's edge. "By the compression of the foliage, it seems likely her body was laid there."

Enara's smile faded as Jai delivered the bad news. "Let's hope she gave them hell first."

"I did make some positive observations, though," he offered. "It would take them all night to travel to Thorncrest. Between Soren and their master, they would struggle with the extra weight."

"That's good," Baz said as he took a swig of water. "Means they wouldn't waste the energy to come back for us."

"That's a fair point," Enara replied. "We can probably forgo the night watch for the next day or two, anyway. Give us all a chance to rest."

"Sounds good to me."

"I'm in," Jai said.

As they drifted along the water, their thoughts remained with Soren and the hope that their friend was okay.

After two days of traveling on the river, apart from the night in Eldrin, Baz was thankful to be back on dry land. Though narrow bodies of water didn't strike fear into his heart like the ocean did, it still had him feeling unsettled.

He had loved the ocean as a kid. The memories were faint, but he did remember the joy of being in the water, floating amongst the fish and becoming part of their underwater world. His mother and father would always be on standby with a towel and spiced pork sandwiches.

A pang of sadness struck the cords of his heart. It was crazy to think that he had been only six years old when he'd lost them. The new regime of Xian-Dao had enforced totalitarian rule over all things. This included regulations against relations between the people of Nuraka and those of the southern towns along the Vakari border. His parents had not hesitated when they'd decided to steal a skiff to cross the ocean in search of a better life. They had been traveling to the seaside town of Ilastead, just north of the Esinian Isles, when the storm had broken out.

He remembered watching his parents bail water out of the boat, his father yelling, "Stay down," so he wouldn't fall out when the vessel rocked. They had made it about three-quarters of the way across when a swell had caused the boat to capsize.

He could still feel the salt scratch at his lungs as he screamed for his parents. His father had been nowhere to be seen, swept away by the current. His mother had used all the strength she had left to lift him onto the broken side panel. She'd lost her grip when a series of waves knocked her back and pulled her under. He had never seen them again.

He had spent the next six hours screaming for help until his throat was raw when, finally, just past dawn, a fishing boat had come to his rescue. The captain had patted his head as he wrapped him in a blanket and gave him a canteen of water.

"You're okay now, son. We got you."

"Where are my parents?" he'd asked, choking on his words.

They had searched the seas between Saipea and the Esinian Isles for two days after taking Baz back to Ilastead. He'd cried for weeks.

The captain had taken him in as a foster while they searched for a good home for him. It was sheer luck that Laraline and Alondra had been traveling to visit some family when they had come across each other at the market.

"Would you look at this handsome guy?" Laraline had said. "What's your name, sweetheart?"

"Um … Baztien."

"Alondra, isn't he adorable?"

"Sure is," her wife said, grabbing her hand.

"He's yours if you want him," the captain had joked.

The two women had looked at each other, and then at the captain, and then at Baz, smiling. They had been trying to adopt back home, but no one was willing to let two women raise a child.

"It's just not right," the woman at the orphanage had said. "A child needs a man in their life for stability." She had turned them away without a second thought.

It had broken Laraline's heart. They had always wanted a family, but closed-minded people always seemed to get in their way. Fortunately for them, the captain had been accepting of their marital status.

They had made a plan to meet a few times throughout the course of their visit to make sure Baz was comfortable. When the captain had deemed them worthy, they'd been elated. They'd packed up his meager belongings and traveled back to Draestel. It had taken Baz another month or so to open up to them.

He missed his real parents, but over the years, his love for them had grown.

Laraline had cried the first time he'd called her mom, and Alondra the same shortly after. He vowed to go back one day to thank the captain who had given him a second chance.

He blinked back the tears and steadied his breathing.

"You okay?" Enara asked, noticing the sheen in his eyes.

"Yeah, just thinking of my parents."

"They would be proud of you, you know."

"I know." He gave her a small smile and pulled her to him, kissing her head. "They would have liked you."

"I think we should settle down here for the night," Jai said, returning from his jaunt around the edge of the lake. "It seems they went east from here, so our journey isn't finished yet."

"Dammit, " Enara swore, kicking a rock with her boot.

"It's okay." Baz rubbed her back. "We're getting closer."

"And Maker knows what they will have done to her in the meantime!" Enara lashed out, pulling away from him.

"We're trying out best …" Baz replied.

"Well, your best isn't good enough!" she yelled, walking off into the trees.

The tracker looked at him through raised eyebrows. "You gonna go after her?"

"Not when she's like this." Baz sighed. "It will only piss her off more. She'll come back when she's ready."

Enara returned an hour later, as the shadows of the day stretched across the water.

"I'm sorry, guys," she said, hanging her head.

"Don't worry about it. We get it," Baz replied for the both of them.

Dinner that evening was quiet. They huddled around the fire, a chilled breeze skipping off the water. It was much colder here than back home, and they were thankful to have picked up some thicker clothing in Eldrin. The weather was only going to get worse, and they wanted to be prepared.

They curled up in their makeshift lean-to.

"I'll be back here," Jai said as he scooted past them to the back of the shelter. "I would hate to be in the way in case you two decide you want to have makeup sex."

Baz laughed, and Enara reached over, smacking the tracker on the head.

They were all out in no time, weary from their travels. Their bodies fell into the depths of sleep as the crickets chirped from the lakeside.

CHAPTER
TWENTY—TWO

Soren pulled the fur cape tighter around her shoulders as they walked through the courtyard. The pathways ran out in all directions but converged at the base of the manor. Well-manicured bushes flanked the sides and rose vines snaked overhead, the thorns looking menacing against the lightness of the sky.

They had barely spoken a word to each other, apart from Rook grumbling when she had slipped on the stairs that descended onto the patio.

"Must you always be so careless?" He caught her arm to stop her fall, and she responded by berating him for his bad attitude.

"What's got your panties in a twist?" she asked as she ripped her arm away.

"Nothing." He scowled at her before stomping away, leaving her to stare at the back of his head.

She jogged to catch up, her breath puffing out little white clouds in the frigid air.

They crossed an old stone bridge that ran over the creek behind the property. The frozen waterway opened up into a large lake that bordered both mountainsides. The different shades of blue glinting off its surface reminded Soren of Rook's eyes.

They looked out over the frozen landscape, taking in the sight of the mountain range that loomed across from them.

"It really is beautiful out here," Soren said.

"Yes, I suppose it is," was all Rook could muster.

They continued on in silence, their footsteps making soft crunching sounds in the snow.

"Where are they?" Soren asked, nodding toward the roof. She had noticed on their way back to the manor that the doors and windows had been left unmanned.

"I gave them the afternoon off," was all he replied.

She contemplated this for a moment.

As if reading her thoughts, he said, "Don't try anything stupid."

She glared at him, crossing her arms. "I'll take it under advisement."

"Do you always have to have such an immature response?"

"Fuck you."

He let out a huff of frustration, rolling his eyes. "Fine. Then try to escape. You'll freeze to death before you reach any semblance of civilization," he said, stalking off.

Soren stood there with her jaw on the ground. *Bossy prick.*

She grabbed some snow and squeezed it into a tight ball. *This will show him.*

She wound up and whipped the frozen orb straight at the back of his head. The white explosion caused him to stop dead in his tracks.

"Are you fucking kidding me?" he growled.

Soren simply shrugged.

His glare softened for a moment, and then a sinister smile spread across his lips. "Well, little bird, you asked for it." He bent down and formed a snowball of his own, throwing it smack-dab into her chest and laughing when she jumped around, trying to remove the snow that had embedded itself in her cleavage.

She looked at him, exasperated, and he quirked up an eyebrow in her direction.

"Oh, it's on," she said, grabbing another handful of snow. She aimed for his torso, hoping to have more success, but he ducked and rolled, returning fire.

The battle raged on until they were both caked in war wounds, their fingers on the verge of frostbite, and waltzed back into the manor.

"I'll have the girls fill the bath for you," he said as they walked down the hall, stopping at her door.

"Thank you," she replied, fidgeting with her hands. "For the walk, too."

"You're welcome, little bird," he replied, looking at her. "We can go again tomorrow if you would like."

"Yeah, sure."

"I'll see you at lunch?"

"Yeah, see you at lunch."

Soren contemplated the morning's events as the steam from the bathwater chased the chill from her body. She hated to admit it, but she had enjoyed her time in the courtyard. The fresh air had felt wonderful, and the manor had a beautiful property. Not to mention how satisfying it had been to smoke Rook with a few snowballs. It had seemed to melt away some of the tension between them. They could hit each other and release some of their anger without causing any real damage.

She realized with a sigh that she no longer had an incessant need to meticulously plan his death, though it was not off the table.

The bath was a godsend, and once she had chased the last of the chill away with the warm water, she applied some of the soap the girls had left for her. She appreciated the scent of lavender and lemongrass coming off her now soft skin.

She slipped on a powder pink dress with long sleeves and a boat neck that showed off her collarbone. She looked herself over in the mirror, tying her hair back in a braid. She looked much healthier now. Her skin held a soft glow, and her curves were a little more filled out now that she was eating properly and not drinking every other day. She was happy to find a simple pair of ballet slippers by the door and donned them before heading down to lunch.

Her stomach cheered when she found out they were having soup again. It was filled with noodles and beans, and they paired it with cheese-dusted rolls. When there was nothing left but broth, she picked up her bowl and downed the liquid, licking her lips with satisfaction.

"That was delicious," she said, placing the bowl down.

Rook gave her a sideways glance and lifted his bowl, following her lead. He patted his lips dry with his napkin. "I'll thank Meena and Evie for you."

Soren found herself staring at him. Every one of his movements was graceful and fluid, like his body and mind were perfectly in sync.

"Hey, do you happen to know what day it is?" she asked, trying to clear her thoughts. "It would be easier to orient myself if every day didn't feel like an endless winter."

"Today is the first of the autumn tide."

"Oh." Her face fell.

"What? Do you not like the season of the fall, either?"

"No, that's not it." She bit her lip, wishing she had never brought it up.

"What's wrong, little bird?" he asked, almost sounding genuinely concerned.

"Today's my birthday."

His body went straight as a board. "Oh."

"Yeah."

Rook seemed conflicted, unsure of how to respond.

"I'm sorry." The apology tasted like ash on his tongue.

"Yeah, it's not exactly how I thought I would be spending it." Soren's chest tightened as images of past birthdays flashed through her mind.

Rook said nothing, knowing his words would be of no use, considering he was the cause of her grief.

"Anyway, it's fine," she said, not wanting to break down in front of him. "But, if it's okay with you, I would rather take dinner in my room."

"I understand," Rook said. "Let me know your favorites, and I'll have the girls prepare them for you."

"Oh, really, they don't need to. I'm fine with whatever." She clenched her hands below the table to hide that they were shaking.

"It's the least I can do, given our current … situation," he replied, his voice strained.

He's not going to drop it until I give him an answer.

She sighed. "Do they know how to make Vakarian food? That's my favorite."

"They have been trained in all the world's cuisines. What would you have?"

"Maybe just some spiced lentils or chicken, with rice, is fine. I'm pretty simple."

"You are anything but," he said.

Her cheeks pinkened as he skimmed her frame.

She tugged on the waistline of her dress. She was used to the male gaze and often used it to her advantage. She was not normally one to shy away, but those eyes … those eyes made her tremble every time he looked at her like that—like he wanted her.

"And for dessert?" His voice had gone a tone deeper, and his eyes were searching for the secrets behind her own.

"Oh, I don't do cake," she said, trying to calm her racing heart. "But I am a sucker for cocoa bites and frozen cream. I can only have it a couple of times a year back home. The weather doesn't usually get cold enough for the cream and sugar to freeze."

"Done."

She headed for the door, needing to escape.

"Rook?" she said before leaving.

He tilted his head, waiting.

"You're not so bad when you're like this." Then she pulled the door shut behind her.

Dinner was more than anything she could have asked for. Soren nearly fell over when Meena and Evelyn brought in tray after tray of all her favorites, complete with fragrant yellow rice, crispy wheat rounds, and sweet mango sauce.

"You guys didn't have to do all this!" she said, hugging them before sitting down at the small table they had set up.

"Of course we did, silly." Meena giggled. "Rook said it was your birthday. Besides, we love Eastern food, too."

"This is everything," Soren gushed as the richness of the butter and tomato sauce filled her mouth. The pheasant was bathed in it, and her eyes rolled back. "You two are going to have to design a pully system to get me out of this chair."

"Well, make sure you save some room," Evelyn replied. "The cocoa bites are in the oven, and the frozen cream will be ready shortly."

"You didn't?"

"We did," they replied in unison.

"Thank you, guys. You know, even though I can't spend it with my friends from back home, I am glad you two are here."

"Aw ... well, we're happy to oblige," Meena said, squeezing her hand. "It's been nice to have another person in the manor."

"I hate to admit it," Soren said between bites, "but it's not all that bad being here. It has its perks." She gestured to the steaming trays.

The girls chuckled, and then Evelyn said they would return shortly with dessert.

"Thanks again!" Soren waved as they walked out, bits of spiced potato stuck to her fingers.

The knock on her door came twenty minutes later.

"Come in," Soren said, too full from dinner to get up.

To her surprise, Rook walked in, holding a tray. He paused for a moment before setting it down in front of her.

She stared at him as he lifted the silver top to reveal a plate of gooey cocoa bites with a crystal bowl of frozen cream. It smelled heavenly, and Soren's tongue quivered in anticipation.

He proceeded to whip out a candle and lit it, waiting. She leaned forward, pursing her lips, and blew it out, keeping eye contact with him the whole time.

His gaze flicked from her eyes to her lips and back, darkening.

She took a bite, and her lids fell shut. The girls had outdone themselves. The cocoa bites were decadent and moist, and the tang of the salted caramel sauce had her tastebuds exploding.

"Happy birthday, little bird." His voice was husky, and the sound of it made her shiver.

"Thank you for all this," she said, gesturing to the excessive amount of food.

"No one should have to be alone on their birthday." His eyes were distant, and it gave Soren the distinct feeling that he knew by experience.

"Do you want any?" she asked, pointing to the cocoa bites.

He said nothing but took a clean spoon from another tray and lifted a piece into his mouth. Without breaking Soren's gaze, he pulled it out slowly, dragging the metal across his lips.

Her chest flushed, and a spark of pleasure warmed between her thighs. She pressed her legs together and pretended to adjust her neckline.

"There's one more surprise when you're finished."

"Huh?" she asked, refusing to make eye contact.

"Meet me in the sitting room when you're done. I have something I want to show you," he reiterated.

"Okay," she said, needing a moment to calm herself. "I'll be there in a minute."

She pressed a damp cloth to her chest and the back of her neck, mentally chastising herself.

What the hell are you getting all heated about? His father murdered yours.

Her body's reaction to Rook's felt like a betrayal. *Maker, help me.*

Soren's hand hesitated as she stood at the threshold of the sitting room. She had no idea what to expect. She had never liked surprises. The idea of the unknown had her hair standing on end.

She shook off the nerves and walked in to find Rook sitting in a chair, fingers clasped around a glass of whisky. He stood when she entered, downing the contents then crossed over to her.

"Ready?" he asked.

"I guess so."

He held out his arm, and she hesitated before taking it. *Ah, what the hell?* She linked her arm with his and let him lead the way.

She could feel the muscles of his biceps flex as they walked, and the heat of his skin was seeping through his shirt. He smelled like a pine forest on a cold winter morning.

"We will go in from the bottom level so you can get the full effect."

Soren's eyebrows shot up, but she didn't respond, wanting to let the surprise speak for itself.

They took the stairs and crossed the main entryway of the manor. There was a twin staircase on the opposite side and both wound up in wide arcs along the walls.

The double door was solid wood with wrought iron details, making it look like a doorway to a secret garden. Soren took note of the dark shadows through the windows. The kestrels were back.

Shit. I should have tried to leave when I had the chance.

They stopped in front of a large door, and Rook fished an old brass key out of his pocket. He fitted it into a keyhole that was hidden behind a false doorknob and turned it counterclockwise until the bolt shifted.

Why is he showing me how to get in?

"After you, little bird." He stepped aside to allow her to enter first.

She swallowed, looking at the doorframe. For some reason, the whole thing seemed to instill an innate sense of fear in her.

"Don't worry. It's just the dungeon." Rook was leaning against the doorframe, watching her, a smirk resting playfully on his lips.

"That was a joke." Soren was baffled. "You're making jokes now?"

"Maybe." He shrugged.

It was a noncommittal gesture, but Soren could see the twinkle in his eyes. She pulled her jaw off the floor and entered the room, not wanting him to see her smile.

Soren gasped audibly. The library was breathtaking. The literary collection took up the entirety of the west wing, standing two stories tall. The fixtures boasted some of the most intricate woodwork she had ever laid eyes on.

The ceiling was made of domed glass and allowed the whole room to be bathed in the light of the sun. It was decidedly cozier than the rest of the house, feeling more like a home than a black and white painting.

The shelves were a soft gray with dark walnut inserts, each one filled to capacity. The bars of the railings were made of rose-gold, capped with the same walnut, and spiral staircases sat in the outside corners on either end of the room.

Across from her was a circular inlet with stained-glass windows from floor to ceiling, a grand piano tucked into the center of it.

I wonder if he plays.

"Is the piano for decoration?" she asked, tilting her head in the direction of the instrument.

"I play on occasion."

"I see."

They fell silent, and Soren let her eyes wander. She scanned the bookshelves, soaking in the smell of ink on parchment. The books lined every inch of the walls, and an assortment of furniture was propped around the center of the room on patterned rugs. The amethyst and turquoise cushions begged to be sat on, and the walnut tables shone as if they had just been polished. It was the most stunning collection of literature Soren had ever seen, and she had to pinch herself to be sure she wasn't dreaming.

"May I?" she asked, reaching toward a shelf.

"Of course. You may read anything you want, apart from those ones." He pointed to the left of the piano. "Those are the most loved in my collection. If you want to see them, I only ask that you consult me first."

"I can be pretty protective of my books, too," Soren said, running her hand along the leather spines on the closest shelf.

"Good. Then you will understand why I only allow access while I am present."

"Of course."

She selected a book and sat down in one of the garish armchairs. Rook opted for the chaise across from her, propping his feet up. Once he was truly entranced in his story, Soren took a couple of moments to look at him.

His posture and face were relaxed. It was obvious this was an escape for him. A break from the ongoing duties his father thought him responsible for. He looked younger, almost boyish, and she couldn't help but find it alluring.

"It's rude to stare, little bird," he said without looking up.

"Sorry," she replied, refusing to be embarrassed. "I was just thinking that you seem happy in here." She paused. "If that is even within your realm of capabilities."

He placed his book down on the table and sat up, his blue eyes pinning her in place. "Books are my only way to escape this world. They take me to new places, they teach me new things, and they show me to appreciate all different types of relationships."

His face was more vulnerable than she had ever seen it.

"When I am reading, it is just the characters and I enjoying our next adventure. These books," he said, looking around the room, "are the home I never had but always wanted."

Soren was surprised at his admission. Normally, she would have said something like, "*What? Your daddy didn't love you enough?*" Instead, her heart ached for him.

"I understand exactly what you mean," she said, exchanging her current read for something more exciting.

A faint smile peeked out from the corners of her eyes when he noticed the racy title she had picked up.

An hour or so later, they called it a night, and he walked her back to her room.

"Thank you again," she said, clutching the unfinished story to her chest.

"It was my pleasure." He paused awkwardly at the threshold. "I'll see you at breakfast?"

"Yes, I'll see you at breakfast," she replied, shifting back and forth.

He lifted his hand as if to touch her but then dropped it, looking conflicted. "Goodnight, little bird," he said, turning on his heel, heading to his room.

She watched him go and wondered what would have happened if he had touched her. *You know exactly what would have happened*, she scolded herself. If he had touched her, it would have been her undoing because, somehow, some way, she was started to feel something for him.

She went into her room, hoping the cold water from the basin would shock some sense into her, to no avail. Then she crawled into bed, pulling the blanket up to her neck, and slammed her eyes shut. She wished Enara were here to slap some sense into her, or that Baz would pop in to cause a well-timed distraction.

Every time she closed her eyes, all she could see was Rook's face, and all she could think of was his mouth and how it would feel on hers.

She cursed her traitorous mind.

"Happy birthday to me."

CHAPTER TWENTY—THREE

Over the next few days, Soren and Rook fell into a system of sorts. They would join each other for breakfast, walk the grounds at mid-morning, and then stop for lunch. Then they would part ways until dinnertime. Every evening, they would go to the library and pick the shelves before settling into the same seats as the day before. Some days, they barely talked and just enjoyed the quiet solace of each other's company. Others, they would share stories about their lives, and Rook would look at her with admiration as she talked animatedly about her friends.

It was a double-edged sword. She was happiest when talking about the times her and her friends had together, but a shadow of sadness would contort her features when she mentioned their names. She would go quiet or, on the bad days, skip dinner and cry in her room. He hoped that, with time, she would learn to move on from them.

To distract her, he suggested they try the billiard room for a change. They played pool a handful of times, and Soren was pleasantly surprised to find that he was a formidable opponent. He had deft fingers and astounding control over his shots. After a tiebreaker, she shook his hand firmly, disappointed she had lost, and said, "Good game."

They went still as their hands touched. Soren could feel his breath tickle her shoulder, causing her to tremble, but unlike the last time, it was not in fear but with anticipation. She thought he might kiss her, but he pulled away and bent to sink the white ball.

Soren blew a raspberry and went to pour herself another drink. "You want one?" she asked, raising the bottle.

"If you're buying."

She smirked and poured him a glass, too. His humor was flat and sarcastic, but she liked it that way. She loved Baz, but comedians were never her type. She preferred one-liners and quick quips to poke fun.

They retired to the sitting room, bringing the bottle with them, and sat in their designated seats. Rook plunked down in his chair, and she stretched out like a cat on the sofa. Soren was starting to feel buzzed and enjoyed the numb feeling of her mouth.

Feeling brave, she sat up and sauntered over to the chair beside Rook, proud of herself when she saw him stiffen as she sat. She leaned over, putting her hand on his knee, and his whole body went rigid.

"Ever heard of stop and go?"

He eyed her hand as he shook his head.

"So, the goal is to see who taps out first. I slide my hand up your leg, and when you can't take it anymore, you say stop. Then we switch, and you do it to me."

"This is ridiculous."

"Aw … is little Rooky scared?" Soren joked in a baby voice, twirling her finger in slow circles on his knee.

"I am not scared," he said, leaning toward her, his eyes locking on hers. "Try me."

She slipped her hand up his leg at an agonizing pace. His eyes burned into hers as she reached his inner thigh, causing him to twitch. A smug smile painted her lips before he grabbed her wrist.

"Stop," he said, trying to hide his elevated heart rate. "My turn … unless the lady protests?"

Soren leaned back, letting her legs fall open. Her dress was long, but the slit in the side rode up, exposing her leg and upper thigh. "Your move."

Rook shuffled forward, placing a hand on her knee, and Soren's eyes lit up, challenging him. He moved slowly. Her smooth skin was soft and delicate. He sucked in a breath as he reached her inner thigh, hoping she would stop him there, but she didn't. She was breathing heavily now and looked hungry. He grazed her skin inches from her delicate area and stopped, pulling his hand away.

"Is that blush I see?" she goaded.

"If I wanted to sleep with you, I would," he said, standing to leave. "I'm not doing this."

"Not doing what? It's just a game." She laughed it off, feigning innocence.

"You and I both know that is not true. And if I am going to have you, little bird"—he leaned in, inches from her face—

"it will be because you beg for it." He grabbed the bottle and took a swig, sitting back in his chair.

Any desire she had felt moments ago had been erased the moment the words had fallen from his mouth.

"I do not beg," Soren seethed, snatching the bottle from him. She downed the contents then stormed out of the room.

How dare he? She thought, pacing her room. *Narcissistic asshole.* Did he honestly think she would beg for his touch? *Who does he think he is?*

She tore off her dress, her body suddenly oversensitive and too hot. She could still feel his touch lingering on her skin and was ashamed of herself. *Play stupid games, win stupid prizes, Sor.*

He was always so stiff, and she had just wanted to get him riled up, but now she was the one left wanting more.

"*Ugh*," she groaned in frustration.

She was in the middle of washing her face when a knock on the door made her jump and her heart thump in her chest.

She stomped over, ripping it open more aggressively than necessary.

Rook stood there with a book in his hand.

"You forgot this," he said, taking in the sight of her unapologetically. "Have I come at a bad time?" He smirked, leaning against the doorframe.

She wrenched the book from his hand, tossed it angrily onto her nightstand, and then stormed back over to face him. "What is your problem?"

"What do you mean?"

"Isn't the whole point of this for us to get involved with each other?"

He chuckled, making her feel stupid. "The mating bond is not about sex."

"Then, what is it?" she asked, not caring that she was accosting him in her undergarments. *I want answers.*

"From what Father told me, the bond falls into place when you truly and fully give yourself to one another."

"So, what? I am supposed to fall in love with you?"

The question was blunt, but she needed to know if she had any chance of getting out of there. If she could trick the mating bond, then she could give them her blood and go home.

He shook his head. "He did love your mother once, but that was not why their bond formed."

Soren's eyes darkened, fury filling her at the mention of the man who had killed her father. "He would not know love if it smacked him in the face."

"I am inclined to agree, but they did form the bond, and that is not something to be ignored."

Soren crossed her arms over her chest.

He let out a breath, thinking of a way to try to make her understand. "The bond only forms when the mental, physical, and emotional connections are in sync. It is not something that can be forced."

We will see about that.

"Fine, fine, I get it. That still doesn't explain why you all but run away anytime we get close to each other. You always find an excuse to leave."

"I do not want to force something that isn't there."

That had been the wrong thing to say.

Soren's nostrils flared, and she raised her voice. "Well, if that's how you feel! What? I'm not attractive enough for you? Or would you rather sleep with your little servant girls?"

She knew the comment was unfair, but her ego was bruised, and she wanted to hit him back just as hard. The girls were just collateral damage.

That had struck a chord.

"Do not bring them into this. I have touched neither, nor do I plan to. They are like sisters to me."

Soren could see the muscles of his jaw tighten as he clipped out the words.

"Then, what is the fucking issue?" she yelled.

"I do not deserve to have you!" he shouted back. Then he hung his head, his hands laying limp at his sides.

Soren wanted to keep fighting, but she had no idea how to respond. *Doesn't deserve me? What does that mean?*

When he spoke again, his voice was soft, defeated. "You are one of the most attractive women I have ever laid my eyes upon, but I can never have you the way I want to."

He wants me?

She shook her head. *Why the fuck do you care?*

Soren's internal battle continued as she fought to hate him.

He is your enemy! Her mind hissed angrily. She wanted so badly to hate the man who stood before her but, if anything, she just felt sorry for him.

"I never wanted any part in this," he admitted. "But, as you saw before, my father can be quite convincing."

She found herself wanting to reach for him, to comfort him, but she steeled herself.

You will get close enough to earn his trust. Then you will cut him down.

"Then, why even bother to spend time with me?"

He thought for a moment before answering, "I find your company ... refreshing."

"You're not so bad yourself," she replied, closing the few steps between them.

He looked down at her, one eyebrow raised. "What are you doing?"

Soren never thought of herself as a seductress by any means, but she knew well enough how to get a man into her bed when the need arose.

"Giving your father something to talk about." She traced a finger along the lines of his chest and heard him inhale through his teeth.

"What are you doing?" he asked again.

She said nothing as she lifted onto her toes, letting her hand glide up the back of his neck. Rook's eyes were molten as she tilted her head, brushing her lips against his. As she waited for him to respond, she could see the war raging behind his eyes.

Try harder.

She pressed into him further, whispering against his mouth, "Please."

A low groan escaped his throat at the word. He lifted his hands to her waist, his skin heated, and … promptly pushed her away.

"What the fuck is your problem?" she snapped. *What the fuck just happened?*

He grimaced. "I don't take women unwillingly. Men who do so are cowards."

Bafflement pushed through her anger. "What part of that"—she waved her arms—"read, *I don't want this?*"

"The fact that you are still trapped here. If the circumstances were different, you would not choose this."

"What happened to *you will beg for it*?" she imitated the timber of his voice. "I all but laid myself bare for you, and you still turned me away!" Soren's voice elevated with her frustration.

"That was a game. If I am to have you, it will be because we both want it, not because there is a prize to be won."

Soren was gobsmacked. She had never had a man treat her with such respect. She might have chosen whom she went home with but never had they stopped to ask her what she wanted. They knew the drill—drink, party, fuck. Then she would kick them out before her morning coffee. Easy as that.

This man … this beautiful, terrible, insufferable man stood before her, wanting but caged himself until she permitted him. She didn't want to play anymore, either. All plans had washed from her mind with a few simple words from his too-perfect lips.

She caught his eye so he could see the seriousness of the words when she said, "No more games, then."

She closed the distance between them, grabbed his face, and kissed him hard.

He pushed her away and looked into her eyes, his grip tight on her arms. She didn't know what he was searching for, but when he found it, he pulled her into him and kissed her back twice as hard.

He picked her up, and she wrapped her legs around his waist. He kicked the door shut, walking toward the bed like a viper ready to strike.

He dropped her onto the mattress then reared back, ripping open his shirt. The buttons flew out in all directions, and Soren became drunk on the sight of his bare torso. Her hands lingered as she shrugged the broken article of clothing off his shoulders.

Their lips crashed together once more, so hard it was almost painful, their tongues colliding. He was on top of her, his desire obvious, and Soren ground against him, her fingers digging into his shoulders.

He pulled away, nipping and sucking at her neck, and unclasped her bra to reveal her breasts. He took them one at a time into his mouth, and she lifted into him, moaning as his tongue circled the peaked flesh. He trailed down to her navel, leaving little bite marks on the edges of her hips. Grabbing her by the thighs, he pulled her to the end of the bed.

His knuckles grazed over the thin lace, causing her to writhe. He pulled the garment aside, kissing up one leg then the other, taking his time to mark her with his teeth as he went. He then kneeled before her and made slow circles with his tongue, wrapping his arms under her legs to hold her in place. The heat in her surged through her veins, and she cried out, covering her mouth, hoping the girls didn't hear her.

Rook looked at her, his eyes blazing, a predatory smile on his face. "Don't worry, little bird. These rooms are soundproof, apart from the doors."

He resumed his assault on her senses and, within minutes, she found herself climbing again. But, just before she could reach her climax, he pulled away.

She whimpered in frustration. "Don't stop."

"Tell me what you want," he ordered. "Beg for it."

"I don't beg," she said, but the response was halfhearted.

He pressed his lips back between her thighs and continued to circle her slowly, flicking his tongue until her breath hitched. Then he stopped again.

"Maker, damn you," she said, her flushed chest falling as fast as it rose.

He lifted her farther back onto the bed and kissed her, letting his hands resume the work his mouth had been doing, bringing her up and letting her fall until she was shaking uncontrollably.

"Beg." His teeth grazed her ear.

"Please."

"Please, what?"

"I want you," she blurted out, angry with herself. "I know it's wrong, and I shouldn't, but I want you," she admitted.

His voice was primal when he responded, "Then you shall have me." He stepped back, removing the rest of his clothing, baring himself to her.

She was impressed with what he had to offer as he leaned over, lining up with her entrance. He hesitated to look at her seriously. "Have you had a contraceptive tonic recently?"

"Seriously? That's what you're thinking about right now?"

He shrugged. "Better safe than sorry."

She rolled her eyes. "Yes, I am not due for another until the week after next."

"Good," he said then slammed into her.

She cried out as he filled her, loving the feeling of him.

He grabbed the sheets, groaning in pleasure as he moved back and forth, biting at her neck and shoulders. Then he pulled out suddenly and flipped her onto her front as she let out a yelp of surprise. He struck her left cheek then palmed it, soothing the spot he had just warmed. Then he lifted her hips to meet him.

She backed into him impatiently.

"Dirty little bird," he said, burying himself back inside her.

She rocked back against him, their bodies moving in tandem as the heat built to an inferno. He leaned forward and wrapped his hand around her throat, pulling her up to her knees so her back was pressed against him. Their skin was slick with sweat, and they glided against each other.

His hand that was holding her waist creeped around to her sweet spot as he bit into her shoulder. The sensation had her vibrating against him.

His breathing became ragged as he hardened inside her, finishing as he growled her name. He then pulled out of her and stretched out on the bed, tracing lines on her back as the last tremors of pleasure left her body. He pulled the blanket over them as her breaths softened, and when he was sure she was asleep, he slipped out of the room.

Soren woke up in a slight haze from the last night's ventures. She reached over to find the other half of her bed empty. *Probably for the best.*

She got ready for the day and went down for breakfast. The spread was as immaculate as always, and she savored every bite, pausing to lick her fingers dramatically.

"If you're wanting to go for round two, all you need to do is ask." Rook's voice traveled across the table, his eyes wandering.

"Maybe another time," she said, a knowing look curling her lips. "I look like I got attacked by a wild animal."

He snarled, and she winked at him.

"For the record, just because we fucked, does not mean I like you." She wanted to make that fact clear.

"Whatever you say, little bird."

They fell back into their routine with the occasional tumble in the sheets here and there, reaching something like normalcy, given their situation.

Rook returned unscathed from reporting to his father, so Soren assumed he had told him about their "progress." Occasionally, she would lock herself in her room and cry, feeling torn between the man she hated and the one she knew now, wishing the world wasn't so cruel. She hoped that Baz and Enara were safe and happy somewhere.

Rook never asked questions when she showed up for dinner with her eyes rimmed red and her face puffy from crying. It was a small mercy.

As they enjoyed a quiet evening in the library, General Corvus interrupted. He rapped on the door a second time.

Just as my story was getting good.

Rook slammed his book shut and walked to the door, talking in hushed tones with the creature. Soren strained to listen but came up short.

Rook walked back to her, running a hand through his hair. "I'll be right back."

"Do you want me to leave?" He had still never left her alone in the library.

"Just don't touch anything, okay? I won't be long. Something's caught the kestrels' attention off the grounds, and I need to hear his full report."

He trusts me. The thought warmed her.

She had given up on being angry in an attempt at self-preservation. Being furious all the time was exhausting and gave her a headache.

He had grown tolerable, and the fact that he was good in bed was a plus. She had chosen to enjoy her time as she waited for an opening to escape, and now the time had come.

"Okay, I'll be right here," she said, waving her current read at him.

"Behave yourself."

"Do I ever?" She smirked, returning to her book, wanting to avoid suspicion.

He gave her a look then followed the general out.

Soren finished the couple of pages she had left in her chapter then got up, stretching, knowing they were now out of earshot.

She ran to the windows, hoping to find one of them cracked, keeping an eye out for movement beyond the glass. They were all sealed shut, apart from a few on the ceiling that had a hook mechanism attached. She would need a really long pole to open one, let alone the semantics of reaching it. It wasn't like she had a thirty-foot ladder in her back pocket.

"Dammit."

She paced the room, huffing her annoyance. *He's going to be back soon.*

She scrapped the plan to smash through a window with a footstool, knowing it would garner too much attention. Instead, she decided to take advantage of the opening to check out the library without Rook breathing over her shoulder.

She walked over to his collection, figuring it was the best place to start. She didn't want to risk touching anything—he would know if any of the books were out of place. Many of them were first editions, hundreds of years old.

These have got to be worth more than the manor and the property combined.

Though she speculated that was not why he had added them to the collection. He was one of the few people she knew who could appreciate the literary stories of old.

Finding nothing but dust, she moved on.

She shuffled over to sit on the piano bench and flipped open the piece of wood that covered the keys. Rook had played for her a handful of times and had done so beautifully, but she had shied away at the opportunity to return the favor.

She tested the keys, hoping to find something out of place, but then thought better of it. She did not want to look like she was on the hunt if Rook walked back in. To cover her intentions, she played a song Enara had taught her back at Voxridge. The tune was meant to teach you the different ranges of the piano and was conveniently designed to hit every key.

Her fingers traveled along the ivory as the music drifted through the room. However, the song came to an abrupt stop when she hit a dead key.

She tapped it a few times to see if it would give, but it gave her nothing in return. Finding it hard to believe that it was a coincidence, she pushed up on the key from underneath to see if maybe it was a hidden compartment. To her surprise, the key lifted, and she turned as the wall behind her creaked open. The wall of Rook's collection had been a door to a secret room. He would probably kill her if he found out she knew, but she would never get this opportunity again.

She sucked in a breath of courage and walked through the dark doorway.

The room was small and dimly lit by a couple of enchanted torchlights, mostly filled with priceless pieces of art that had likely been stolen. Everything in the room had a fine layer of dust on it, apart from the Oculus that sat shining on a stand atop the table.

I thought Adriel took you back to Anistera? It was as if it were calling to her blood, as her veins hummed the closer she got. *I have to hide it.* She reached out her hand, but before she could touch it, she noticed a journal resting on the table.

It was bound in fine black leather and had a single red rose hand-painted on the front, the flower petals pooling at the base of the stem. It was the only other thing not covered in dust, so she took the opportunity to crack it open, wanting to see what secrets lay in its pages.

The book was full of poems and passages, many of which recounted horrible depictions of torture and abuse that would have even Enara pitying him.

How could his father let Corvus do this to him?

Her hand shot to her mouth as the contents of her stomach threatened to paint the walls. *No wonder he follows Adriel's orders.* And then in understanding. *I would do anything to escape if it were me.*

She placed it back down just as she'd found it.

Knowing she was running out of time, she turned to leave, vowing to come back for the Oculus. As her hand touched the edge of the doorway, however, something caught her eye. She turned her head, curiosity getting the better of her as her gaze landed on a thin chain of gold.

There was a wedding band hanging from it, and even covered in dust, it shined through the dark. She would recognize it anywhere. *That's Mother's ring.* Her throat constricted as tears stung her eyes, blurring her vision. *How does he have this?*

Her father had worn it on his neck every day since she could remember. He'd had it on him the last time she'd seen him.

She snatched up the chain and walked out just in time to see Rook stepping back into the room. He turned, his eyes blazing when he saw she had found where he kept his secrets.

"Where did you get this?" she yelled.

His eyes fell to the chain, the ring swaying back and forth like a pendulum. "It's not what you think."

"Then, what the fuck is it, Rook? How is it that you have this?"

"He showed up unannounced on my doorstep, looking for my father."

Her eyes narrowed as anger surged through her whole body. He was about to impart an explanation, but she held up a hand to silence him. She had only one question, the only piece of information that mattered.

"Did you kill him?"

He gave her a resigned look and opened his mouth, letting one syllable fall out. One syllable that changed everything.

"Yes."

CHAPTER
TWENTY—FOUR

Baz zipped up his trousers and took in the view of the lake. It was a still morning, and the surface was as smooth as glass, reflecting the image of the mountains and surrounding forest.

Jai sauntered out from the tree line to the left, giving him a wave. "Good morning."

"Good morning, man. Out for a jaunt in the woods?" Baz asked.

"Just clearing my head."

Baz gave him a skeptical look. "Can I level with you?"

Jai raised a brow. "Sure, buddy, what's up?"

"You see, the advantage of being a joker is that you tend to be overlooked. I am a lot more observant than people give me credit for." Baz put his hands in his pockets.

"Okay, man, not sure what you're getting at here." Jai cocked his head to the side, brows furrowing.

"Your hands were covered in sand when you returned from the beach, and I noticed that that handy little box of yours is missing, so you can beat around the bush, or you can give it to me straight. Either way, the truth will come out, and I won't hesitate to act if you put Enara in danger."

Jai's features shifted from surprise to anger to resigned acceptance, and he let out a sigh as he sat down on the sand. He picked up a handful of the crushed rock and let the granules sift through his fingers. "You're right. We do not give you enough credit," he said, patting the spot beside him.

Baz sat down, waiting for answers.

"It wasn't trade papers in the box," he admitted, wringing his hands together nervously.

"I figured as much."

Jai squinted out at the water, tossing a stone and watching the surface ripple. "They were photographs of the Patrovian princess, and some of my mother's belongings." He looked pained.

"Seriously, dude? You want me to believe that you were being so secretive because you had the hots for the princess?"

"Not exactly," he croaked out, crossing his arms. "I was in love with her, but that's not the whole story."

Baz allowed him to gather his thoughts, wanting to give him the benefit of the doubt.

"I grew up in the castle. My mother was one of the queen's handmaidens before she passed, so I lived there until I was old enough to go off on my own. The princess and I grew up together and fought as siblings do. I left when I was old enough to join the tracker program in the flatlands. I didn't see her for four years. When I returned, I found out she had been taken, and I did everything I could to get her back. We traveled for a few weeks together and became very close. By the time we made it back to Edras Mora, we were inseparable."

Baz nodded to acknowledge that he was still listening.

"When my mother fell ill, she stayed by my side the entire time and supported me while I grieved her death. My mother shared something with me before she died."

He held his breath, knowing that there was no turning back now. "The princess was adopted. The late queen was not able to carry a child to term, so they paid a young woman to keep her child as their own. Given the girl had similar physical qualities to the queen, her heritage was never questioned, But that meant that Adaryn is not the true heir to the crown."

"So, who would be next in line then?" Baz asked, not knowing much about court politics.

"The king's brother, in normal circumstances, but my mother shared with me that there was another heir. The king had many affairs throughout his relationship with the queen, one of them being my mother"—he sucked in a breath then blew it out—"making me the rightful heir to the Patrovian throne."

Baz considered the statement. "So, that makes you what? A prince?"

"I guess it does. But it is not a life I ever saw for myself. I did not want to risk Adaryn's life being turned upside down, so I left. I broke her heart and never looked back. I couldn't. If anyone found out who I was, she would be removed from the line of succession and thrown to the wolves, so to speak.

"The king and I came to an agreement. There is a document with my mother's things, signed by him, confirming my lineage in the event that anything happens to his daughter. He may be a greedy prick, but he cares for her in his own way. We agreed that no one would know."

"And what about Adaryn?"

Jai fisted a rock in his palm, his knuckles turning white. "She is set to marry the Duke of Stelonbriar. An arrangement of sorts, but her father tells me they get along famously. I still track for him on occasion, and he ensures my coffers never empty."

"Dude."

"Yeah."

"You're a prince."

Jai sighed. "Yeah."

"I'm sorry about Adaryn."

"So am I," he said solemnly, tossing the rock into the water.

"Hey, you guys are up early. What are you two chatting about over here?" Enara asked, coming out of the tree line.

"Oh, nothing. Just guy talk," Baz said, looking anywhere but at her.

Jai stood up, chuckling. "I appreciate your discretion, man, but I think it's best that we're all open with each other going forward." He clapped him on the shoulder and stood to greet Enara.

Her head swiveled back and forth between them. "Am I missing something?"

Jai reached out his hand, and she shook it, her face a mask of confusion.

"Pleasure to meet you. I am Prince Ashwood, the true heir of the Patrovian throne."

"Nice to meet you, Your Majesty," she said, bowing with a flourish. "I'm Princess Liliana of the Esinian Isles."

Her smile broke when she saw the serious look on his face. "Wait—you're not joking, are you?"

"Not even a little."

He recapped the story he had told Baz about his mother and the princess of Patrivah while Enara sat in silence, hanging on to every word.

"Wow," she said, shocked. "That's … a lot."

"Yeah."

"So, no one else knows who you truly are, apart from the king?" she asked.

"Just my good friend, Everett. He was the stable boy at the castle. We've been close since we were kids. I trust him with my life."

"That must have been hard," she said, eyes full of sympathy.

"It was … It is … but I'd do anything for her to be happy." He gazed off into the distance, his throat tight.

"Why couldn't you just claim the throne and marry her, anyway?" Baz asked, trying to problem solve.

"There are rules to these things," he said, his voice gravelly. "If she was of any royal heritage, we could make it work, but her mother was a young servant girl who got knocked up near the end of her studies. She was not of noble descent. The country would revolt and possibly turn on the monarchy. I can't let my feelings risk putting her in danger."

"You are a good man," Enara said, touching his arm.

"I try to be," he replied, shifting away from her. "We should get going. Keep the furs handy; we will be in mountain territory soon."

They packed up camp then headed east, following the trail that led up the base of the mountains of east Thorncrest.

The air was thinner and caused their cheeks to pinken as they trudged along the rock-strewn path.

They kept up a steady gait as the snow started to float down from the sky in little wisps. Enara snuggled closer to Baz, relishing in the warmth of him as they went. Jai only had to veer off track a handful of times, and the three of them had agreed to resume night watch after he had reported more kestrel tracks than usual.

"So, what are your plans after this?" Baz asked Jai when they paused for refreshments.

"I hadn't thought that far ahead, but after everything, I'm not sure I want to go back to Patrivah. For the last two years, I have hidden in the shadows to remain close to Adaryn, but I worry if I stay, I will try to stop her upcoming nuptials." He poked at the ground with a stick.

"Hey, if we get out of here unscathed, I'll be the first to help you wedding crash." Baz winked as he threw his pack back over his shoulder.

"I'd tag along, too, but only for the free wine," Enara joked.

Jai smiled, thankful for their support.

They continued on the winding path up the mountainside, their pace slowing as they reached the midway point. They decided to stop by a stone ledge that blocked out the wind from the west, giving them some semblance of protection at their backs.

They made a fire, but kept it low, not wanting to risk sending smoke signals to their enemies. They huddled in close to keep warm and took turns warming their palms on the embers, the heat chasing away the cold with a torch and pitchfork.

Enara's hands prickled as the flames danced in her eyes. The closer they got to Soren, the more her anxiety took hold.

She had no idea what to expect and was jumping at every sound, worried kestrels were going to rain down on them at any moment.

"Hey," Baz said, pulling the cover back over her shoulders. "Where did you go off to just then?"

"I just have a bad feeling. We don't know what comes next. Hell, we don't know if there is a whole army of those things waiting for us." She shivered, but not from the cold.

He scrunched his face, not quite knowing what to say. Instead, he just held her tighter.

They went to bed early, putting the fire out before nightfall could give them away. Baz took the first watch.

The next morning, they had a quick breakfast and continued their ascent.

Mother Nature was angry, and the wind howled through the cliffs, causing tears to run down their faces. The snow had been a permanent fixture for a few miles now, and their eyelashes and brows were frosted.

The furs were enough to regulate their temperature, but they were heavy, and the steeper parts of the climb were a struggle. When they crested the first peak, the gale threatened to teeter them off the side, and Enara had to plunge her staff into the ground to keep steady. Still, they pushed on, determination driving them up each frozen step.

As they switched paths from one edge of the peak to the next, they found themselves in fresh powder that sucked them up to their knees. They practically had to swim their way through.

They paused to break when they had reached a section of hard pack, daring to have a small fire to warm their fingers and eat something above freezing temperature. They had acquired gloves, but they had been cut off at the fingertips and did little to protect their hands from frostbite.

Jai was finding it hard to track from here, as the blowing snow left the landscape flat and untouched. Without that, they were going in blind. The goal now was to get to a high enough vantage point to see what they could and pray they didn't walk smack-dab into a den of teeth and talons.

The mountains started at the coastline and jutted up and down like an accordion, midway to Ventshire, the capital of Thorncrest. The highest peak was about twenty thousand feet above sea level. The peak they were heading toward was around fifteen thousand feet or so.

They continued along the mountaintop, trying to plan out where to stop for the night, when a loud crack split the air and had their heads whipping around. They could hear a distant rumble, and the ground beneath them began to shake.

"Guys," Baz said, a tremor in his voice.

"That's not what I think it is, is it?" Enara asked. Worry spread across her face like spilled ink on parchment. "No, not when we're this close." She shook her head in defeat.

The rumble of the mountain grew louder. In the distance, they could see a large, white cloud forming, moving at incredible speed.

They started running toward the edge of the cliff, hoping that the overhang would protect them and the snow would just flow over top.

Their lungs screamed as the cold air choked them while they ran. The water from their eyes tried to freeze before it dropped to the ground.

"Hurry!" Jai yelled from a few yards ahead.

Another boom broke through the sky, and they looked up in horror to see that the avalanche had crested the peak and was crashing toward them like a frozen tidal wave. Jagged pieces of ice, trees, and rocks gnashed at them like sharks' teeth.

They were all quick but not quick enough. Their feet lifted out from under them as the frigid wall came crashing down.

They stretched their arms out, trying to keep a hold of each other, but the frozen current was too strong. The cliff loomed closer, and if they didn't do something soon, they would be thrown to their deaths.

Enara lost her grip on her staff, but Baz grabbed it before it was carried away and swung it as hard as he could at the trunk of a passing tree. He gripped the middle around the raven's beak and held fast to Enara's wrist, yelling out as his arms strained beyond their normal capabilities. His fingertips screamed as the enchanted weapon blazed to life at the foreign touch. Pain lanced thought him but he refused to let go.

Jai was farther down, grasping a fallen log. He looked around desperately for something to slow himself down. However, snow clouded his vision, and the ice crystals scratched his throat as he was dragged blindly out of Enara's line of sight.

"Jai!" she cried, but received no answer.

Baz was losing grip, his knuckles rubbed raw from the icy drift. "Hold on!" he yelled to Enara, trying to keep them both afloat. His body was being hammered with large chunks of trees and other debris, his fingertips all but singed off.

He stared in horror as a large chunk of frozen earth barreled toward them, knowing there was no way to get out of its path.

"Whatever happens, I love you!" he yelled to Enara, who was holding tight to his waist.

It was a direct hit, and his shoulder gave out with a sickening pop. His scream echoed off the mountain peaks as his strength gave out.

Seizing the opportunity, the cold hand of winter dragged them under, and all went quiet.

CHAPTER
TWENTY—FIVE

Soren screamed. The guttural sound shook the dust from the bookshelves as tears screamed hot down her face. *He is a dead man!*

She swiveled her head around, looking for anything she could use as a weapon. She threw the chain over her head, the ring lifeless and cold against her chest, then ran to the piano. With one swift kick, she broke the lip prop loose and charged at Rook.

He was already walking in her direction, trying to say something about how it wasn't what it looked like, but she couldn't hear over the blood filling her ears.

"How could you?" The sound tore from her throat, more animal than human. The active volcano of rage exploded, releasing itself from her body. "I confided in you!"

She swung the wooden rod, and he blocked it with his forearm, grunting as she swung again, taking out his legs. He landed with a *thump* on the hardwood floor, gasping for air when the wind withdrew from his lungs.

"I should have known all along. It was just a game, wasn't it?" she shrieked, cracking the shaft against the floor again and again. Rook rolled out of the way as the force of her blows rang off the walls.

"It wasn't like that."

"You murderer!" she screamed as she sloughed off the wooden outer layer that had cracked from the force to reveal a metal core. She hunted after him, ready to continue the assault. *Father killer!*

He moved out of the way just in time for the rod to thud into the heavy armchair.

"Soren, listen."

"I'm done listening to you! You are poison. You deserve every punishment your father ever gave you."

He stepped back, the words hitting him harder than any strike she could ever dole out.

"I can see now there is no coming back from this." He kneeled before her, his arms out, defeated. "I am sorry, little bird."

She stood before him, her chest constricting as she readied her swing. The metal cut through the air and sunk until the floor inches from Rook's face.

He looked up at her, his eyes wide, his chest heaving.

"You do not deserve a quick death," she spat the words in his face. "You are not some tortured animal. You are your father's beast, raised only to cause harm. I will let him have you, and when I return, I will put you down myself." With that, she left.

Soren ran out the main door, clawing at her throat as the noose of grief tightened. Her heart shattered. The shards of betrayal stabbed and tore at her insides until all that was left was a shell, broken and bleeding. *I trusted him.*

She ran blindly down the road, toward the main gate, screaming in frustration when she found it locked, the cold of the metal stinging her hands.

The kestrels were circling, watching the events unfold.

She ran around the side of the house and down the path of the courtyard, the tree branches cutting into her pink flesh and leaving behind trails of red. *I let him put his hands on me.*

A wave of nausea filled her, but it was quickly replaced by the frenzy of red that invaded her vision. She kept running through the haze, her body hot with rage amongst the winter landscape.

Logically, she knew she couldn't survive out here for long, but she would rather die out here than be in that house for a moment longer.

You should have killed him, her mind shot at her.

She had wanted to. Maker knew she wanted to. But when he had kneeled before her, she couldn't finish it. She needed time to think. Her mind was a warzone, and coherent thought was nonexistent.

She crossed the bridge and edged her way down to the water, taking a tentative step onto its clear surface. When it held fast, she continued, thankful that she at least had her house slippers on.

She wiped the tears from her eyes and wrapped her arms around herself as she walked on. If she could just reach the base of the mountain, she could make a fire and figure out her next move.

She gave up yelling to conserve her energy, but rage boiled hot in her veins. *How could I have been so stupid?* The nausea had returned, and she got sick on the ice, her stomach heaving any semblance of nourishment from her body. *You let his pretty face blind you. You let him in. You left yourself vulnerable. Now look at you.* She kept coughing, her stomach muscles flexing painfully. *You cared for him.*

The final thought was her undoing, and the panic took hold. She did not know how she had any tears left, but still, they came. Her chest ached, and she struggled to catch her breath.

A boom in the distance shook the ground beneath her, and her eyes turned to saucers. She scanned the ice for any fissures and sighed in relief that it had held. Then she looked around, trying to gauge where the sound had come from. *There.*

A wave of snow was falling from one of the peaks, heading east.

Deeming the crossing was still safe, she continued until another boom stopped her in her tracks. She looked on in horror as a part of the wave broke off, heading in her direction.

She froze in terror as she watched the wall of snow come down and crash along the lake's far edge. There was a deafening crack as the ice split, and a whimper escaped her lips as she turned back toward the manor.

She struggled to keep upright as the fabric of her shoes slid on the blue sheet of ice, her lungs resisting the cold air she tried to inhale. She cried out as the fissures got closer, reminding her of the kestrel's taloned fingers.

She jumped over the smaller cracks, her body swaying awkwardly as she danced with death. She had almost made it back to shore when a large gap appeared in front of her, forcing her to change her course.

As she turned, a chunk of ice reared up as she stepped on it, causing her to lose her balance. She fell onto her backside, head whipping in all directions, looking for an escape route.

She went to stand, but the ice below her shifted and cracked, so she remained on her hands and knees, trying to redistribute her weight.

She crawled toward the other side of the shore, taking her time not to disturb the ice, when a creature landed on the edge of the water in front of her. The kestrel's hollowed eyes were filled with what she guessed was humor.

"Stupid girl," it said.

"Fuck you!" she yelled as she gave it the finger.

The movement caused her other hand to slide out from under her, and she slipped, her face smacking into the frozen surface and making her see stars.

She looked up to see the unnamed kestrel put pressure on the ice in front of it, the ground fracturing as it flashed its sharp teeth.

"No!" she cried as the surface began to split open.

The cracks split off in all directions, cutting off any hope of escape. She could see the blue-black water roiling below, waiting to swallow her.

"Soren!"

Across the ice, she could see the body of the kestrel twitching on the ground, its head laying a few feet away. Its black blood leaked into the water, darkening it further.

Rook stood beside the body of water, a knife in his hand. Soren could faintly see something dark dripping from it. He opened his mouth to say something, but before the words could reach her, she fell into the icy depths.

She tried to swim up to an opening, but a current was pulling her under. She banged against the underside of the glassy surface as ice filled her veins and her brain became fuzzy. Her limbs went numb as she fought the current.

She looked up through the ice to see wings overhead as her body went limp and she waited for the end. The last thing she saw before death took her was a flash of white with glacier eyes.

EPILOGUE

Rook's chest sank as he looked out at the broken expanse of ice. The lake's surface was a shattered mirror against the night sky.

He flashed back to the moment when he had seen Soren's tiny frame disappear into the water below.

He had followed after her, anger burning inside him when he had seen one of his father's beasts taunting her. He had run out of the manor with incredible speed, a dagger in his hand.

The creature had been laughing at her, if you could even call the sickening sound a laugh. The noise was somewhere between a caw and a human voice, the two battling each other for higher ground.

His anger had peaked when he had seen the creature's taloned foot press into the surface, creating more fissures in the ice.

Rook had rounded on it without a second thought. *No one hurts little bird but me.* With one hard swing of his blade, he had cut off the kestrel's head, the dagger slick with ichor.

He cast his gaze to the lake. Soren had fallen hard on the ice and was trying to crawl her way to safety.

"Soren!" he called to her.

He wanted to run to her. He observed the ice, trying to find a way to get there.

He opened his mouth to speak again, but he was too late. They made eye contact for only a breath before she plunged into the frigid water.

"No!" he yelled.

Throwing caution to the wind, he sprinted onto the cracked surface, only putting his foot down long enough to propel the next one forward. He slowed when he reached the spot where she had fallen, stepping gingerly from one section to another, searching.

He fell to his hands and knees, wiping the surface to get a better view of the underwater world. *Where are you, little bird?*

"Soren!" he yelled again, knowing the effort was futile. The water would dull the sound, even if she was coherent enough to respond.

A shift in the water caught his eye a few feet away, and he scrambled across the surface. Soren's hands were pressed against the ice, and he could see the fear in her eyes before they closed. He watched as the last of her breath escaped her mouth, the bubbles caught between her lips and the ice ...

In the present, he pressed his eyes shut, pushing the thought away. He released the death grip he had on the railing. His knuckles had healed, but he could still feel the ghost of rawness they'd held from when he had beat on the ice, try-ing to get to her.

This is all your doing.

It had been one week since the avalanche, and his mind had spent the majority of the time torturing itself. The look on her face when she had attacked him in the library had his heart constricting. *She was right. I am a beast.*

He looked around his bedroom, disgusted with himself. When the realization had hit him that she was gone and never coming back, he had gone on a rampage.

The curtains were ripped from their hooks, and the dress-er had broken into pieces during his assault. Feathers from his pillows littered the floor, along with splinters of wood from his nightstand.

He ran his hand through his hair, crossing the room to leave. He grimaced at the mess one last time before walking down the hall.

He had been sleeping in Soren's room since the day he'd lost her. The sheets still smelled like the lavender soap she fa-vored, and everything was just as she had left it.

He fingered the nightgown that rested on the bathroom hook before washing his face.

He couldn't even look at himself without turning away in disgust. *It's your fault she's gone.* He hated to admit that he missed her, but in those few short weeks they had spent together, he had grown to care for her.

Originally, he had wanted nothing to do with her. She had been crass and immature, barely able to rein in her emotions. She'd vexed him to no end, and he had constantly been infu-riated by her.

Though none of that mattered because he'd had a job to do. Rook had known it would be an impossible task. She'd been stubborn and violent and thought him the enemy.

My father is the real enemy, he thought as he dried his hands then sat down on the edge of the bed. He had never intended for this. For any of it.

He thought, at least if they could just get along, then life in the manor wouldn't be so tumultuous. He'd never meant to develop feelings for her, though that was exactly what Adriel wanted.

He just wanted to hide in his library and live in the worlds of his books, away from prying eyes. But he had been raised by animals, so he had become one.

He did not know where his father's creation ended and the real him began. He had started to with her. She had brought out parts of him that he had so often hidden away for fear of condemnation.

She is never coming back.

He knew his end was coming. He had failed in his mission to secure a mating bond with Soren and now, without her, completing the task would prove impossible.

In a few days, Adriel would come down from Anistera and see to it that Rook was duly punished. He knew his father would likely kill him. Rook was sure he would find another way to enact his plans to destroy Entheas. He had accepted that his solitary existence would come to an end sooner rather than later. *I deserve to die.*

He hated what his father had made him to be. He had caged his little bird, chained her, fought her, and lied to her. He had killed her father. He had let her slip through his fingers, just as something had started to form between them.

His broken little bird had warmed a piece of his frozen heart. The shred of warmth but a sliver amongst the ice.

He held on to that piece, the silent reminder that she had been here, that she had been real.

He strode to the balcony, casting his eyes to the sky. It was a clear night, and the stars blinked back at him as he whispered to her, "Until we meet again."

ACKNOWLEDGMENTS

First and foremost, I want to thank myself. You heard that right. I know it sounds conceited but bear with me. I am always basing my self-worth on the opinions of others, and that is a dangerous path to be on. When I started writing this story, I was telling my husband how worried I was about pouring my soul into these pages and having it fail.

He just looked at me and said, "Who cares? Do it for yourself. No matter what happens, it will still be amazing just to say you wrote a book."

So, here I am, so incredibly proud of all the effort I have made these past few months to get to this point. I wrote a whole ass book!

But, in all seriousness, I want to thank my husband, Sheon—pronounced *Sha-on* (you can thank my mother-in-law for that. *Love you, Mandy!*)—for the countless hours he spent on baby duty so I could write in peace.

Peanut, you are my sweet baby angel child, but you're also half-pterodactyl and those noises are simply not conducive to writing.

Thank you to my mother for being my cheerleader and emotional support in all things. Thank you for never making me wonder if you were proud of me.

As a whole, I want to thank everyone—family and friends alike—who have shown support throughout this journey and who constantly checked in on me. Your kind words and feedback did not go unnoticed.

Huge shoutout to Kristin Campbell, my amazing editor, who fixed my horrendous grammar and helped to make my story the best it could be for all of you.

This leads me to my final acknowledgment. Thank YOU. Yeah, you over there reading this damn thing. Even if you hated it, thank you, anyway. You took the time out of your life to celebrate a piece of my own, and I am forever grateful.

Love always,
N.J. Rodman
May 30, 2023

ABOUT THE AUTHOR

N.J. RODMAN WAS BORN IN EDMONTON, ALBERTA, AND CURRENT-
ly resides in Cold Lake with her husband, Sheon, and their
daughter, affectionately referred to as Peanut. She has been
an avid reader since childhood and loves to immerse herself in
other author's fantasy worlds. Writing was something she had
always been passionate about but never pursued until recently.
She looks forward to what the future holds for her newfound
career as a self-published author.